Island Stories

Edited by

Melissa McCann

DEDICATION

For all the brave souls who live with their hearts on their sleeves and their blood in their pens.

MISTRESS OF HEMLOCK COTTAGE

By Delinda McCann

Anderson Island WA

Hemlocks punctuated by the occasional western red cedar lined the small clearing. Their branches brushed the ground creating hidden fortresses where the little creatures of the wood could watch for hawks and bald eagles before dashing across the drive in search of seeds and berries. The dark green trees drew their shadows around them like winter coats and whispered among themselves.

Mrs. Hemlock leaned over the driveway and watched the cars leaving the clearing. "Did he pass over the rainbow bridge?"

Young Cedar scratched an old empty cone off the end of a branch. "They live such short lives. Are you sure he's gone?"

Old Hemlock nodded his head. "This is their way. They go out laying down, then lots of people come and carry away what they've hoarded."

Old Grandpa Cedar had the last word. "Aye, they're like us in this way. When they go out layin' down, they're done for and aren't ever comin' back." The trees settled down to wait for a new master or mistress.

Los Angeles CA

Audrey sat at her desk and slid the binder onto the monthly financial report. *There, both reports are done and the old bitch isn't even in yet. I wonder if I can sneak some time off to make up for coming in early?*

Audrey didn't have to wait more than five minutes before her boss bustled up to her desk. "Audrey, I want the itemized totals on my desk in a half hour." Mrs. Hardy, who insisted on being called Gloria as if she were Audrey's friend instead of her step-mom's, brushed against Audrey's desk, knocking the ledgers she had spread out in front of her askew. Audrey wondered how often Mrs. Hardy reported her activities to her parents and if the reports were as critical as Mrs. Hardy was. Audrey asked herself for at least the thousandth time, *Did Dad tell her that I have mental problems?*

"Here they are." Audrey handed the folder with the sales by category and item to Mrs. Hardy. "Here's the monthly statement if you want it, too." She picked up the recently completed report and held it out in her other hand, and there she sat looking up at her supervisor, a report in each outstretched hand. She wanted to look at her clock to see how long Mrs. Hardy would make her wait before taking the reports.

Mrs. Hardy fluttered her hands. "Oh, done already? How on earth did you get them done so early? I just unlocked the doors five minutes ago."

Audrey shrugged, "I had them ready to go last night. I just had to plug in the numbers from Hawaii and hit calculate, then print." Audrey knew better than to tell Mrs. Hardy that the janitor had let her into the office at six. She'd have a fit and maybe get the janitor fired, worse she'd call Step-Monster, and she'd tell Dad, and Dad would say Audrey gets confused and can't tell time.

Mrs. Hardy adjusted the rings on her fingers. "I want accurate numbers. If you're done already, you can't have had time to double-check. I want you to go back through and double-check your figures. We can't make sound decisions if we don't have accurate information. The numbers from Hawaii are the most likely to skew the results. Garbage in garbage out, as they say." She walked away without taking the reports with her.

Audrey sighed and set the reports aside, then searched her drawer for different-colored binders. She'd learned long ago that Mrs. Hardy would reject finished reports on a whim, but changing the binders would be enough to satisfy the old witch. She stifled tears as she sat at her desk wondering why her best was never good enough.

She watched from behind her computer screen while Mrs. Hardy harassed the company's sales representative, Michael. As soon as the supervisor disappeared into her office, she made a break for the restroom. Locked in a stall, she blew her nose and let the tears slide down her cheeks. She chided herself for being so sensitive. Mrs. Hardy, Glooooria, just likes to be in control of everything. She's insecure. Her behavior has nothing to do with me. Audrey repeated the mantra her counselor helped her make up for Mrs. Hardy.

Her phone emitted the whoop, whoop of a British police car. She looked at the thing, then answered. "Hi Mom. What's up?" She really wanted to call her step-mother by her name, but Daddy had insisted she call her new mother Mom. She didn't really remember her birth mom very well.

She was six when a drunk driver ran up on the sidewalk in front of their apartment, killing her mom and injuring two other people from the building. She'd tried to remember her real mother and had even gone to counseling where the brilliant psychologist told her, "You're blocking those memories," charged her more than she could afford, and sent her home.

Her step-mom sounded cross. "Did you get the letter about your grandfather's will?"

"Yes, it came yesterday. I haven't gone through the complete inventory yet."

"I don't know why the attorney insists on including you when you didn't come to the memorial. Your father was very hurt that you didn't care enough to come."

"I told you, Gloria wouldn't give me the time off from work because the monthly financial reports need to be in today. If you'd scheduled the service for tomorrow, I could have been there. Is there something I need to do about the letter and inventory?"

"No. The attorney wants you to write him a letter saying you don't want anything from the estate. I can write it for you, but it has to be notarized. I'll get in trouble if I just sign your name. You'll have to send me your signature with a notary stamp on it, and I'll staple it to the letter for you."

"I don't know that I don't want anything. I saw Grandma's Limoges china listed. I might like the china. Who gets the beach house?"

"We told the attorney nobody wants it and to cash out the whole estate. If you start picking this and that for yourself, it will make it harder for us to do that. It's going to be hard enough to settle the estate because it's so isolated, and some idiot started rumors that the house is haunted."

"Whatever. Listen, I've got to get back to work." Audrey disconnected the call and returned to the office.

Mrs. Hardy fluttered her hands and called to Audrey the minute she came through the door. "There you are. Where did you go? You should tell me before you step out. I didn't know where you were."

Audrey returned to her desk and pulled out the chair. "Urgent call of nature. In fact, I don't feel real well today. Was there something specific you wanted?" She wondered if Mrs. Hardy had missed her and called her step-mother to say she wasn't at her desk. *Maybe I'm just paranoid. Maybe a different counselor could help me.*

"I just didn't know where you were. Now you've made me feel bad by saying you're sick. How was I to know you weren't feeling well?" She sniffed. "When you don't tell me things, I'm not going to figure it out on my own, then you say you're sick and make me sound mean for expecting you to work when you're sick."

"I double-checked the numbers on these reports. Do you want them now?"

"I don't need the monthly report, just the itemized sales. I don't even know why you do the monthly report. It's a total waste of time."

Audrey had long since given up explaining that the monthly report needed to be run before the itemized report and the two reports needed to balance. She pulled the keyboard toward her, brought up a spreadsheet for her own private project, a company she was forming with her friends, and turned her back on her boss, knowing Mrs. Hardy couldn't tell one spreadsheet from another. A great lump swelled in her throat. *Maybe I really am sick today. I wish I could have been at Grandpa's service. I wish Dad had put it off until today. Just sending those flowers didn't feel like enough.*

Shortly before lunchtime, Grandpa Singer's estate attorney in Washington called Audrey. "I understand you don't want anything from the estate, is that correct?"

Audrey pursed her lips. "No. That isn't correct. I want my grandmother's good china, and I want to know what will happen to the beach house."

"The beach cabin can be sold if nobody is in a position to live there. I understand you have a good job in LA and hate the Washington rain."

Audrey kicked at the side of her desk. Obviously the attorney had been talking to her parents. "My job sucks. It's my step-mom who hates the rain. I don't mind it. What's the deal with the beach house?"

"It goes to any immediate family member who wants to live there. Your dad wants to stay in Arizona, and your brother wants to stay in Bellevue. If you want to stay in California, we have the option of selling the house and splitting the proceeds."

"How soon can I move in?" She asked the question mostly to show the attorney that he didn't know everything and that her step-mother didn't make decisions for her.

"Are you serious? The only way out to that island is by ferry, and it doesn't run after nine at night. There are rumors the house is haunted, too."

Audrey looked up to see Mrs. Hardy coming toward her. "How soon?"

"I guess I can have the paperwork…well…really…according to the will, you can move in as soon as you want. You don't have to wait until the estate closes, in fact, you should move in before then."

Mrs. Hardy stopped beside Audrey's desk and opened her mouth.

Audrey said into her phone. "Cool. Is the key still in the well house? I can be there Friday." She disconnected the call, ignored Mrs. Hardy and fished a shopping bag out of her bottom drawer. She scooped all her personal items from her desk into the bag.

Mrs. Hardy nattered on about needing the monthly report, "I don't know why you always forget to give me the monthly report. You should give me both reports every month. Mr. Bigly is very specific that we have to have…"

Audrey interrupted, "I quit." She stifled the urge to call Mrs. Hardy a crazy old bat because she knew she might need a recommendation to get another job if her project with her Cal-Tech friends didn't work out. "I'm needed in Washington to deal with my grandfather's estate. I can't take care of the house from here." She turned and walked out the door.

Mrs. Hardy shrieked. "After I've treated you," sniff, "like my own daughter," sniff, "you're going to abandon me?"

Audrey struggled to open the door with her hands full of her possessions.

Mrs. Hardy paused then tilted her head to one side. "You're just upset over your dead grandfather. You shouldn't be driving. You might panic and run up on the sidewalk." She shrugged one shoulder.

Audrey fled.

On Wednesday, Audrey's friends helped her pack her car. Susan wedged a cooler in the back seat and gave Audrey a hug. "You'll be fine driving by yourself. Your imagination isn't going to run away with you. Check in with us. I'll be up there as soon as my office finds someone to replace me."

Phil closed the trunk. "Do you have enough money? We can make a distribution from our R & D fund. A free place to work and live is a valid expense."

Audrey hugged Phil. "Thanks, I think I'm okay. I got a deferment on my school loans and have all my deposits back on the apartment." Audrey hugged Susan. "I'll send updates. Keep me posted on how your presentations go." She turned and seat-belted a chubby cabbage patch doll with red hair like Audrey's into the passenger's seat. She straightened the doll's frilly dress and checked that the seatbelt was secure.

Anderson Island, WA

The trees around the clearing listened to the rustle of trees farther up the road. "She's coming."

A young Douglas Fir tossed his topmost branches. "That's what everybody has been saying for the past week every time a strange car comes on the island."

The maple at the Y sent the message through his roots to the nearby Hemlock. "She kept left."

Mrs. Hemlock nodded. "This is her. I feel it in my sap."

The old cedar sounded as excited as a sapling. "There she is. I can see her. She's coming this way."

A stately hemlock by the road waved her branches. "She's slowing down. Oh, I'm so excited."

Old Cedar whacked the hemlock next to him with a limb. "Everybody look sharp. Get your branches up. Clear the driveway. We have a new mistress."

5

The youngest cedar flipped his tiptop from south to north and checked the contents of the small hole near his roots where a tiny little girl had left a small bear behind. Nothing remained of the bear except some fluff and a red glass heart, buy Young Cedar had kept the heart safe.

Audrey double checked her directions and turned left down the drive between the thick trees. She'd expected the drive to be more overgrown. The branches formed a cathedral arch over her head but didn't encroach on the drive.

Weary beyond belief, she pulled her car up to the front door of the craftsman-style house. She'd been fascinated with the house perched almost at the water's edge on the few times her father had taken her to visit her grandfather. It had a large river-stone fireplace. Grandpa called it heat-a-later, because it had air vents that took in cold air near the floor, circulated the air around the firebox and pushed the heated air out between a lacework of holes in the stone face. She'd spent hours stuffing popcorn kernels in those holes, hoping the popcorn would pop when nobody expected it and scare everybody in the room. The popcorn didn't pop, but her mother had made her spend what seemed like hours with the vacuum cleaner sucking the popcorn out of the rockwork. She smiled. The house had brought back a good memory of her mom.

Audrey carried her purse, computer bag and overnight bag with her to the door while she fished the house key from her coat pocket. The attorney had assured her there were no keys in the well house and she must stop at his office before setting foot in the beach house. She scowled. He had emphasized several times that she actually had to live in the house before it could be transferred into her name. "You can't just vacation there then go back to California. You'll have to stay here even when it rains. Commuting to work on the ferry will be challenging."

"I'll be telecommuting. Are you sure there's nothing in the will preventing my business partners from moving with me?"

He shuffled some papers. "That should be okay. You know the house is a bit remote. There've been reports of unusual activity around it." He leaned back and furrowed his brow. "I'm concerned about your mental health history. Your dad told me you've experienced phobias and hallucinations. I should warn you that if you get into trouble living alone, he can have you declared incapacitated. If you get spooked and move out, the house will be sold according to the default clause in the will."

Audrey nodded and didn't try to argue the whole mental health thing. She'd heard this line before. The attorney had kept Audrey busy with paperwork until she barely had time to grab a few overpriced groceries at a small store and run to catch the last ferry at nine.

"Stupid man, nattering about haunted houses," she said as she unlocked

6

the door to the house, shoved it open and reached for the light switch. She winced as a blast of cold air hit her. "I told him to be sure someone kept the heat on. It's freezing in here, and the light is burned out." She dropped her belongings on the floor in the entry hall and fished out her phone to use as a flashlight. She kicked the front door closed behind her.

She finally found another light switch, but it didn't turn on any lights. She made her way to the kitchen, wondering how every single light bulb could be burned out. The kitchen lights didn't work either. *Has someone turned off the electricity? What am I going to do if the power is out?* She opened the refrigerator door, and the warm glow of the refrigerator light spilled out accompanied by the stench of rotted food. She quickly closed the door.

She'd begun to worry about her phone battery by the time she'd found the thermostat for the furnace and set it at seventy-five, then climbed the stairs to the bedrooms where, of course, the light bulbs appeared to be burned out. *I wonder where the breaker switches are?* She considered facing the dark basement and shuddered. Finally, the stress of quitting her job, her step-mother's hysterics and threats over her quitting her job, business with an attorney on her mother's side of the family, the long drive up from LA, and finding the house cold and dark overwhelmed the last of her courage. She sat down on the edge of the bed in the smallest bedroom and let the tears roll down her face.

Audrey sniffed and concluded that since the house was cold and dark, she might as well find a blanket and go to bed. The trees parted outside her window allowing fitful moonlight to fill the room. She found a blanket in the closet, stripped the dusty cover from the bed, kicked her shoes off and, using her sweater for a pillow, promised herself that it would be easier to deal with the basement, breaker panel, lights, and housekeeping in the morning.

Sweat covered Audrey's forehead, and she'd thrown off her blanket by the time the first morning light found its way between the hemlocks and into her bedroom. She smacked her lips and grimaced over the thick fuzzy feel on her teeth. *How hot is it in here?* She sat up and pulled at her tee shirt to let her skin breathe. *At least I can see a little.*

Feeling much more hopeful now that the house felt warm, Audrey wondered if she should unload her car first thing or go to the beach first. She went down stairs to the entry hall. Her stomach gurgled reminding her she hadn't had a decent meal in a couple days and that she'd left her groceries in the car the night before.

She stopped at the base of the stairs. Where was her bag? Her computer? She glanced around and found the overnight bag and computer sitting on a sturdy bench in the hall beside the stairs. She scrubbed her face. *I must have absentmindedly put them there before I went upstairs.* She stared at the two bags, trying to puzzle out what was wrong with the way they looked.

Oh well, I was tired. I better get those groceries out of the car and find a bath towel. Where's my coat? She turned in a circle. *I remember I took my coat off and dropped it on top of the bag before I went upstairs.* She scowled at the bags again, clearly remembering leaving them in the middle of the floor. *I haven't had memory troubles for years. Is it this house?*

Audrey searched the kitchen for the coat, circled through the dining room and through the living room and back to the front hall through the room Grandpa obviously used for a TV room. It still held his recliner and a big plasma TV. The other rooms contained a sparse assortment of wood tables and chairs, but nothing big enough like a sofa to hide a coat. *Did I leave it in the car? No. It was raining. I remember pulling the coat on before I got out of the car.*

She climbed the stairs and searched the four bedrooms and bath upstairs but didn't find the coat. Back downstairs she looked out at the morning fog and shivered. Maybe someone had left a sweater or coat in the front coat closet. She opened the closet. There, with only a few spider nests for company, hung her down coat. She stood and stared. *I'm absolutely certain I didn't hang that up because it was too dark to see.* She looked around her, expecting someone to appear out of one of the too-many rooms. After several minutes of being rooted to the same spot, she pulled her cell phone out of her pocket and wondered what this small island might have for police protection. She glanced at the screen. She wouldn't find out. She'd forgotten to charge the battery during the night.

Finally, Audrey talked herself into enough courage that she could move. *Nobody has jumped out of a cupboard and chopped me up with an axe yet. Whoever was here must have left.* She opened the front door and stepped out into the morning mist. *Look at that. I left the front door unlocked. I bet I left my car unlocked, too. I bet the person who was supposed to be keeping an eye on this place stopped by found the front door unlocked and picked up my things. It was probably just the caretaker. I'll have to find out who that is.*

She soon found herself in one of those loops of interlocking chores where she couldn't eat because she couldn't put the groceries in the dirty refrigerator, and she couldn't clean the refrigerator until she found a garbage bag for the rotted food. She could use the garbage bag her pillows were packed in, but all her clothes and necessities were packed on top of the pillows. She finally carried, sorted, and threw out until she felt somewhat organized and could at least feed herself. *Next up, I'm going to go buy every light bulb on the island.*

She went out to her car and turned the key. Nothing happened. She scowled at the dash and tried again. She checked the overhead light. It wouldn't come on. The battery couldn't be dead. It just couldn't. She released the hood latch, got out and lifted the hood as if she knew what to do about a car that wouldn't start. Everything looked the same as usual. She wiggled a battery cable, it didn't move. She wiggled the other cable. It slid off the terminal. "This, I can fix." She spent the next half hour tightening the bolt on the battery cable with a pair of pliers that were never intended to tighten battery cables, but she got the job done, started the car and left on a quest to get light bulbs.

The local store on the main road had six light bulbs--four sixty-watt and two forty-watt. She picked up a roll of paper towels and a box of garbage bags and placed her purchases on the counter. "Hi, I'm Audrey Singer. I'm staying at my Grandpa's place. Do you know who took care of the house after he went to the nursing home?"

The woman behind the counter bagged the few items. "Nobody has said anything. Nobody bothers much out here. The local kids are afraid of the place. Rumor is that an old Indian haunts it." She put the last of the light bulbs in the bag without looking at Audrey. "Could be Brad Stewart checks on the place. His mom used to take care of your grandpa."

Audrey chatted for a few more minutes then went home to change light bulbs and make a list for a trip to Costco.

Old Cedar tossed his head. "Guess who's coming. Again."

Mrs. Hemlock pulled her branches close around her. "I don't like him poking around here with a new mistress in the house."

The trees threw their shadows across the drive and reached their limbs out to grab at the mirrors on the man's new truck.

Young Cedar knocked his branches together with a creaking and groaning. "I got some of his paint this time. Maybe I can get a mirror next time."

Late in the afternoon, the doorbell interrupted Audrey as she was sweeping spider webs from the walls. Leaving her broom in the living room, she strode to the front door hoping to give the caretaker a piece of her mind for coming in when she was home. She opened the door and came face to face with a Nordic God, with blue eyes and golden-red hair. Her heart raced. Her brain turned to mush, and her stomach developed butterflies.

"Hi. I'm Brad Steward. Folks up at the store said you were looking for me." He peered at Audrey as if he were near sighted.

"I'm looking for the person who's been taking care of this house. Is that you?"

"Nope. Don't know as anybody has. Your dad checked things over when he was here after the memorial service last week. Is everything okay?"

"Someone came in during the night and moved things around. Nothing serious, but I didn't appreciate the intrusion."

A muscle twitched in Brad's cheek. "Uh. The neighbors are summer people. Nobody's living out here much, and your drive's not that easy to find." He turned as if looking for intruders in the clearing. "Um…you sure you didn't imagine things moved? Nobody out here to bother you really."

"Is there a locksmith on the island?"

"No. Nobody locks." He grinned. "Hey, you'll be fine. Nothing to worry about. Probably your imagination." He looked around the clearing, and Audrey thought he shuddered. "Hey, I'm a bit late, and my dog will be wondering where I am. I just stopped 'cause folks said you wanted me."

Audrey watched the Nordic God climb back in his red mustang and drive too fast down the drive. She watched the trees sway from the force of his retreat as she backed into the house. She closed and locked the front door then shuffled to the living room.

She fanned her face. *I didn't know they made men that look like that.* She looked down at her dusty jeans and tee shirt and rolled her eyes. *Of course the first time he sees me, I'd have to be a mess.* She scowled. *Other people didn't help by telling him I wanted him to stop by. He probably didn't like being told to stop by as if the lady of the manor was summoning him. Mm, mmm, I'd like to do more than summon. He's easy on the eyes, for sure. He has got to have the most perfect body I've seen in a long time.*

She picked up her broom, swept down another dusty spider's nest and imagined looking her best when she stopped for dinner at the country club, and he'd just happen to be there. She'd smile and wave before asking to be seated at a table where she could see the lake. She'd pretend to be supremely uninterested while he couldn't take his eyes off of her. *Yes, that's how it would be.*

Audrey ignored Brad's comments on nobody locking and locked all her doors securely before she climbed the stairs to her room, propped her doll up in its rocking chair, patted its head and went to bed, leaving all six lights on.

Old Cedar twisted and turned in the dark. "I hear his truck again."

Mrs. Hemlock said, "Oh seed and root, that one is up to no good."

Old Cedar nodded, "Aye, he was always a bad sapling with his cutting and burning."

Mrs. Hemlock shook her branches, then poked and shook her husband who only pretended to be asleep. "That bad sapling is coming back. Do something."

The old hemlock said, "What do you want with me, woman. I'm rooted to the ground. I can't do much."

Young Cedar stood beside Old Hemlock. "I'll help." He whacked Old Hemlock hard with one of his biggest limbs and knocked a hemlock branch across the road.

The approaching truck slid to a stop.

Young Hemlock swayed to one side allowing the lights from the house to reach the

10

drive.

The truck backed out of the driveway.

The phone woke Audrey shortly after seven. "This is Jim from Atlas Moving. We'll be on the next boat. We have your address in our GPS."

"Cool, I'm going to park a green Studebaker out on the road at the end of the drive. The GPS is about five hundred feet off here. Look for the car."

Audrey ran out in her robe and slippers to move Grandpa's car. It wouldn't start. She poked around the garage and found a battery charger. Next, she sent a picture to Phil. "How do I start this car? I found the key and am charging the battery."

She poked and prodded at the old car. She ran in the house and dug her duct tape out of her sewing basket and read Phil's return email. She sent him a thank you and found the hammer in the kitchen junk drawer to whack the round coil thingy as instructed. As she worked, she wondered what to do with the car. *It isn't worth much, and I want to put my car in the garage. Would anybody even want to restore this? Nobody else in the family seems to want it.*

Audrey was still in her pajamas, slippers and robe with her hair standing on end when she parked the Studebaker, checked to see if it was completely off the road and started to walk back to the house.

A mustang convertible with the top up stopped beside her. Brad rolled down his window. "Are you okay?"

Audrey wondered why he only showed up when she looked a mess. "Oh sure, I'm just making room in my yard for the moving van. You told me there's nobody out here, so I thought I could do one little chore without anybody seeing me in my robe." She winced and tried to hide her greasy fingers from view. Scolding him might not be the best method for creating a good impression. "I need some coffee." She turned and marched briskly back toward her house, wishing the trees would swallow her up and hide her.

Mrs. Hemlock fluffed out her lower branches like skirts, hiding Audrey from view before she'd gotten around the bend in the drive.

The moving van arrived and two men unloaded the few pieces of furniture and boxes Audrey had needed in her four-hundred square foot LA apartment. She spent an hour directing the movers. "Set up my bed in the little bedroom over the porch. That's my sewing table. It goes in the big bedroom overlooking the water. Books go in the small room off the entry hall. Can you move the TV to the living room for me? That's not my dining set. Did you pick this up at Susan's?" She stroked the real wood table and wanted to do a happy dance. Susan sent some of her stuff.

By ten, the movers were gone again and Audrey faced the next major project-finding her way to Costco. She took her coat from the closet and thought about her disconnected battery cable. "This house and the garage need some serious deadbolts. I'll stop at a hardware store if I can find one."

Audrey was starving by the time she returned to the ferry dock with a car full of food, supplies, and a couple dozen light bulbs. Once in line for the ferry, she took a brisk walk back up the hill to the little restaurant. "Hi. I'm in line for the ferry. What can I get before it loads?"

The hostess said, "Half the people in here are getting something before the next boat. If you want to wait in the bar, we can get you some chowder or fish and chips to go."

"I'll take a pint of chowder if you can box it to go." Audrey peeked into the bar, hoping for an inconspicuous table in a corner.

A dozen men turned to look at her.

She ignored them and perched on the edge of a chair at a small table near the door.

A chubby man with a round baby face set his beer down on the table in front of her. "We don't bite." He pulled up a chair from another table. "You're Audrey."

She nodded.

"You look about the same. Hair is still red and curly. Remember me? I'm Bill Evans. I used to hang with your brother Chris every time he came out. We had great fun the summer he lived with your Grandpa. Say, I'm sorry for your loss. Grandpa Singer was a good man. Did a lot for the community and was better to his neighbors than some of them deserved."

Audrey broke into a smile. "I do remember you. You had the most amazing bicycle with a light and a bell and a back seat, and oh, I don't remember all."

Bill turned toward the bar. "Hey, did you guys hear that. She remembers my bicycle." He turned back to Audrey. "Yeah, that was something. Weighed a ton. After riding that as a little kid, I was the best football lineman our high school had ever seen. I went to Washington State on a football scholarship thanks to that thing."

"Once, I rode on the back of your bike all the way up to the lake."

"And you patched the hole in my pontoon boat with chewing gum, a paper clip, and a rubber band."

Audrey laughed, "That hole was at least five-eighths inches long. It was a good thing you had the paperclip in your pocket. How long did the patch last? We played on the lake all afternoon."

"I don't know. The boat's deck rotted out before I left for college, and the thing has been out of the water since. I'll have to turn it over and see if the patch is still there."

"You have got to be kidding."

"Nope, it never leaked again."

Bill's smile caused Audrey to laugh. "My brother will be thrilled to hear that I met you. Do you still live on the island?"

"Yeah, I built a house on our Lake Josephine property. My folks still have the farm. Don't have animals anymore, but they still cut and sell hay. I have a law practice in Lakewood. Hey, if there's anything I can do for you, let me know." He started to stand.

"Maybe you can help. Do you have any idea who's been taking care of the place since Grandpa got sick? I had an intruder my first night. No harm was done, but I didn't like someone coming in while I was there alone."

"Nobody's been officially watching the place. My dad said something about tire tracks in the drive and thought your dad had been there. Lock up good at night. You're a little isolated out there."

A waitress appeared with a tray covered in to-go boxes and bags. Audrey paid for her chowder, waved goodbye to Bill and returned to her car still smiling. Bill had always been kind. He used to take her in his boat when the boys went fishing. All her brother's other friends seemed eager to leave the little girl behind, but Bill included her.

After unloading her car and putting away most of her supplies, Audrey felt more than ready to sleep in her own dear bed set up in the smallest bedroom. "Bed, I missed you." She pulled her comforter up under her chin and sniffed its familiar scent of lavender and fabric softener.

As she slept secure in the small bedroom, a shaft of light appeared out on the water, casting a beam that traveled up the outside of the house and into the window of the big bedroom. The light shifted and wove its way across the room. As it neared the center of the back wall the amorphous beam took on the shape of a grotesquely distorted head with a long thin lower jaw and a large bulbous forehead. The light moved closer to the center of the wall and features of a human face coalesced as the head changed shape becoming more round, while the edges of the face still wavered and rippled, as it crept its way along the wall. Finally the face reached the center of the wall. The eyes glowed green, and the mouth opened wide as if to devour the soul of any living thing. The face slowly grew huge, covering four feet of the wall. The open maw in the face grew wider, a black hole in the eerie light. It might have been terrifying if anybody had been in the room to see it. A moment later, the whole apparition disappeared.

First thing the next morning, Audrey grabbed her camera and ran down to the beach, determined to capture the trailing fog and sunrise on the water. The tide was out beyond the rock shingle, exposing a few oysters in the mud. *I wonder if I can encourage more oysters to grow here?* She knelt where the barnacled rocks met the silt of the bay bottom and pointed her camera toward Olympia. *I wish I could see the mountain from here. I bet I can get a shot of the morning sun on the Olympics if I walk up to that point.* She turned north then glanced down to watch where her feet were going. A shallow, water-filled groove ran up the beach toward her house from where she stood. She stared at it and calculated how long ago a boat could have been hauled out of the water here. She followed the indentation until it ended just above the last high water mark. She squinted toward the house. "Oh ho, Mr. intruder, so this is how you come in. What do you want?"

She studied the house. The land sloped down toward the water so that the basement was ground level on this side. A deck off the living room on the upper level disguised the solid concrete basement wall. Double wood doors at one end of the basement could be opened where two rails ran down to the water for a boat ramp. Weeds and small trees between the rails indicated that it hadn't been used for years. She imagined launching a boat with Susan and Phil and how much fun they could have out on the water. She promised herself that she'd attend to the basement door and intruders later. Right now, she wanted to photograph the mountains because Susan and Phil had demanded pictures of their new home to be.

The basement door turned out to be discouraging. She was able to easily pull it open far enough to slip inside. The wood was so rotted, Audrey couldn't find a place solid enough to hold a nail if she had something to nail across the door to reinforce it. The basement smelled musty, and unidentifiable heaps of refuse or treasures huddled in the corners. The old sailboat didn't appear to be in much better shape than the rotted door. In the dim light from the open door, she scowled at the old washing machine sitting beside the stairs and noticed water stains on the floor around it. She didn't see an outlet for a clothes dryer and remembered Grandma hanging clothes in the basement to dry. Flipping the light switch did nothing. Squinting at the ceiling, she saw the one light socket was empty. She climbed the stairs to find a new light bulb.

She shuddered as she entered the main hall. There was absolutely nothing to stop an intruder from entering the house through the basement. She left her wet, sandy shoes at the top of the stairs and crossed the hall toward the kitchen. She stepped in something wet. Looking down, she found a smear of water under her stockinged foot. Where did that come from? Another wet spot closer to the front door still held the imprint of the bottom of a shoe. Audrey looked toward the stairs, then her eyes darted toward the living room and kitchen. She listened. She slipped silently into the kitchen, wondering where she'd left the knives. She found the hammer. Holding the hammer like a baseball bat, she puzzled for several minutes before deciding, *the intruder hasn't been violent before. Maybe I should take the car out and drive around for ten minutes to give him time to leave safely.*

Instead of getting her own car out of the garage, she started the old Studebaker and left the yard, making as much noise as possible. Her house was on a side road that formed a loop off of the main road, so after leaving the yard, she turned left to drive in a circle back to the house. She didn't see anybody until she reached the highway, where she saw Brad turning off in his mustang. She waved, then turned right and went on home. *Maybe I need to get a dog.* The house seemed empty when she returned, but she did a walk-through, carrying a big screwdriver with her because she couldn't find the hammer she'd been carrying earlier.

After replacing the basement light bulb and determining that the washing machine only leaked a little, Audrey decided to focus on reinforcing the door at the top of the stairs. She fetched the sack of deadbolts and latches out of the back of her car, then spent an hour installing the deadbolt. *It isn't the best deadbolt in the world, only big enough to go into the molding, but it might at least slow someone up.* Three feet up from the floor on each side of the door, she attached a small black box that contained the laser sensor from her garage door system. She'd spent more time than she liked modifying it with a bluetooth computer chip that would tie into her central control system. She'd installed a simple on/off switch to set the detector.

She descended to the basement door. Maybe a hook in the basement would deter her intruder even if the wood around the screws was mostly rotted. She drilled holes in the rotted wood, filled them with superglue, then put in the screws to hold the hook to the door. She wished for bolts, but she didn't find any among the odds and ends on Grandpa's workbench. More superglue and screws held boards across the door to keep the rotten thing from falling apart. After reinforcing the door, she spent another hour organizing things to her satisfaction in the basement. She felt grubby and sticky when she finished. *I'll tackle the washing machine in the morning.*

Feeling too tired to fix herself something to eat, Audrey showered, washed her hair and pulled on a silk pantsuit to take herself to dinner at the country club. She remembered her fantasies of encountering Brad when she was actually looking decent. *Nope. I only encounter Nordic Gods when I'm looking like something the cat dragged in.*

Audrey picked up a file folder on her way out the door, intending to stop by Bill's house before dinner.

Bill met Audrey when she pulled into the driveway of his contemporary-style house overlooking the small lake in the middle of the island. "What is this you said on the phone about embezzlement? Oh, come inside."

Audrey followed him inside. "You'll be able to see the whole thing from these papers. My mom's parents' attorney is working on the case since the trust was set up in Maryland where they live. There are copies of emails in here. Those aren't…um…legal. They can't be used in court, but we've used them to track where the money went."

Bill scowled at the file as he opened it and flipped through several pages. "What exactly do you want me to do with this?"

"Hold on to it. I've kept logs and detailed incidents other than the money thing."

Bill glanced over a few more pages. "Good God, Audrey. This just goes on and on. What's the matter with him?"

Audrey shrugged. Her voice wavered. "I think I remind him of Mom."

A muscle clenched in Bill's jaw as he turned toward Audrey. "I'm going to look this over. We should at least get a restraining order. Listen, I remember what people said after your mom…uh…after your mom died. If you have any trouble, promise me you will call me."

Audrey looked past Bill to the lake. "I don't want to impose, but those papers need to be someplace safe."

"You're not imposing. I've got your back on this." He tapped the file with his finger.

Audrey nodded and took herself out to dinner.

The restaurant was empty when Audrey arrived. "Hello? Are you open?" She peeked around the corner from the door into the bar area, which was just one wall of the garage sized restaurant.

A girlish voice from behind her said, "We're open. Are you here for dinner, or do you want to sit in the bar?"

"Dinner, please. May I sit by a window where I can see the lights on the lake?"

"It's kinda cold by the window. Will anybody be joining you?"

"No. By the way, I'm Audrey Singer. I just moved here from California."

Dropping Audrey's menu on a table by the window, the hostess/waitress/random belligerent adolescent/or whatever she was turned to walk away. "Oh, you're the gal that moved into that haunted house."

"I'm fairly certain it isn't haunted. It's been in the family since it was built and nobody has died there."

The waitress left, calling to someone Audrey couldn't see. "Cal, are you driving to the game next week?"

Audrey seated herself and picked up the menu, feeling slightly sorry for herself that there was absolutely nobody here to see her when she looked somewhat pretty. She read the limited menu and decided she might as well have the house hamburger if the special didn't sound good.

An older couple entered the restaurant. She looked up at the sound of voices, and the couple nodded at her, so she nodded back. Her dinner arrived to interrupt her enjoyment of the ducks on the lake. Before she'd organized her plate and cut her hamburger in half, a passably attractive man entered and sat nearby at the bar. *Too young,* Audrey thought. The lights in the restaurant were now brighter than the outside light so Audrey had to look through reflections of the room behind her to watch the ducks. She saw Brad before he saw her. She kept her head down so he would have the opportunity to see a presentable woman before he recognized her.

Audrey counted to thirty before she looked up to acknowledge Brad's presence. She blinked. He'd slid onto a high stool at the bar next to the younger man. He hadn't paused to admire her. She snorted at the silliness of her own thoughts, then choked on the water she'd just sipped. She looked back out the window, feeling slightly disappointed. *What is the matter with me? I've seen all sorts of attractive men in LA. I even stood next to George Clooney in the grocery store. Okay, Brad is right up there with the best of them when it comes to looks, but I don't know anything about him.*

"Miss Singer?"

Audrey looked up at a woman in her late seventies who wore polyester pants and an acrylic sweater. She wondered if people had access to real clothes in this remote corner of the world.

The woman had a pleasant enough smile. "Oh, I don't want to interrupt your dinner. I'm Alice Sanders. Your grandma Chloe was in my Bible study classes for years. I just wanted to say welcome to the island. We're the only Sanderses in the phone book. Feel free to call if you need anything."

"Thank you. Do you have a recommendation for a carpenter? I have a long list of minor repairs that I'd like to have completed before friends arrive." In the small, almost empty room, other diners couldn't help but overhear the conversation. Audrey wondered how long it would be before everybody on the island knew she wanted a carpenter.

"I'll send one of my grandsons over. They usually work off-island, but they'll be happy enough to have work that doesn't require commuting for a couple days."

"Thank you." As her neighbor returned to her own table, Audrey caught the waitress's eye and raised her hand slightly. She wanted to ask if the restaurant served dessert. After a hard day working she deserved a sweet treat, maybe cake. *Or, should I ask for pie and ice cream?*

Before the waitress made her way to Audrey's table, Brad came over and dropped into a chair. "That house is in good shape. What are you planning to do with it? I do odd jobs sometimes."

Audrey looked into Brad's impossibly blue eyes. *He wears blue contacts. How vain is that? Is he insecure?* She glanced at the waitress who was on the phone, then back to Brad. "The basement door is rotting out and some boards on the front porch need replacing. I want a chair rail in the dining room and to uncover the wood floors in what was the TV room. Just little stuff like that."

Brad twisted an extra napkin the waitress had left on the table, then shifted his weight and changed the subject. "Mrs. Sanders was my first and second grade teacher." He leaned back in his chair and crossed one knee over the other then uncrossed them. He glanced toward his friend at the bar.

Audrey turned in time to see Brad's friend nodding and making 'move on' motions with his hands. Was Brad trying to get the courage to ask her out? *Where do people go on dates here?* "Seems everybody knew my grandfather."

"Uh yeah, about your grandfather. He was real good to me." Brad paused and looked around the room then leaned forward. "Um…the thing is, I never knew my dad. People talked about me, or…well, my mom and your grandpa, but mom said…anyway, your hair is kinda red like mine. Do you think your Grandpa could be my dad?" Brad leaned back in the chair and avoided meeting Audrey's eyes.

Audrey blinked at Brad. The edges of a memory tickled her brain. An image of her mom yelling at her dad surfaced from the hidden recesses of her memory. "No. It wasn't Grandpa who…" Her mind went blank. She blinked again trying to find the elusive memories that seemed so clear a moment earlier. Gone.

The waitress hadn't come with a dessert menu, so Audrey stood, not sure why her knees wobbled and her gut twisted. "I'll see you later. I still have a day's worth of chores waiting at home." She shook her head to clear the cobwebs as she ran for her car.

Brad returned to his bar stool beside his best friend. "Well, I screwed that up. She looked like she'd seen a ghost. I shouldn't have blurted it out like that."

The maple at the crossroads shook his limbs. "She's on her way home."

The alders in the hollow swayed and asked, "Who?"

"The Singer girl. Pay attention."

The alders whispered and giggled among themselves.

Maple sent the message through his roots. "Danger, she's headed home, and he's following."

The willows didn't understand but passed the message through root and bough.

The fir grove picked up the message and sent it down the island on the breeze.

The trees in the clearing heard the message before Old Cedar said, "Aye, she's coming. I hear her car." The trees all fell silent, listening.

Mrs. Hemlock whispered, "Is that his truck I hear?"

Old Cedar swayed. "Aye, I can see her now, but the fool behind her is driving with his lights off."

Audrey parked in the garage and ran into her house locking the door behind her. She double-checked the locks on the kitchen window and basement door then went upstairs to change into jeans and a tee shirt. Her fingers shook as she unbuttoned her silk shirt. "Hello, Marianne. Did anybody come in while I was gone?"

The Cabbage Patch doll sitting on the bed answered, "Nobody entered the house while you were out."

Audrey went back downstairs and logged onto her computer. She shook her head and tried to remember what Brad had said that upset her. *He talked about his schoolteacher. Why would that be upsetting? I must be upset about him telling me the house would be cold with no carpets. No, I think I remember something about Mom."* She scowled as she tried to remember what happened. Her email started to download, so she shrugged. *Dr. Psycho said if I try to force memories they'll just go deeper and become more symbolic. Still, did Mom know Brad? It's like a hole.*

To: Audrey
From: Susan
Subject: Moving/News!!!!

First, I won't get there until this coming Saturday at the earliest. The stuff I'm sending UPS might get there Thursday or Friday. The pictures you sent look fantastic. Such a beautiful place to live.

Now, for the important stuff! The reason I will be delayed is that I just happen to have to stop at the Tesla headquarters on my way up!!!! Gary liked our electrical storage idea and thinks it might work. Phil and I will present the whole concept to them on Friday. I'll leave from there to drive up. I'm so nervous and excited I'm afraid I'll pee my pants.

Phil said your pictures look wonderful. He's stuck in his lease until Jan. first but hopes to be able to move in with us before Christmas.

Love you.

Audrey grinned and bounced in her chair, forgetting Brad's existence and anything to do with her dinner. *Yes. Tesla is a good enough client for our engineering firm.*

As Audrey imagined laughing with Susan and throwing great handfuls of money in the air, she heard a soft scratching sound and paused in rereading her email to listen. It could be waves on the beach or wind in the trees. She went back to savor her email. *Tesla.* Tears of joy filled her eyes. *Should I fly down and be in on the presentation? Would Elan Musk be there? I could drive back up with Susan.* A creak from below the living room window interrupted Audrey's fantasy of shaking hands and chatting knowledgeably with Tesla engineers. She listened, but all was quiet. She typed a reply full of exclamation points and smiley faces.

The distinct scuffle of cardboard boxes falling over startled Audrey as she was searching for the link to the ferry schedule to send Susan. She stood and tiptoed to the basement door. She listened and heard the swish of taffeta or was that just waves on the beach? She placed her hand on the doorknob, listening again. Finally, she turned the knob, still locked. *Good.* She pulled the door toward her, double-checking the security of the dead bolt. She checked the switch that turned on the laser sensor, then quietly grabbed her coat from the closet on her way to the front door. She paused and took inventory of her situation. *I have my phone and a good coat. Hopefully, the intruder will think I'm not home.*

She slid out the front door, locking it behind her. Her heart raced as her stomach turned over. Trusting the intruder to still be battling her defenses in the basement, she ran across the grass to the line of trees along the drive.

As she approached the trees, their branches swayed and parted. She ran for the darker shadow between the dark trees, hoping to find the place she remembered. She ducked under branches and around behind the Douglas Fir. She inched her way forward. Despite her fear, she smiled at the trees. She'd always loved these trees and imagined they each had their own personality. She parted the branches of the old hemlock and descended a short slope where a small, shallow stream ran under the driveway. Across the stream and up the other side, the trees were thickest here. She slipped and would have slid back into the cold water, but she instinctively threw out her hand and found a cedar branch to catch herself on. "Thanks," she whispered to the old tree. Using the cedar branch for support, she pulled herself up the small slope and felt the empty space before her with her hands as she inched forward in the dark.

The phone in her pocket pinged. Shielding the screen with her coat and the trunk of the cedar tree, she looked at the message. SOMEONE BROKE THROUGH THE BASEMENT DOOR. She whispered, "Marianne, turn on the TV." She put the phone back in her pocket and moved farther from the drive, guiding herself along the cedar branches and testing the ground with her toe before placing weight on her foot. The cedar branches came to an end. She felt for the hemlock. Taking a firm grip on the branch before her, she worked her way toward the trunk. She stepped on a dead branch that broke under her foot sounding like a gunshot in the quiet night. The branches above her rustled and swayed.

After what seemed like forever, but in real time could only have been a minute, she reached the trunk of the hemlock and pulled out her phone.

"Marianne, turn on the stereo." She should have turned on the stereo earlier to cover any sound she made. Maybe the TV was loud enough to cover the sound of her passing from limb to limb in the woods. She worked her way from the trunk of the hemlock toward its outer branches deeper in the woods.

The ground under her feet turned spongy. She knelt and touched the earth. Yes, here was the deep loam she remembered. She inched forward until a cedar branch brushed her face. She grabbed the cedar branch, using it for a guide. Remembering the hump of the rotted log beneath her, she felt her way with her feet and held onto a cedar branch beside her. Turning to face the branch, she edged sideways along the rotted log. Her life line soon rose above her reach, she lost her balance and fell, almost bouncing on the deep mulch under the cedar tree. Standing, she felt around her for the rotted log and the younger cedar at the base of the nurse log. She found a root wrapping around the rotted log. Yes, she knew where she was. Crouching down, she hoped she was still in range of the house. "Marianne, turn on the house lights."

Audrey slipped her phone back into her coat pocket and inched forward, crouching low to reach the tiny cave where the roots of the young cedar hid the hole where the old rotted tree once stood. Secure now, she pulled out her phone. "Marianne, show me what moves. A rough floor plan of her house appeared on the screen. A green dot moved quickly from the area of the front door toward the back of the house. As the dot moved around on the waterside of the house, Audrey guessed the intruder was in the master bedroom. She smiled and nodded. "Marianne, play the Indian drums."

The dot on the phone screen froze then moved slowly to one side of the screen, paused then moved to the other side of the screen. *He must be checking the side bedrooms.* Audrey wished her drawing was more accurate. The dot moved toward the center of the screen. "Marianne, say, 'Hello, nice man. Do you want to play with me?"

Audrey waited, wondering if she was out of command range. The dot didn't move. Audrey waited. The dot started to move. It disappeared off the top of the screen then appeared again moving fast toward the bottom of the screen. It paused at what Audrey guessed was the front door at the center bottom of the screen. She heard a crash as the front door of her house hit the wall. The dot still showed up on her screen. The screen scrolled, and the dot moved quickly toward the bottom. She heard footsteps on the front steps. The screen scrolled again, and the dot continued down the screen again. In the quiet night, footsteps crunched on gravel. *Hm, I should tell Susan that our range may be too big to be practical in the city?* She watched her screen as she contemplated how to set limits on the motion detectors. *Perhaps commercial motion detectors would come with a range.*

The dot continued to move. Audrey's stomach rolled over. The dot was coming toward her. Did he know about her secret hiding place? Had he found it the same as she had? Had someone told him she had a secret cave in the woods. She watched the screen with the dot coming toward her. He would be very angry at her tricks. Could he find her? More green showed up on her screen. Tree limbs swayed causing green lines to flicker around the edges of the screen.

Old Cedar shook his head. "Hide her. He's coming this way."
Mrs. Hemlock said, "I think he's just running away from the house."
Old Hemlock shook a limb at her. "Think, woman, he'll be back if we don't do something now. He won't leave her alone."
Doug Fir spread his branches and swayed. "Stand back, everybody. I've got this."
He swayed backward. "Watch."

Audrey watched her phone. The green dot moved toward the bottom of the screen. A mass of green appeared in the upper right hand corner of the screen. The crack of splintering wood and the crashing of tree limbs rent the night. The big green blob fell down the screen obscuring the green dot. The screen went blank.

Doug Fir stood up straight. "Ah, that feels much lighter. My roots feel like they can think again without all that top-weight pressing down."
Mrs. Hemlock reached out a branch and touched the broken stump where Doug Fir's top third had been. "Does it hurt?"
"Not at all. It's the way of my kind. We have to lose some weight now and then."
Old Cedar leaned over to examine the pile of branches and splintered wood. "Good shot. You got him square."

Audrey shoved her phone back in her pocket as she crouched under the cedar and wondered what to do. The cold seeped through the soles of her shoes and up her legs. She got a cramp in her calf. *I need to stand. Nobody can see me here.* She grasped the woven roots at the entrance to her cave to keep her balance while she eased out of her hole. Her fingers met something glassy smooth wedged between the roots. She braced herself against the roots and stood to stomp her feet. She fingered the odd, smooth stone and listened to the noises of the night. The trees whispered above her, but nothing stirred along her drive.

Well, what now? Do I try to go back to the house? Should I check on whoever is under the tree? What if the intruder is just standing in the dark waiting for me to come out? If it's who I think it is, he would wait. She shuddered and rubbed at the smooth stone stuck in the tree roots.

Curiosity overcame her caution, so she pulled her phone out of her pocket. Shielding the phone's light with her coat, she held it down close to the smooth stone. The light lit a piece of red glass. Audrey played her light around the little hollow right at the base of the tree. She found some fluff and a few synthetic fibers. She pried the red heart out from where it lodged in the roots. Memories flooded back. She felt again the lump filling her throat when she handed the bear back to Bill. "Daddy says I can't keep a gift from a boy."

"It isn't a boyfriend gift. It's just a friend gift, because your mom was killed, and your Dad's been…um…gone."

Audrey remembered the summer after Mom died. Hiding had been her lesson that summer. She'd hidden the bear in her room until she could bring it to her hiding place in the woods. She'd set it in the hollow above the cave. "Stay here in the woods where bears belong."

She glanced at the road. *I can't hide anymore. I can't live like this.* She glanced down at her phone and scrolled through the contacts, until she found the one friend who hadn't lied or pretended. She hit dial and hoped Bill would pick up on the other end. "Hi Audrey. What's up?"

"I don't know. I need help. I think. Someone may be hurt or dead, or they may just be standing in my driveway waiting for me to show myself," she whispered into the phone hoping nobody heard her.

"Stay where you are. I'll send help and be there as soon as I can get there." He disconnected, so Audrey crouched down below the tree roots again.

She waited maybe five minutes before she saw car lights in the trees overhead and heard a car pull off the road causing loose gravel to ping against its bottom. The car stopped. In the quiet night she thought she heard an engine idling not too far away. A car door opened. "What the hell? Oh my God. Oh my God."

Brad? What was Brad doing here? Audrey shuddered. *Brad. Mom yelled at Daddy about That Woman. Yes. Mom said she was leaving, and Daddy could have his piece of fluff and her poor son.*

Above her, on the drive, the car door slammed again, and the car reversed out to the paved road. Audrey could still see its lights in the treetops. She waited. More cars came. She watched almost hypnotized as the red and blue lights reflected off the tree trunks above her. She felt cold and just wanted to curl up and sleep. She tried to get comfortable in her cave as she held the little red heart in her hand.

Finally, Bill's voice drifted down to her hiding place. "Audrey? Audrey, can you hear me? Come out now. It's safe. Come on out."

Brad's voice joined Bill's. "I checked the house and garage. Her car's in there. Somebody definitely broke through the basement door. The house is a mess. You think she's inside?"

"No. She called me. Audrey! Audrey where are you?"

"I'm here, under the young cedar. Can you hold up a light so I can find you?"

Audrey heard crashing as tree limbs snapped and crunched under heavy footfalls. She slipped the red heart in her pocket, then tried to climb out of the hole where she'd been hiding. *This was easier when I was six. I was six that summer, wasn't I. Why did Daddy think a six year-old wouldn't understand or remember?* She hauled herself up on top of the old rotted log. *He did his best to make me believe my memories were just make-believe. That was his word, Make-Believe.* Her lip curled. *"How could anybody forget watching their father murder their mother?"*

Within minutes, Bill reached the cedar tree and lifted his arms up to help Audrey down from the nurse log. "There you are. Are you sure you're okay? Do you know who is up there on the road?"

"I think so. Did the tree get him?"

"Yeah, it's bad. Are you going to be okay with that?"

Audrey sobbed and leaned on the person who had been kindest to her when she was terrified before. "Bill, I was in the back seat of the car when he ran mom down." Audrey continued to lean against Bill. "He tried to make me forget. He told me lies. I've been afraid of him all my life."

Brad stood at the side of the drive and pushed tree limbs aside to clear Audrey's path. "The sheriff is here. Come on. Let's get her inside. Uh. Audrey don't look."

She sniffed, "Maybe I'll feel better if I see he's really gone. You have no idea how frightened I've been almost all my life. How I've hidden everything from him. When I was young, he called my teachers and my friends parents and told them I told lies and not to believe me. I never told him that I went to college or that I have a masters degree from Cal Tech." She scowled at the mess of fir limbs blocking the drive.

"Miss Singer, can we get a statement from you." A county sheriff stepped between Audrey and Brad.

Audrey sidestepped the sheriff and continued stumbling on numb feet toward the house. She stepped over a large limb and shuffled forward on a bed of broken branches. She glanced down when she passed the trunk of the broken fir in the drive. Her father's face was fully recognizable, resting in a nest of fir boughs. She scowled thinking he didn't look dead enough, then saw his legs and an arm sticking out from under the tree trunk ten feet from his head. She glanced away and covered her face with one hand. *I guess that's dead enough.*

Bill stepped between Audrey and the sheriff who attempted to follow her. "I'm Miss Singer's attorney. She'll give you a statement, but she's in shock. It's pretty obvious that this is an accident."

Audrey half turned, "I have to get warm, and someone should call my brother." She fished in her pocket for her phone. "Marianne, turn on the yard lights."

Bright lights on the porch roof lit up the clearing, and strings of Christmas lights shed enough light on the drive that she could see her way to the house.

Brad looked at Bill. "Who's Marianne? I didn't see anybody when I checked the house." His eyes darted around the clearing.

Bill shrugged and kept close to Audrey in case she tripped again or fainted or something, and he'd need to catch her.

Fortified with hot cocoa and a blanket, Audrey sat on her sofa with Bill beside her. Brad sat on the floor at her feet as she told the sheriff her story. "Basically, he ran out of the house and down the driveway. The tree broke and fell on him. That's all there is to know about that."

She sipped her cocoa and stared into the empty fireplace. "He murdered my mother. Every body said Chris and I spent that summer here because he was working in Saudi Arabia. When I was about nine I wanted to read about Mom's passing in the paper, so I looked it up at the library. That's when I found out he served ninety days for involuntary manslaughter. I guess we moved across country to escape the scandal." She stared at the wall then huffed out a breath. "He's been hanging around here since I moved in. I think he wanted to scare me off. He told the estate attorney he intended to have me declared incompetent."

Bill stroked down Audrey's hair that had frizzed in the night air. "No way could he do that."

Audrey snorted. "I graduated suma cum laude with my masters, so no, but he could make my life miserable. All this recent stuff with the threats and the lies is because he embezzled a quarter of a million dollars from a trust my mom's parents set up for me. My mom's brother was investigating that. Dad wanted to sell this house and use the money to hide the embezzlement. Would he have killed me?" She shrugged. "He killed mom because she was going to divorce him."

She glanced down at Brad, and her voice softened. "I heard my parents arguing after we came come from visiting Grandma and Grandpa. She'd discovered Dad had an affair and…" she paused. "Brad, um… to answer the question you asked at dinner, it was my father who…. Mom intended to divorce him because of the affair, and because he refused to support you. I remember your mom had lost her job, and you were sick or something. I guess people thought you were Grandpa's son because of the red hair, but anyway dad wasn't going to help your mom, so Grandpa did."

"You're my half-sister?" Brad looked up at Audrey with his eyebrows raised. "I never believed any of those…um…stories about Grandpa Singer until I saw you the other day. We have the same eyes."

Bill stroked Audrey's hand. "How long have you known all this?"

Audrey shrugged, "I knew about most of it as it happened. I went to counseling because I had nightmares about running over people with the car. Sometimes when driving I'd have to pull over and stop because I was afraid I'd hit people on the sidewalks. I guess I'd repressed most of my memories like the argument about his affair." I only just remembered that tonight." She swallowed, "Now, I remember seeing Mom's face as he drove into her." I had nightmares about that for years. Audrey looked at her fingers as a tear slid down her cheek. "Anyway, I was always afraid. I started hacking his email when I was ten. That's how I knew what he was saying about me and how I learned about the embezzlement." She blinked then sniffed. "It was like I was split in two, I pretended to be stupid when he was watching, I was smart when I was at school and away from home." She sighed and glanced sideways at Bill. "I wonder how much to tell Chris. He idolized dad and never knew any of this, but I do want to go after the money he stole from my trust."

Bill kissed Audrey on the temple. "Whatever you think is best."

"Knock it off Bill. That's my sister." Brad grinned. "I have a brother and a sister. How cool is that? Uh, I think. This is going to take some getting used to-not being an only child, but having family is good."

Delinda McCann is a mostly-retired social psychologist. During her professional career she worked with at risk youth and individuals with disabilities. Her research in the field of Fetal Alcohol Syndrome led her to become an advisor to several governments. To ease the stress created by working in the disabilities field, she took up gardening. Never one to do things in a small way, Delinda now runs a small farm and sells cut flowers. She writes general fiction based on her experience as a social psychologist. She has published five novels. She expresses her sense of humor in many of her short stories. She's also published numerous professional articles on Fetal Alcohol Syndrome and Youth At-Risk. The professional articles are rather academic and dry, but Delinda pulls what she knows about human behavior, disabilities and youth into her fiction.

You may purchase her books at:
http://www.amazon.com/s/ref=nb_sb_noss_1?url=search-alias%3Daps&field-keywords=Delinda+McCann

You may view her flowers, gardens and personal blog at:
http://delindalmccann.weebly.com/index.html

HERE & BEYOND LLC.

By Anna Shomsky

Having returned from Venice with a sense of unease about the dwindling novelty the earth had to offer, Borgan booked a ticket for a tour of the island of the hereafter. The bus, which would travel by ferry to the island of the land of the dead, was scheduled to leave in four days. Borgan began packing.

What does one wear in the afterlife? He brought a yellow rain parka and some Mardi Gras beads.

Borgan woke at three in the morning to drive to the ferry terminal, which doubled as an abandoned factory perched atop a stagnant inlet of the ocean. A ferry boat floated on the slurry.

A few people milled about in front of the squat, dreary building. Some took pictures of the defunct smokestacks. Something about the freshness of their polo shirts, the pleats on their khaki shorts, the bulkiness of their camera bags told him they were fellow tourists.

A woman wearing a vintage air stewardess uniform shoved a clipboard into his hands. "You're Borgan, correct?"

"Yes."

"You haven't signed the waiver."

The paper in Borgan's hands declared that he was aware of the dangers of entering the island of the hereafter, and, should he by accident or act of God find himself unable to leave the afterlife, neither he nor any beneficiary would sue Here & Beyond LLC. He signed.

The stewardess clicked her pen. She raised a bullhorn to her grey lips and called the tourists to attention. "In a matter of minutes, our bus will arrive. The portal to the hereafter is just beyond the chained doors of the abandoned factory. Please stand at least thirty feet away from the entrance."

The tourists shuffled in various directions until they'd cleared a swath of moonlit grass. The chains on the rusted door rattled, a revving came from within the derelict building, and a tour bus with a bent hood and two flat tires emerged from the ether.

The stewardess ushered the tourists into the bus. She pulled the microphone from beside the driver's seat. "Can everybody hear me? I'm Patricia, and I'll be your guide. This bus will be your home base for the next four days. Each day you'll have an excursion into an area of the hereafter, followed by a meal, then a night at a hotel. You will return to the bus in the morning. Do not be late."

A man in the back called out, "What if we're late?"

Patricia spoke heavily into the microphone. "Then you're late."

She covered the mic and whispered to the driver, a hunched, bearded man whose most prominent feature was a bulbous red nose, then returned to her charges. "We're about to depart. Please buckle your seat belts."

From the back of the bus, the man called out, "There aren't any seat belts."

The bus chugged onto the ferry. The boat disappeared into the space between molecules, where souls go when they slip out of matter.

It emerged a second later inside the factory, run aground on the dirt floor.

"You may now unfasten your seatbelts."

Out the window, Borgan saw the remains of the factory. Conveyor belts lay silent on rusty treads and empty hoppers loomed. In the far back, a single light illuminated a sign that read *gift shop*.

Patricia said, "We'll be entering the hereafter through the gift shop. You'll have ten minutes to browse. We'll then head to the Sorting Room."

Borgan browsed the gift shop. T-shirts and tunics, hastily folded, lay on a shelf. A few faded postcards sat idly on a spinning rack. He chose one that showed the ice fjords, which were on the itinerary for day two.

He approached the cashier, who was in a discussion with Patricia.

Patricia, tapping her clipboard, said, "You should have restocked."

"I've been working the till alone for thirty hours straight. I haven't had time."

"Were you not informed that a tour bus was coming through?"

"It was on the d-sheet, but Maurice didn't drop by with the schedule until a few minutes ago. We're understaffed."

"Don't I know. This is my fifth tour this month."

Borgan cleared his throat.

The cashier, without looking away from Patricia, rang up his postcard and told him to have a nice day.

She finally looked at Borgan as she handed him his receipt. "And be good, or you'll end up here again."

Back on the bus, Borgan asked the woman in the seat beside him,

"What did the cashier mean, that if I'm not good I'll be back there again?"

The woman held up her copy of the guide book. "All the staff in the hereafter are from purgatory. While they're waiting for their cases to be tried, they attempt to prove their merit."

She handed him the book. The cover portrayed two decorated Day of the Dead skeletons.

Borgan leafed through it, stopping to gaze at pictures of endless beaches with soft pink sand, of rolling hills, of forests and fern groves. "I take it the guidebook writers didn't visit any hells."

His neighbor tapped on a picture of a bustling city inside a massive tree stump. "All those places can be heaven or hell, depending on who's there with you."

Borgan skimmed the introduction, which welcomed mortal souls to the Island of the Hereafter, a place of many natural wonders that, some fifty millennia ago, bubbled out of the infinite sea where eons of cetacean souls have gone to rest.

The bus zipped through a tunnel, a deep black surrounded the windows, and the occasional white gash whizzed by. The bus stopped in front of a sand dune under a night sky. On top of the dune stood a shack with a crooked roof.

"We've arrived at the Sorting Room," announced Patricia into the microphone.

The tourists emptied from the bus, some complaining that the oppressive darkness made taking pictures untenable. "Shouldn't the afterlife be clouds and light?" one asked.

In the cramped Sorting Room, a pile of wet organs pulsed beside a gilded scale. Before it stood a woman in a blue nightgown. Her grey hair flowed around her ashen face. Borgan recognized her. She was an old neighbor of his, years ago. She'd once confronted him over something he'd found inconsequential, and he couldn't quite shake his disdain for her.

Anubis, his hawk face sullen, clawed the heart from her chest. He placed it on the scale, opposite a feather. The scale teetered.

"This," said Patricia, "Is the Sorting Room. Anubis here determines which afterlife to send people to."

Anubis turned his black eyes onto Patricia. "Been seeing a lot of you lately."

"We're understaffed."

Anubis smiled with his Jackal mouth. "Fancy that. Can't say I mind."

"Well I do."

"Purgatory must be rotten." Anubis watched the scale rhythmically rise and fall. "Doing the same job day after day. I can't imagine."

"I'm sure humanity will destroy itself soon and you'll be free of your godly burden."

"Yeah, but I'll have to do a lot of overtime right up to the end."

"Listen, I have twelve chits left for Valhalla Casino Night. If you can get me a reduced workload, they're yours."

Borgan focused on the scale, the way it bobbed up and down.

Anubis adjusted the heart, leaving his thumb on the scale a moment longer than necessary.

The scale ceased to bob, and the side holding the heart clunked down.

"So sorry, ma'am. Don't look so glum. Purgatory's not that bad. Just ask Patricia. She'll set you up with a job."

"But I'm a good person!"

"Was," corrected Anubis. "You can file an appeal if you'd like."

Borgan's old neighbor picked at the edge of the hole in her chest. "How long will that take?"

"Compared to how long you were alive or how much time you've got left?"

"Don't bother trying to answer," said Patricia. "It was a rhetorical question." She motioned for her goslings to turn around and scoot out the door.

Anubis called out, "Next!"

Borgan peeked over his shoulder as he exited the Sorting Room into the desert night. Two jackals escorted his neighbor through a back door.

The tour bus awaited. Once everyone was settled, the bus revved its engine and toodled over the sand dunes. The falling sensation made Borgan nauseous. He opened a window, and a scarab crawled in. It scuttled the length of the windowsill and hopped onto Borgan's shoulder, then up to his ear. It whispered.

The woman beside Borgan leaned over, her head practically touching his, and listened. "It's reading the Book of the Dead. Not all of it, just the relevant parts. The questions the dead are asked and the answers they should give. Illiterate people were buried with scarabs to help them manage in the afterlife."

"So It's a cheat sheet?"

"Pretty much. Must have missed its mark, though. I wonder what poor illiterate soul is on its own down here without it."

Borgan considered his former neighbor, unfairly judged. "The afterlife is more bureaucratic than I expected. I figured, without a body, the gods would read your soul."

"Even the gods can't communicate in pure ideas without some mediating language. And besides, what you do and say is who you are. There's no pure you underneath it all."

Borgan flicked the scarab away.

"I'm gonna take a nap before our next stop. Feel free to borrow my guide book." She passed the book over to Borgan. He leafed through it

30

briefly, then stuck it in his cargo pants pocket and rested his eyes.

Patricia spoke into the microphone. "We have a few more stops in the Intake Station, which is what the locals call this section of the afterlife. Next stop, ash extraction."

The bus halted in front of an oasis. Starlight twinkled on the water pooling around a spring that bubbled between palm trees.

The woman beside Borgan pointed. "That's a tributary of the River Styx."

The tourists spilled out of the bus and stood by the spring. In front of them was a concrete building, brutalist and blocky. A pump and a series of hoses siphoned water from the spring and directed it to the building.

"This is the Extraction Center," said Patricia. "It's where souls are brought out of ash. If you choose cremation as your final rite, this is where you'll enter the afterlife." She motioned toward the building, with its many inert smokestacks and boarded windows.

"Come, let's watch the magic happen." Patricia beckoned them with the controlled gestures of a flight attendant.

Their footfalls echoed as they entered the building. The only light came from a furnace, which sat under a tub of boiling water. Beside it, a man in a welding helmet studied an urn, kinking and unkinking a hose in brief intervals.

"To reconstitute a burnt soul, water from the spring is combined with the ashes," said Patricia. "Notice how the operator is controlling the amount of water? If he used too much water, the soul would end up as vapor, a ghost, if you will."

"Hey Erlik," Patricia called out. "When you gonna have a soul to show us?"

The operator removed his welding mask and wiped away the sweat that was dripping down his leathery blue skin, his piggish snout, and his tusks. "Just about done with this one." He replaced his mask and continued filling an urn with water.

A soothing sigh filled the room as a being emerged from the urn. The sigh was followed by a scream. All the tourists looked at Borgan.

"Mom!" Borgan called out. He ran forward, but Patricia stopped him.

"No interacting with the dead," she said.

"But that's my mother!"

"I gathered that. She can't hear you. If she could, you'd be dead too."

Borgan struggled against Patricia, reaching out his hands, flailing with his feet. "When did you die? How did you die?"

"Erlik, could you call for backup, please? I'm having trouble containing this guy."

Erlik slipped out of the light and crossed the cavernous room. He reemerged under a distant lamp, which hovered above a red telephone. He made a call, then returned.

The doors of the Extraction room flew open, and a host of security roared in. Among them was Borgan's old neighbor, standing toward the rear, hunkered and uncertain-looking.

"Take him back to the bus," Patricia ordered them. "And you," she said to the old neighbor, "report to me in the break room tonight after my shift. I want to get a jump on your paperwork so we can start your tour guide training early."

Security dragged Borgan to the bus and shoved him into his seat. Without a word of reproach, they left, vanishing into the dark.

The scarab scuttled along the bus seat in front of Borgan.

"Hey you, talking beetle, how do I speak with my mother?"

The scarab approached his ear and spoke.

Borgan sighed. "Of course you don't speak English."

The scarab walked back to the bus seat, then climbed up the wall. Borgan followed its movements until it reached the emergency exit in the ceiling.

Borgan piled suitcases and trunks atop each other until he could reach the exit. He twisted the door handle, and the hatch popped open. Out into the eternal night he fled. He hid in a shadow as the tourists emerged from the extraction room. Just after the last tourist had left, he scurried into the building, slipping through the door before it slammed shut.

"Hello?" he called out.

"Hello?" came his own voice as an echo.

"Mom?"

"Mom?"

A heavy hand fell on his shoulder and he jumped.

"Buddy," said Elkin, "I've finished with your mom and sent her on to processing and judgment. I've got a lot of work to do here. I've got an earthquake and a collapsed parking garage to deal with. If you don't mind, I'd appreciate it if you got back on your bus." He turned Borgan toward the exit.

Borgan left the building and stood outside, watching the taillights of the tour bus rise and fall as it scaled the dunes.

The tusked god had said his mother was being processed and judged. That must mean she was with Anubis. He'd just have to go back the way he'd come. Borgan looked around him. The desert was a uniform mass, dark, forbidding, and the stars weren't the ones he'd grown up with and gave no indication of which direction was north.

The scarab flew to Borgan, then landed on the tracks the bus had made.

"Smart little bug," said Borgan. He followed the tracks until the sand was too windswept to retain marks.

After an hour under the unmoving stars, Borgan's tummy rumbled. "I don't suppose the dead eat," he said. The scarab, perched on his shoulder, shook its rectangular head.

"I don't suppose they drink water, either?"

The scarab hopped up and waggled a feathery antenna in a direction perpendicular to Borgan's path.

Borgan turned a hard left and walked over a dune and down, where he found a hovel half-covered in sand, In front of the ramshackle mess of bricks, sticks, and shingles, was a barrel with a hose leading in through a broken window.

"When's the last time the afterlife got fixed up?" asked Borgan. "Has it always been such a dump?"

The scarab crawled down to Borgan's pocket, then back up to his shoulder.

Borgan felt in his pocket. "Oh, I still have that lady's book. I'm looking up *maintenance*. Says here that the hereafter is filled with the souls of the dead, so paradise is as good as the people who inhabit it. Says no one sees upkeep as a priority because it's not like anyone would die if a ceiling collapsed on them. Anyway, what's this building about?"

The scarab scuttled off his shoulder and onto a dusty plank. Borgan blew the dust away. The sign out front read *Break Room 12*.

"Index says that's on pages 89-90. Let's see. Ah. This is the break room for grim reapers. Apparently, there are millions of reapers, but they're all emanations of the same being, sharing their thoughts, memories, and feelings." He put the book back in his pocket. "Well that's convenient. One of them must have met my mother. That means all of them met her."

Borgan pushed open the saloon doors and entered the break room. A few reapers were throwing darts at a picture of Fidel Castro. The rest sat around in silence, drinking water.

One reaper regarded Borgan when he entered the room but returned to its glass. Borgan approached. "Excuse me, sir? Or maybe ma'am? Your grimness?"

The reaper looked up, her hood falling back to reveal a skull containing two eyes, one a ruby, one a swirling black hole.

"I...I was wondering if you could tell me about my mother."

The reaper took a sip of water. Finally she spoke, in a voice like paper crinkling. "Who was your mother?"

"Marybell Anderson."

"I've had a few of those. How did she die?"

"The thing is, I don't know. I just saw her in the Intake Station, and I was wondering what happened to her."

The reaper stroked her chin with a skeletal hand. "She may have fallen off a horse in 1847."

"Unlikely. She died within the last few days."

"Then it was either a heart attack or heartbreak."

"Can people really die of heartbreak?"

"People can die of anything."

"She lived in Wisconsin. Did one of the Marybells die in Wisconsin?"

"The heartbreak one. Was holding a postcard at the time. Had a bunch of gondolas on it. Said *wish you were here.*"

"I find it hard to believe that my postcard killed my mother."

"Yes, that would be ridiculous. It was your distance and lack of connection that did her in. Also she'd always wanted to go to Venice and was sad you didn't know that."

"How could I have known that?"

"She had two posters of Venice and a carnival mask hanging in the living room."

"Why didn't she just tell me she wanted to come with me?"

"I only knew her for a few brief minutes, but I'd guess she wanted you to figure it out yourself. She thought she'd raised you to be perceptive, thoughtful, and inclusive. The postcard just hammered it in that everything she thought she'd done right as a parent she'd done wrong."

Borgan shook his head. "She always was emotionally overindulgent."

"Also she had pneumonia."

"So I didn't kill her!"

"It's debatable." The grim reaper pushed her glass toward Borgan. "Anyway, the past is in the past. I've harvested thousands of souls since her death. You look thirsty."

Borgan took a long drink of water. "I was wondering, how can I find her?"

"Have you tried the Sorting Room?"

"That's where I'm headed."

"If that fails, just find the heaven that would best suit her particular tastes."

"She'd probably like the ice fjords." Borgan consulted his itinerary. He could visit the Sorting Room, then catch up with his bus at the hotel.

"I wish you the best of luck."

"Thanks."

"Hasta mañana." The reaper reclaimed her glass and drank. The water spilled down her jaw and onto the dusty floor.

Borgan left Break Room 12 and returned to the desert. The sky had a twilight glow, and little animal footprints zigzagged over the sand. He pulled out the guidebook. The first page folded out into a laminated map that resembled the courtesy map given out at the zoo. It depicted the entrance to the afterlife as a white gate floating atop a cloud beside a calm bay. From the gate, a path curved through the hereafter, broken up by various attractions, such as a pagoda labeled Tian and an ominous cloud called Sheol.

Borgan located Break Room 12 and plotted the shortest path, which passed conveniently through Valhalla. That ought to make for a story to tell the neighbors when he got home.

The sun, perched in a chariot, rose over the horizon. A bedraggled horse tugged on the yoke, and the sun made a halting progress across the sky. The charioteer lay slumped over his horse's behind, the whip in his slack hand tangled around the horse's hooves.

The sun's heat burned Borgan's balding head. He regretted leaving behind his luggage, especially his straw hat. Perhaps Valhalla would have a gift shop? They'd likely only sell caps with felt lightning bolts protruding from the sides. Borgan kicked at the sand.

The sun had made it to about ten o'clock when the horse laid down. With its hooves, the horse pushed its blinders over its eyes. No amount of prodding could convince the beast to move, so the charioteer curled up in the shade under the chariot and dozed.

During this interminable morning, Borgan arrived at Valhalla, a stucco castle flanked by neon lights that must have gleamed and flashed in the dark night, but looked sallow under the desert sun.

Borgan pushed open the faux-wood door and found himself in a casino. Directly in front of him stood a row of slot machines. They dinged and jingled invitingly. Borgan checked his pockets but found no coin to play with. He passed up the slot machines and approached a blackjack table.

The players turned to Borgan. He found himself being assessed by four sets of eyes. A striking young goddess appraised him with her pale green eyes. A fellow with mossy antlers and crooked, bandaged deer legs had the empty grey eyes of a gambler. An athletic god who was shirtless yet wearing a helmet shot Borgan an impatient look with his piercing blue eyes, which then dulled with a look of utter boredom. The dealer had red eyes to match his wild red hair.

"Cernunnos," said the dealer, "stop messing with your horns and choose."

"Hit me."

The dealer slapped a card in front of the Celtic god. "A nine. Too bad." He scooped up Cernunnos's pile of coins.

"I swear you cheat," said Cernunnos.

"And yet you play." He dealt a hand to the assembled players, plus one extra.

"Now you're just miscounting," said the young goddess, who had a pile of gleaming apples in front of her instead of coins.

"Not at all, Iduna. We have a guest."

Borgan fished in his pocket and pulled out a penny.

"Very well," said the dealer.

"Don't do it," said Iduna. "Mortals shouldn't play cards when Loki deals."

"Don't listen to her. She's just has a grudge against me."

Loki dealt Borgan a three face up and a card face down. "Well? Would you like another card?"

"I guess?"

Iduna leaned over to him and whispered, "Then you have to say 'hit me.'"

"Hit me."

Loki dropped a queen atop Borgan's cards.

Borgan flipped over his card to reveal a nine.

"Such a shame," said Loki.

"Well, thanks for the game."

"Going so soon? Stay and see how it plays out. Find out who'll go home with your coin."

"I really ought to go find my mom."

"The oldest excuse in the book," said Loki. "It's not that you don't want to play with us. It's just that your mommy's calling you." He pouted theatrically.

Borgan sat. He watched as each player lost to the dealer.

"Another round?" Asked Loki as Borgan stood.

"Sorry, I don't have any more coins."

Loki flipped a coin in the air. At its apex, he blew on it, and it floated down and landed in Borgan's hand. "Now you do."

Iduna whispered to Borgan, "Don't accept gifts from Loki."

"It's all for fun," said the dealer. He dropped two cards in front of Borgan, one face down and one face up, a one-eyed Jack.

"That's lucky," said Cernunnos.

"Bloke's probably got a four face down," said the shirtless god. He tossed a coin onto the table.

Borgan peeked at his face down card. It was the ace of hearts. He dropped his coin onto the table. "I'm good."

Loki said, "And what about you, Cernunnos? You've got a five showing."

"Hit me."

Loki flipped a card in the air. It turned end over end nineteen times and landed face up atop the five.

"Twenty two," said Cernunnos. He pushed his cards away as if they were a plate of spaghetti and he was full. "I swear you cheat."

Loki cupped his chin in his hands and rested his elbows on the table. "And my fair Iduna with the nine? What will you do?"

"I think I'll keep my apples and drop out of this round."

"A shame. And you, Thor?"

The shirtless god rubbed his chin. "I should get back to work. I've gotta make a lightning storm at the ice fjords for a tour group. And all I've got are a four and a two." He flipped over his card and chucked a coin at Loki. "I'll win it back at backgammon." He nodded to Iduna and left.

"It's mortal against dealer," said Loki. "I wonder who will win?" He flipped over his cards. "Two kings."

"Twenty-one," said Borgan.

"Fancy that," said Cernunnos. "He let you win."

Loki pushed the pot of winnings to Borgan.

Borgan handed one coin to Loki and kept the rest. "Thanks for loaning me a coin. I best be off now."

"Come on, my mortal friend. The fun's just started. Where could you possibly need to be?"

"The Sorting Room."

"Then I'll likely see you around soon," said Loki. "I've told Anubis that we need more busboys around here."

"Oh, I'm not dead. I'm just visiting."

"Sure, sure." Loki waved a hand. "But everyone comes back eventually."

Borgan stood.

"Ta-ta!" called out Loki as Borgan left.

The blackjack tables gave way to poker and finally, at the back of the room, a bar. A barmaid leaned on the counter, polishing a glass. Best get something to drink when the opportunity struck. Who knew when he'd pass another break room. "Excuse me, ma'am?"

The barmaid looked up.

"May I have a glass of water?"

She turned around and filled the glass she'd been polishing with murky tap water.

Borgan gulped it down. "Do you sell anything to eat?"

The barmaid plucked a menu from behind a napkin holder and placed it in front of him. A variety of sandwiches were on offer, mostly made with elk meat, and a few potato dishes looked enticing.

Borgan pulled out his winnings. "What could I get with these?"

The barmaid pulled a bag of peanuts from a rack and chucked it at Borgan. She took one of his coins and dropped it in the till.

Borgan tore open the bag and ate handfuls of peanuts. His mouth full, he picked up his glass and waved it at the barmaid.

She refilled it.

Borgan washed down the peanut dust he'd licked from the bag. He then took a moment to inspect it. *Persephone's Peanuts* it read in the blue and white blocky font employed by Greek restaurants. He pocketed it to keep as a souvenir.

Around the corner from the bar was the exit. Borgan pushed on the metal door and landed back in the desert.

The horse and chariot trotted along, and the sun burned directly overhead.

Borgan consulted his map and followed the path toward his destination.

When the sun hung at two o'clock and the sky horse stopped to drink from a thin cloud, Borgan spotted the Sorting Room. He rushed to it.

Once inside, he hopped from foot to foot as Anubis placed a bloody heart on his scale. The feather across from it thunked down.

"Well done," said Anubis. "Take the second door. It leads to the Assessment Room where you'll be assigned an appropriate heaven."

Jackals escorted the new soul from the room as Anubis sprayed his scale with glass cleaner and wiped it with a rag.

"Next!" He cawed out.

"Excuse me," said Borgan. "If you don't mind a brief interruption, I was wondering if you'd seen my mother?"

Anubis glanced over at Borgan. "Who was she?"

"Marybelle Anderson."

"Just had her in this morning. Her heart's still in the pile."

Borgan glanced at the bleeding mess of organs in the corner of the room. He shuddered. "I was wondering where you sent her."

"Purgatory."

"And where's that?"

"All over the place."

"I mean, where can I find her?"

Anubis waved over his next customer and ripped out her heart as he addressed Borgan. "I sent her to work the galley on Charon's boat along the River Styx."

The heart on the scale teetered just below the feather.

"Thank you," said Borgan, and he backed away as the jackals descended on the newly deceased.

Once outside, he consulted his map. The River Styx meandered through the desert and drained into the ocean where, judging by the cartoonish drawing of a spout and tail fin, whale souls swam. A dock was located only a few miles from the Sorting Room. He folded the map and stuffed the guidebook in his pocket. The scarab, who'd been snoozing in the pocket, scurried out and perched on his shoulder.

"Well, my bug friend, soon you'll get to meet my mother."

Borgan walked in the direction of the sky horse. His face burned. He cast his eyes down, but the light glared off the sand. His head hurt. He wanted more water.

The sun dipped behind a dune, and Borgan sat to rest. He closed his eyes. Dreams bobbed in his head. Quick images floated into his attention and sank away. He remembered his mother and stood. He then opened his eyes to find he had only dreamed of standing. He stood again, then again found he'd only dreamed it. Why couldn't his mother come to him? She always had when he was a child. She'd wrap a blanket around him, pet his hair. He could smell her when she leaned down to kiss him, a scent that was almost sour.

Borgan opened his eyes and stood. He was sure that he was truly awake now. He could feel the sand under his feet. He crested the dune and there shone the sun again. The horse had picked up speed and was racing toward the horizon.

Borgan crossed another mile of desert, his shadow an elongated smudge behind him, until he came to the dock. Barnacles covered its pilings, and an algae bloom turned the water around it green. A familiar figure stood at the end of the dock skipping rocks. With each toss, a skeletal hand emerged from its black robe.

Borgan approached. "Has the ferry of the dead passed by yet?"

The figure turned to Borgan. Her ruby eye glowed in the setting sun, and the wisps of red light that emanated from it swirled into her balck hole eye and disappeared. "You're just in time." The grim reaper pointed at a shadow in the distance.

The river snaked in from the dark horizon, and on its flat surface a boat slowly sailed.

"Perfect. Will it dock here, or should I send out some sort of flare?"

"It'll dock."

Borgan sat down on the end of the dock and dangled his feet above the water. A light breeze cooled him. He pulled out his guidebook and consulted the index. "River Styx, page 37." He flipped to the page. "Says here Charon ferries souls to the afterlife. Once you make it through sorting, you get to ride his boat to the other half of the island of the dead. Ooh. And they serve wine. You have to pay him. He accepts all forms of Earthly currency. Well, that's convenient since I didn't bring any Euros."

The boat drew nearer, and Borgan stood. It was two stories tall, with an outside deck on the upper half and a white metal hull. Borgan waved at the souls on the deck; but none waved back. "Where's Mom?"

"Inside," said the grim reaper. "The wind just picked up. It's cold on the deck. And she's probably working her shift now."

The boat docked with a heavy thunk. An aged man, robed, with the weathered face of a sailor, disembarked. He tugged on a heavy rope and tied it to one of the pilings. He nodded at the grim reaper.

"Hello, Charon," said the reaper.

"Good evening. Love the robe. Is it new?"

"Arachne made it for me. Notice the embroidery around the wrist."

Charon leaned in and squinted. "A spider and web pattern. Subtle."

"One of my other avatars got a pink robe with a paisley collar and floral hem."

"I'm jealous. I keep asking her for a new robe, but she's so busy with reenactments."

"Yeah, it's been crazy these days."

"Tell me about it. I keep seeing flashes of light along the riverbank, and I think it's sailors drowning, but no, it's just camera flashes."

"Did you hear about Cernunnos?"

"The guy with the horns?"

"Yup. Got hit by a tour bus."

Charon shook his head. "Poor guy. How's he holding up?"

"He's been hanging out in Valhalla and gambling."

"Now that's a place that could use gentrification. They should send the tourists through there." Charon stretched and cracked his back. "Did I tell you I passed up a steamship the other day?'

"No way. I thought they were sticking to busses."

"They've added a cruise line."

The grim reaper sighed, and the scent of mothballs and mold wafted from her. "Anubis is gonna need a lighter feather if they think they're gonna send enough souls to purgatory to staff an entire steamboat."

"Anyway, who's this guy?" Charon stuck out a thumb in Borgan's direction.

"A hitchhiker. He's looking for his mom."

Borgan's voice cracked as he spoke. "Her name's Marybell Anderson. Is she on your boat?"

"Sure is. I'm taking her to the canals when she finishes her shift in the galley."

"Not the ice fjords?"

"She hates the cold. Said she wants to ride around in gondolas."

"Can I talk to her?"

Charon nodded. "Sure. Price of entry is any Earthly coin."

Borgan pulled his casino winnings from his pocket and handed them over.

"Sorry, those are underworld coins. Not valid fare."

"I had a penny earlier. Loki won it from me. These must be worth far more."

"Them's the rules. If you want on the boat, bring me a proper coin. Not some piece of chintz that's been soaking in Thor's palm sweat."

"There must be some way I can talk to my mother. Can she come out to meet me?"

"I suppose." Charon turned toward the boat and let out a call like an agitated crow. A crewman appeared on the bow. Charon yelled up to him. "Get Marybell out here, will ya?"

The crewman disappeared and returned with Borgan's mother. She wore a long white apron, and her hair flowed in the breeze.

"Mom," Borgan called out.

His mother cupped her hand to her ear.

"Mom!" He called even louder. "I love you."

"You too, son."

"I'm sorry."

His mom smiled. "Tell me about Venice."

Borgan told his mother about the hotel's dingy carpet, the trash floating in the canal, the gelato shop that ran out of ice cream.

"I enjoyed reading your postcard."

"How do you like working the galley?"

"I like stocking the pastry display and brewing the coffee, but the hours are long."

"Soon you'll be free of it," Borgan called out.

"So I hear. I'm just covering for Wendy while she goes to haunt her killer. We pick her up in the morning, and then I can go to heaven."

"My bus does the canals tomorrow. I'll come find you!"

"I'd love that."

Charon untethered the boat from the dock. "Sorry man, gotta get moving." He threw the rope onto his ferry with a flourish, stepped aboard, then turned to Borgan. "By the way, your breath smells like peanuts."

As Charon's ferry sailed away, Borgan's mom stood astern, waving until she disappeared into the night.

A fog horn sounded, despite the clear skies.

"Come," said the reaper. "You have an appointment with Hades."

"Will he help me get back to my bus?"

The reaper, had she a proper face, would have given Borgan a look of compassion. Instead, she clasped his arm. "There will be no meeting your bus."

"Then how do I get to the canals?" Borgan clutched at the reaper's robe. "What if I find Loki and get my coin back?"

The reaper twisted out of Borgan's grasp. "You heard Charon. You can't sail the River Styx."

"Then can I cross it? Is there a bridge?" Borgan pulled out his guidebook and flipped to the index. "There's gotta be a bridge."

"Borgan," said the reaper. "You're not crossing the river."

"But I promised my mother!"

"She'll understand."

"Maybe, but she'll still be upset. I don't want to ruin heaven for her by disappointing her on her first day."

The reaper shook her head. "You have other places you need to be."

"So you want me to get back to my bus?"

"Your bus is over the river now. You can't get to it."

Borgan looked out over the water, which had grown black as night fell. "How do I get back home?"

"My friend," said the reaper, "this is home now."

"Here? In this dump? Couldn't be."

"You've got mopping duty in Valhalla in two hours. And we still need to get you a uniform."

Borgan dropped to his knees. "I'll swim home."

"You'd swim for millennia until you grew tired and drowned. Then you'd land right back here."

The scarab scuttled off Borgan's shoulder and dug deep into his ear. It whispered the answers to the questions asked of wayward souls, gave instructions on how to get to heaven, but Borgan didn't understand.

Anna Venishnick Shomsky lives on Vashon Island with her husband, two daughters, dog, cat, and chickens. She has an MATESOL (Masters in Teaching English to Speakers of Other Languages) and has worked as an ESL teacher for twelve years. She wrote and produced the radio show Whispers of Vashon on 101.9 KVSH. Her writing has also appeared in Women on Writing and the Post Culture Podcast.

CL-CLUNK, CL-CLUNK, CLUNKY-CLUNK

By Marilyn Mosley

This original story appears in Island Dachshund Tails by Marilyn Cochran Mosley. This account was written by Moose II, although he was not one of her regular dachshund authors.

Marilyn over the years had two dachshunds named Moose with the first Moose being her original dachshund "author" in the "dachshund series". The second Moose never knew the first one as he was born much later, although they were half-brothers. Marilyn just ran out of names, or maybe there was something about the second one that very much reminded her of the original one. It certainly wasn't his size as the first Moose got his name because of being larger than the rest of the litter while Moose II was little, almost tiny as a matter of fact.

I'm probably the smallest Moose you'll ever see, and was almost the smallest in my family of five dachshund brothers, but Charlie beat me in that department by almost a pound. He was the runt of the litter.

The winter before Marilyn built her log house she rented a small two-story summer cabin on Magnolia Beach two houses down from her friend's historical five-story home including the attic and named Marjesira. That's on Vashon Island, for those of you who have never heard of that beach. Even long-time residents of Vashon don't know where it is. At one time it had been a post office, general store, and overnight guest house. A long dock had extended out into Puget Sound but most of it has since been removed. Sometimes when we went over the house was a little spooky.

The cabin did not have any heat except for a fire place that had limited use by us. Marilyn didn't have any wood except a few sticks she had managed to find nearby. We were there in the cold part of the year. The wind came up the channel at times like you wouldn't believe. I shiver just thinking about it.

My three brothers were there with me as well as our two cats, Harrison and Tasha. My fourth brother Charlie had passed away while we were still in the old house on Burma Road from unknown causes.

When Marilyn was home from working in Alaska, she sometimes built a tiny fire, and I mean it was small. The cats curled up near the chimney for warmth as the bricks retained some heat. As for us, we slept with Marilyn in the big bed. When she wasn't there, all of us had to go back to camping on her new property where her house was to be built the following summer.

We had a big enclosed fence at that site with plenty of room to run and a two-room house of our own. The neighbor man brought over a metal garage door for a roof and put it on top of the two dog houses we had that made up our home. Marilyn had furnished it with lots of straw. She also hauled in an old down sleeping bag and put it into the bigger of the two rooms. The other one was our "dining" area as that's where meals were served. We were warmer there than in the summer beach house.

Back at the cabin we could watch the tide cover our beach from the front room, but more interestingly we could see one of the neighbor's cats. Oftentimes, Stormy, that's the name of the cat, came over to look at us through the porch windows while we looked out at him. He couldn't get in, and darn it all we couldn't get out.

Stormy would rub his tail along the window, and yawn right in our faces. I think he was looking for a free meal. Sometimes Marilyn would set some choice tidbits out for him. Oh, I wanted to go out on that porch with her when he was there. Stormy was definitely a temptation for me.

Our own two cats stayed high up on the mantle near the chimney. They didn't want any part of us. I can't imagine why. Now I didn't chase cats, at least, not while Marilyn was watching. Of course, my brothers didn't either, and I suspect for the same reason.

I think Stormy was lonely despite the fact he had his sister, named Coyote, living with him. Coyote never visited us. The two of them lived in the old historical home that belonged to Marilyn's friend Marian. It was winter time and the caretakers of the house were not there all the time. And Marian, of course, didn't return until the summer months.

Other critters lived in that house as well, and should have kept both cats well entertained. Besides the dog that stayed there, rats were sometimes in the walls of her house. There were rats in the cabin as well, but Marilyn didn't know about them until late March or the beginning of April. Land otters were also hidden under the porch. They kept well out of sight but brought in fish that rotted and left a distinct smell. I never saw them.

Sometimes I walked over with Marilyn to feed the two cats and dog when the people taking care of the house were gone for short trips. Marilyn had agreed she would do this when she wasn't in Alaska. The resident rats remained hidden particularly when we went over there. I can honestly say I never saw a rat on those visits, but my sniffer sure smelled them. I later learned that 38 rats were caught that winter. I mean, 38 rats, that's a well-established colony.

After all it was the "Year of the Rat". Some years are like that on Vashon. They liked to come indoors when the weather turned cold and wet. We dachshunds knew they were there, but then we would go to our "camp" and promptly forget about them while Marilyn was working up North. When she came home, it was back to the cabin and the smell of rat not only permeated the air but quickly reminded us of what we had come to expect.

I'll never forget the first rat Marilyn saw in the cabin. It was causally walking across the living room floor between the windows and the kitchen door. Marilyn was reading a book with me curled up beside her. Its movement caught my eye the same time Marilyn saw it. Her book fell at the instant I leaped stretched out in a running stance when I landed on the carpet. The rat, however, went into a full flight mode and through the door before my feet even touched the floor.

Marilyn followed me into the kitchen. We both searched around. I sniffed here and there, and smelled the rat but it had been here many times before so it was impossible to track it. "Moose, where is it?" Marilyn looked at me expectantly.

I didn't know. The trail led all over the kitchen, up on the table, over the counters, just all over everywhere. The scent was fresh. I knew that rodent had been here before, or at least, one of his relatives had been. Marilyn opened the door under the kitchen sink half expecting it to dart out. I was poised. Nope, no rat! She pulled the refrigerator out a little way. I was on the ready. Nope, no rat! She opened more drawers. I was right there. Nope, still no rat!

Humph! I was disappointed as we returned to the living room. Harrison's eyes were shut tight; he was all but snoring. As for Tasha, she looked down at the two of us from her comfortable perch on the mantle and yawned. Outside I could see Stormy at the window wanting to get in. Yes, he had seen it. His tail swished across the glass. His eyes glowed amber. He raised a paw and scratched on the window's surface. He had definitely seen it, I just knew it. As for my brothers, they stood up, stretched and went back to sleep.

I thought about it. I'll bet Stormy would be fun to play with. He was bigger than I was, but that didn't stop me. Maybe, just maybe, we could hunt that rat together. But Marilyn didn't see it that way. She didn't open the porch door. Too bad!

Marilyn then checked around the kitchen and found a number of rat droppings here and there, a sure sign that more than one rat was in residence. She also found some of their little calling cards behind the couch and under a table in the living room. Yep! They had been there all right.

The "they" rather than "one" was confirmed the next time we saw a live one as it had multiplied into two of them and both of them darted through the room. It was a re-run of the previous scenario except my brothers joined the chase. They soon lost interest, however, when both rats disappeared.

I stuck it out and stood right by Marilyn. I could tell that she was getting a bit worried. "Oh dear, Moose, guess I better let the owners know. We have to be out of here by early May and they should know. After all, they might get the wrong idea if they find rats here."

Marilyn called the next day and told the woman that she had seen a couple of rats.

"Oh my gosh! I'll call the exterminators!" was her immediate response. She all but lost it when she heard Marilyn's news.

I guess she didn't understand the ramifications of living on a beach particularly during a rat-infested winter.

We went back to our camp the next day and Marilyn returned to Alaska for a couple of weeks. The exterminators came while we were gone according to the owners. Our return to the cabin should be rat free, or at least, that is what we were led to believe.

Hmmmm! I wandered around the house. Then I went upstairs. Ah, ha! There was a big fat one right under one of the beds. It didn't move, but I attacked it anyway. I found it was attached to a piece of board with a spring on it. The combination of rat and trap didn't fit into my mouth easily. I didn't care. I grabbed it the best I could and headed for the stairs.

Cl-clunk, cl-clunk, clunky clunk, cl-clunk down the stairs I went. A cl-clunk punctuated each step I took as the back of the trap holding the rat hit the riser! I could hardly wait to show Marilyn my rat. I had caught it. I was now a successful hunter. I knew she would be proud of me. Cl-clunk, cl-clunk, cl-clunk, clunky clunk! Of course, it was very dead. I made it down the entire staircase to the last step where she met me. She had heard the noise. Her eyes were laughing when she saw me.

The exterminators had set rat traps around the house. Marilyn wasn't terribly impressed by them as she could have set rat traps for a lot less than the $250 plus fee the owners had paid. She was, however, most impressed by me. "Oh, Moose, you got the rat. Good for you." She was smiling as she gingerly picked it up.

As for Stormy, who was watching Marilyn remove the rat from the trap, walk out onto the porch then toss it onto the beach for a meal for the gulls, he gave me a big "paws up".

Dr. Marilyn Cochran Mosley is a retired educational psychologist and has worked with children and young adults since 1973. Prior to her career in school psychology she had been a counselor at the college level both at the University of Washington in Seattle and Grinnell College in Grinnell, Iowa. She then returned to Seattle to complete her formal education and began working in the public school system in Washington and later in Alaska. She commuted from Alaska for 20 years before retiring in 2007. During that time she was married in 1975 to O. A. (Bob) Mosley until he passed away in 1995. They adopted two pre-teenage children from Peru in 1986.

Marilyn is a third generation Oregonian. She grew up in the Pacific Northwest, and has traveled extensively throughout the world, including a trip in a single-engine 1948 Beechcraft Bonanza between London, England, and Brisbane, Australia, in the World Vintage Air Rally in 1990 flying on to Papua New Guinea and Guam. She and her seven dachshunds live on Vashon Island in Washington. Her son and daughter live in nearby West Seattle.

Outside her professional life, Marilyn is an avid photographer, and loves animals and the outdoors. She also enjoys gardening and baking. She writes for fun, and has held both a scuba diver's certificate and a private pilot's license.

WATER, WIND AND WHISPERS

By Melissa McCann

Waves chopped the sides of the little boat trundling across the waters of the lower Puget Sound. The motor chugged, and the mast and sail lay folded snugly and secured along the inside of the right hand side of the boat. Crystal could never remember which was port or the other one—starboard. There hadn't been time to put up the mast and raise the sail, so she'd just started the motor and steered out of the harbor toward the west.

She squeezed the backpack resting on the floor between her feet and smiled to herself. A jab of pain made her wince. She probed her bruised cheekbone and the swelling around her eye, finding the crust where Bryson's ring had caught her. Well, he was going to be sorry. She snickered, careful not to move her face too much.

The wind had gotten stronger as the sun got lower. Thick purple-grey clouds were making everything darker than it should be a few hours before night except for a light strip right on the horizon where the clouds ended. It would be totally dark before she got to the other side, and the boat was starting to toss.

Crystal tried to turn the front of the boat toward the waves at an angle. You were supposed to do that, weren't you? If they came at you straight from the side, they'd sink you. The boat was supposed to be unsinkable. It had something to do with foam in the walls or the hull or something. That's what Bryson said, but she hadn't been paying attention. She liked going sailing, or just putting around with him in the tiny boat, but she'd rather lie across the seat and dangle her hand in the water than listen to him talk about bows and keels and tacks and whatever.

She kind of wished now that she'd paid attention. If she turned the boat into the waves, wouldn't that mean she'd be going the wrong direction?

She'd planned to drive the boat right across and…well, she hadn't thought about how exactly she'd get to Mom's house. Hitchhike? It would be pitch dark by the time she got to the shore. Way to get yourself ax-murdered, Crystal. She'd pictured herself showing up, bragging about how she'd found out Bryson and his friends were making drugs and stolen his stash. She'd show Mom all the money and laugh about how screwed Bryson would be when his buddies found out.

The problem was she'd never thought about getting from her and Bryson's apartment to Mom's house. She'd thought of the boat, and it had seemed like such a great idea that she'd laughed with surprise. Bryson wouldn't think to check the marina, and by the time he did, she'd be long gone.

Now the waves were getting big and she had to turn toward the north, but that was no good, was it? The bridge and the narrows were north. The water went so fast under the bridge, could the little boat make it? Bryson had never taken the boat out of the bay. Maybe it wasn't big enough for the open water. She should have thought of that.

She rocked back and forth on the bench seat, trying to think what to do. The light halfway between evening and night made it hard to see clearly. The high hill of an island ahead and off to her left looked like a flat cutout against the yellow-white streak on the horizon. She remembered on sailing expeditions with Bryson seeing a couple cute little doll-sized islands from the shore. They probably had names, but nobody lived on them. Maybe if she could get there and around to the side away from the wind and waves, there'd be a quiet spot, wouldn't there?

She had to do something soon or the boat was going to sink. What would Mom think when Crystal didn't call her next Saturday? Nobody would ever know what had happened unless her body washed up on a beach somewhere.

The boat had to go at an angle to the waves to get to the island. She pushed the tiller in the direction she wanted to go. The boat swerved the opposite direction, and she yanked it back. She kept forgetting you had to steer backwards from the way you did in a car. But now she had turned the boat the right way, which made it rock from side to side. She jerked her foot against the bottom of the boat, unable to do anything to make it go faster and almost jumping in her seat every time the front went up over the top of a wave and slapped down again.

The strip of light from the horizon was getting in her eyes, making it hard to see ahead. As long as she kept the waves coming at her from the front corner of the boat, she would be going the right way, wouldn't she? Water kept slopping over the side of the boat and collecting in the bottom. She didn't know how she would get it out except for scooping it with her cupped hands. She realized she'd been making a little whining sound in her throat. The water around her feet got deeper. She thought she was going to have to stop and empty the boat anyway when suddenly the waves flattened out and she slid into a less bumpy and wavy spot.

The boat still rose and fell and bounced a little, but she must have come into the area behind the island, and she'd been right that it was smoother here. Now she could steer straight toward land right up the middle of the calmest spot.

It wasn't as easy as she'd pictured. The water kept pushing her to the side and trying to turn her around. The motor made little sput-sput sounds like it was running out of gas, and she'd started to whine in her throat again, but the black tower of the island kept getting closer until the waves started breaking close to the beach and pushing her toward land. She wanted to jump out and paddle to the shore, but she held on, rocking as if she could push the boat forward.

Something stuck up out of the water off on her left. She thought it was a rock at first, then she saw another one and realized it was a log sticking straight up. Of course. It was a post where somebody had built a dock a long time ago, and it had rotted or been washed away. She took a deep breath and sat up a little straighter. The posts went straight toward the beach. She could follow them right up to the beach.

Gravel ground and crunched under the boat, stopping it with a jerk, and a wave slopped over the back and soaked her jeans. The motor made a spitting sound and died. She wanted to jump out and run up the beach as far from the water as she could get, but without the boat, she would be stuck, so she wriggled out of the life vest and wrestled the backpack over her coat. She grabbed the rope tied to the front of the boat and waited for the next wave to come up, rattling gravel and shoving the boat a few inches farther up the beach. Then she jumped out and started pulling.

It took her a long time, and the strip of light at the horizon was turning red by the time she got the boat up the beach far enough that she wasn't afraid of it getting washed away if the tide got really high. She tied it up to a post, slogged up to the edge of the beach and dropped down on a big log left there by the high tide.

Now that she didn't have to worry about being drowned, Crystal clenched her hands tight between her knees to stop them from shaking. Her teeth chattered, and her legs shook so hard she wondered for a minute if it was an earthquake. She'd gotten wet, and the wind was still blowing around the side of the island, tugging her hair and sucking the heat out right through her coat. Why had she run out of the apartment in thin sneakers? Her feet were wet, and her toes felt gritty, like the sand had already gone through her socks.

It was all Bryson's fault. If she hadn't been so mad at him, she wouldn't have been yanking all his stupid, creepy bikini underpants out of the drawer and jamming them into the toilet, and she wouldn't have found the stack of hundred-dollar bills and the two big bags of pink crystals that now lay in the bottom of her backpack.

Crystal assumed it was drugs. She didn't actually know much about drugs, but she knew people talked about crystal meth, so bags of crystals hidden in a drawer with a lot of money must be meth, right? And sometimes Bryson would stop when they were going to a movie or something and make her stay in the car while he went into this crummy little falling-down house with a crummy little yard in a crummy little neighborhood. A couple of greasy, dirty-looking guys lived there, and once a big fat guy with a little round bald head like a baby had showed up and yelled at Bryson. Crystal had been too far away to hear with the car windows rolled up, but Bryson had been in a really mean mood when he came back to the car.

It was five years since she'd met Bryson at Skinny's Pizza and Beer. She'd thought he was kinda handsome at the other end of the bar with a bony face and a slouchy walk. Like a cowboy, she'd thought, and he'd bought her a pizza and a beer, so she'd gone home with him and sort of never left. She'd never even wondered what he did to make his money. Now that she thought about it, she probably should have, shouldn't she?

She wondered what baby-head guy would do when he found out Bryson had lost the drugs. She smirked. Suddenly, she felt a lot warmer.

Warmer, but not warm. True, Bryson would never find her here in a million years, but she was also stuck, at least until morning, and she didn't have food or water or even a blanket. She'd better see if she could find someplace better to curl up and wait. Her cell phone lit right up when she got it out of her pocket. Five bars and eighty-three percent on the battery. The clock said seven-thirty-six. Mom would be still up.

She typed in a text: Guess what island I'm on hint no bridge no ferry no dock and super teeny it's so cute!!! Send.

Then she squeaked at the thought that Bryson might call Mom and ask her where Crystal was. Quickly, she tapped: If Bryson calls don't tell him because I don't want him to find me I'll tell you why tomorrow it's super funny. She added three laughing emojis and hit send again.

Putting the phone back in her pocket, she stood and turned her back to the water, tipping her head up to study the island before her. She couldn't really see anything. The last bit of sunset was going out of the clear streak between the clouds and the horizon, and the bank and the trees above it were all shades of grey and black. But if there had been a dock, then there must have been a road or path somewhere, or else why have a dock, right? And if there was a road, there ought to be something at the other end, a house or a building or something, right? Which would be better than sitting here in the wind.

She dug out the phone again and climbed over drift logs to the bank where the trees hung over the beach with their roots showing. Exploring up and down the bank, she used the light from the screen to pick a way over the tilted trunks and fallen branches. Right where the line of pilings came up to the bank, there was a low spot where she could pull herself up by holding onto a branch.

When she could stand upright in a flat spot, she tried to see where she was by the light of the phone. It wasn't bright enough to see more than a little way, but the dock had come right up to this spot, so why shouldn't there be a road or a house or something straight ahead? So she went that way, struggling to get through the ferns and bushes that grew under the trees. After a few yards, the ground started to slope up. Pretty soon, Crystal was trying to climb up a steep pile of rocks and gravel that kept sliding under her feet and carrying her back two steps every time she took three. Finally, a big flat rock slid under her weight. Crystal landed hard on one knee and skinned the heel of her hand. Then all the rocks started sliding, and Crystal skidded down with them like a waterside. She managed to roll over on her back, then she hit a big rock with her tailbone and landed on the level ground at the bottom.

She sat for a second, clutching her backside and hissing through her teeth until the pain started to go down. Then she kicked a stone lying near her foot. She'd wasted all that time getting up the hill as far as she did, and now she had to start all over again.

Except now she thought about it, who would put a building at the top of a hill like that? Nobody could get up it. No, if anybody wanted to get farther back from the water, there'd be another way, wouldn't there? She just had to follow the line of the slope until she found it, right?

She pushed herself up to her feet and probed her butt for bruises, but it didn't feel like anything was broken. Instead of trying to go up the slope, she went along the side, using the phone to look for a place where there might have been a road. At first, she wasn't sure she had found one. The slope was almost as steep, but the trees and bushes grew on it, so it couldn't be rocks like the rest, could it?

So she tried going up between the trees, and the ground felt pretty hard, so it must be a road, right? It was like the roads on mountainsides with a steep wall on one side and a steep drop on the other. The ground dropped so steeply on that side, she could see out between the trees across the water to the lights on the shore.

Using the phone for light made her nervous. What if she used up the battery too soon and needed it later? She turned it off and stuck it in her jeans pocket and looked around. After a second, she could kind of see lighter grey spaces between trees, and as long as she could see the lights from the mainland between the trunks on her right, she couldn't walk right off a cliff, could she? She felt her way along, trying to see how far she could go before she had to take a look around by the light of the screen.

She started to feel smug again despite the cold and the dark. She was sure to find some kind of shelter to hole up until morning. Then she'd get back in the boat and go the rest of the way across to Mom's house. She had enough of Bryson's money to help out with rent and electricity and groceries and things until she got a job and her own place.

The money reminded her that she still had the two bags of pink crystals. She didn't know why she had taken them. She'd been crying and shaking after he walked out and hadn't really been thinking too clearly at the time. She supposed she should have flushed the stuff in the baggies down the toilet, but that had already been plugged up with Bryson's dumb underwear. Anyway, taking the stuff seemed more...personal. She imagined telling Bryson she had it. He'd be so pissed, and there wouldn't be anything he could do about it.

She chuckled. Even the pinch of her bruised face reminded her of what his drug-seller friends were going to do to him when they found out the drugs were gone.

The storm must have gotten stronger while she was on the sheltered side of the island because the wind beating the tops of the trees made a noise halfway between a roar and a whistle. Wood creaked all around her, popping and cracking as the trees bent back and forth in the wind. She paused in the partial shelter of a tilted tree trunk overhanging the path. She'd lost sight of the lights of the mainland and worried for a minute that she'd gotten turned around, then a spat of rain hit her cheek, and she realized there must be rain over the water thick enough to block the lights.

Weirdly, the lack of lights made the dark seem lighter. She must have gotten used to it. The rain looked thicker out over the water than it felt where she was. The trees must keep it out. As she watched, a knot of falling rain seem to twist in on itself and solidify, bending like a live thing to peer in through a gap in the trees in front of her. Crystal caught her breath, and a chill prickled her back.

She stood frozen for three heartbeats, then a harder gust blew the shape apart. Water pellets pecked her face in a blast of spray, making her duck and throw up her hand like it was broken glass coming at her. Then she shook herself and laughed. For a second, she'd imagined that the darker swirl of rain had been some kind of goblin thing that knew she was there. Mom would roll her eyes and shake her head when Crystal told her about it.

She stepped out of the half-shelter of her tree and resumed her uphill trudge. The rain came in spurts, hitting her from the side as much as from the sky. Maybe if she could find a big enough hollow under another one of the tilted tree trunks, it might be smarter to huddle there rather than hoping the road would lead to a house or something.

A low voice whispered something right behind Crystal's head. She turned with a yelp and a jump, slapped instinctively at whatever or whoever had come up behind her. She didn't feel anything, and nothing moved except the wind winding through the ferns.

She held her breath, listening for another whisper, but her pulse in her ears was almost louder than the rain. Failing that, she tried to remember what the voice had said, but either the mutter had been just nonsense sounds, or it had been too quiet to make out the actual words.

Her knees and hands shook. She wanted to run, but the voice had been behind her, between her and the water, so she couldn't run that way, could she? If she ran the other way, the voice would be behind her where she couldn't see it if it came after her.

No, that was silly. A voice couldn't chase her, and anyway, it hadn't really sounded like a voice. The whistle of the wind and and the popping and creaking trees had sounded for a second like somebody speaking, and a cold breeze had touched her neck at the same time as the sound. She took a breath and made her hands and shoulders relax. Don't be stupid, Crystal. She was just jumpy and imagining things. She was tired and cold and wet, and it was dark. Anybody would be hearing funny noises in the wind. She wasn't going to be afraid of a little weather.

Crystal turned her back on the moving ferns and went uphill. She stared into the dark with her eyes as wide as could make them. Her pupils felt heavy. She imagined they must be wide open to take in every bit of light they could to let her find her way between the bushes and avoid bashing her head on branches.

It was weird to be walking around in the middle of the woods. She'd always thought you must have to know something special to be one of those people who hiked around in the woods. Things like knowing what direction you were going by the moss on trees. Turns out it wasn't so hard. She couldn't see what the fuss was about.

She kept her ears open to the sound of the wind. As long as she listened, it couldn't sneak up on her, whispering things she couldn't exactly understand. Pine cones and little fir twigs hit her like rain. The ferns and bushes kept moving and swaying. She jumped every time she imagined seeing something out of the corner of her eye. It got harder and harder not to just bolt and run head first into some low branch.

Bursts of rain broke the sound of the wind into mutters and growls that sounded so much like words that Crystal couldn't completely stop the hair from standing up on the back of her neck.

She stumbled and puffed, rubbed water out of her eyes and stared into the black. It was getting darker. Maybe she should get her phone out again for light. She was still thinking about it when the road made a sharp turn and leveled out. The wind sounded different, and in a second, she figured out she was in a clearing. She thought the air looked a little lighter ahead, so she went a few steps forward with her hand out in front of her. There weren't any bushes or trees, but she couldn't tell much more. She'd about decided she'd better get out the phone when she walked right into something cold and rough and flat that felt way too big to be a tree.

She squeaked with surprise and relief. Then she laughed. Of course, if there was a road, it had to get someplace, and of course there would be a building at the end. The wall was rough, splintery boards that went up as high as she could reach. She felt along to the corner and worked her way down the other side. If she found a door, she could finally get out of the wind and rain and put her back against a corner where nothing could get at her without her seeing it.

Her hand came down on something sharp, and she jerked it back with a gasp. The pain came a moment later. She shook her hand, then put it to her mouth. She tasted blood in a deep gash.

It was one thing to save the phone battery, but a full battery wasn't any good if she didn't use it when she needed it. She reached across into her left jeans pocket to get the phone out. First, she turned on the screen and forced herself to open her shaking hand. The cut maybe wasn't as deep as she'd thought at first, but it went all the way across her palm, and the rain was washing blood off onto the ground. There wasn't anything to wrap it in, so she twisted the hem of her shirt around her hand and squeezed it in her fist. It hurt a little less, and maybe it would help stop it from bleeding so much.

She turned the light on the building. She'd put her hand right down on the spot where a window had been broken and a jagged piece of glass stuck up from the bottom of the frame. She'd probably get all kinds of infections. Lockjaw and gangrene, and there was that flesh-eating stuff that you couldn't cure, and they'd have to cut her arm off. Only blood was supposed to wash germs out of a cut, wasn't it? Maybe it was a good thing it was bleeding so much; her shirt was already starting to feel squishy.

She aimed the light through the window. At first, she didn't see anything, then she figured out she was looking at a heap of wood and shingles. Her heart sank. The roof must have fallen in a long time ago. It would probably be mossy and wet, and if there were any dry spots left, they'd be full of rats or something disgusting like that.

At least the light helped her to go a lot faster without tripping—which was good because walking half bent over her cut hand made it harder to avoid stumbling over rough ground. She rounded the next corner and found where the front door had been. It wasn't a door now, just a pile of cracked and broken wood on the dirt floor inside the cabin. Crystal took a wary step into the opening and played the light around the jumble of beams and boards. She still hoped to maybe find a corner or a nook where she could huddle up and moan. Her hand hurt more every minute, and that whine was back in her throat.

But no, even where the roof beams lay at an angle against the wall, it was still damp and cold-looking. She turned back toward the door, and her light shone on the wall beside the empty, open doorway. Someone had scratched something on the wall. She turned the light back that way and stepped over a spiky, shattered board to look closer at the marks. They had used a knife or something to scrape out, in rough block letters, In the wind.

Crystal squeaked and jumped, almost tripping over the board behind her before she caught her balance. Just what she needed, to fall on a broken board and stick herself through like a spear. It had been safer outside.

Except that the wind was out there. And whatever was in it.

She made herself take a breath even though it shook with the trembling in her stomach. It wasn't any good staying in the cabin. She should go back down and find herself one of those leaning trees with the dry hollows underneath where the rain couldn't get her.

Except that as she shone the light around the clearing around the cabin, she thought she saw a gap in the trees where the road kept on going up. She stood frozen with indecision. At least she knew there was some shelter back down the hill. Only now she thought about it, the tree hollows hadn't really been that big, and they wouldn't be warm at all. On the other hand, if the road kept going, there might be something up there with a real roof. She would at least be warmer if she kept walking. It wouldn't hurt to look and see if the road really did go on.

To get to the gap in trees, Crystal would have to cross the clearing where tall weeds jerked and waved in the wind. It would have been creepy even without the whispers and the rain-goblin thing she'd imagined before. Maybe she should try to explore the cabin some more. There might be at least a little corner she could squeeze into.

No, that was stupid. She straightened her shoulders. She wasn't going to be scared of some wind and rain. Stepping carefully over the broken pieces of the door, she took a deep breath to brace herself and run-walked across the clearing, ignoring the way the stalky plants dragged at her pants legs like water. It was lighter in the clearing than in underneath the trees, so she noticed when the weeds in front of her suddenly jerked and rippled. They swooshed in a wave as if there was a huge, invisible snake slithering toward her. Only it wasn't a snake. A dark spurt of rain had twisted itself together. That's what was rushing at her, spinning around like a top and blowing the weeds out of its way. It rose up over her, its top spreading out like it was going to crash over her like a wave.

In spite of herself, Crystal yelped and bolted into the trees and didn't stop running until the woods closed all around her and she could look back, panting, and not see the clearing or the cabin. She made her breathing slow down. What an idiot, jumping and running like a scared rabbit from something she couldn't even really see in the dark. She'd obviously made it all up and imagined it. She should kick herself. She'd done so good not letting herself go crazy up 'till now. She ought to go stomp her way back across the clearing and kick down all the weeds and bushes she could reach.

She shuddered. Well, that really wouldn't be any better than running away in the first place, would it? She'd still be getting all worked up over something she imagined. It would really be a stupid waste of time. After all, she was definitely on the road again. The trees hung over her on either side, but the path was pretty much clear straight ahead. The ground still slanted up, but not so steep, and it still curved a little, going around the top of the hill instead of straight up. Crystal waited until she was sure she wouldn't run like a scared cat, then faced the road and started walking again.

The sky flashed white, and Crystal jumped and scooted under the nearest tree and crouched at its foot. A second later, a boom shook the air and seemed to even make the trees shiver. Another flash lit up the woods, and Crystal realized she'd been spooked by nothing but lightning. The thunder came a second later and Crystal let out a deep huff of air. She actually liked lightning and thunder. It was like Fourth of July, only bigger and wilder and more exciting because you knew that lightning could kill you, but, of course, it wouldn't because you were usually inside a building, not outside in the rain under a tree near the top of a mountain. You weren't supposed to go under a tree when there was lightning, were you? Lightning could hit the tree. She jumped up and darted back out into the middle of the overgrown road.

The sky forked into white-hot bolts that seemed to walk across the clouds, followed by cannon booms of thunder. Crystal rubbed rain out of her eyes. At least the flashes gave her glimpses of the road ahead if she could remember what she saw in the millionth of a second. But the flashes were big enough and close enough that they made those funny black and white film negative pictures that stayed in your eyes for a while after the light went out. She could see a pretty clear picture actually, clear enough to see that the road was mostly clear except for a small tree fallen right across the way. Holding her unharmed hand out in front of her, Crystal went straight ahead, found the tree and stepped over. She chuckled. The lightning turned out to be lucky.

Another bolt, then a fork, lit up the road. After that, she never had to walk more than a yard or so before the light showed her a new picture. The thunder was coming right behind it, which meant it was really close, didn't it? You were supposed to count how many times you could say "pretty little pony," and that was how many miles away the lightning was. On the other hand, how often did people get hit by lightning anyway? And it would hit the trees first, so she was probably safe.

The wind switched to long, low hoots like an owl or a gigantic flute or something like that. At least it wasn't talking anymore, which was a big improvement. The lightning came so fast it was practically like walking across the floor in a club with a strobe light.

She had started to feel a little pleased with herself again when the road turned and opened up on a level place big enough to park a car. There weren't any of the big trees, but it wasn't a clearing like the one with the cabin. It was more like the flat spot by the water when she'd first climbed up off the beach. It was all rocks—a cliff about twenty feet high in front of her. Piles of broken rocks lay around like something somebody might have dug up and thrown aside. Whoever it was could have been digging for rocks for building maybe, but that seemed stupid. There were plenty of rocks on the mainland, and you'd have to put them on a boat and carry them away, so that didn't make any sense.

She risked stepping farther into the open, using the cloudlight and the lightning flash to study the cliff face that went up about twenty feet. Somebody must have come up here for something, or why else would they have the road? Why would they even come here at all?

Then another flash-boom lit up the ledge. She blinked, trying to figure out what she was seeing in the crazy white and black negative picture in her eyes. The only trees were bushes about twice as high as her head. She couldn't tell what kind they were. Mostly what she cared about was that they weren't big enough to keep the rain off. She had wasted all this time coming up here, and she'd have to go all the way back down past the cabin and the clearing and see if she could find a dry spot under a tree. She'd better go soon because the rain that whipped back and forth in the wind was starting to twist around in one of those whirlwind things that she'd seen in the clearing and further down when she'd first started to come up the road.

She was just about to turn around when another giant lightning bolt flickered across the sky and lit everything up, and she was looking exactly in the right spot to see a black opening in the cliff kind-of half behind a holly tree. The shape was too square not to be made on purpose. She couldn't go back without at least looking to see if she could use it to get out of the rain. She hitched her breath and ran toward the place where she had seen it. The whirlwind rushed at her, and she screamed and put up her arms to cover her face.

Rain slapped her, then the rain-goblin fell apart and she came up against the side of the opening and almost bashed her head on the top of the doorway before another flash came just in time to warn her to duck. She ran straight in and fetched up in a corner where she pressed her back into the angle between the rock wall and something that felt like wood. She slithered her butt to the floor and squeezed herself into the smallest ball she could and stayed there waiting for something to come in after her. Finally, her heart started to settle down. She'd really scared herself that time. She started to giggle and clapped her hand over her mouth to stop it because it felt like something crazy was going to come out, crying and screaming all at the same time, and she didn't know how she'd stop it if it did.

She took deep breaths until the giggle went away like a sneeze when you held your finger on your upper lip under your nose. When she could think about what was going on around her, the first thing she noticed was just the wonderful feeling of not being pecked on her head and face with icy wet raindrops that all seemed to have a speck of ice in the middle. Then she noticed the cold. It wasn't really any colder here inside the cave. It just felt that way now that she could forget about the rain itself and feel the wet. She was soaked from her shoes to her knees, wet hair sticking to her neck and cheeks, shoulders wet where rain had beat all the way through her canvas coat and its inner lining right through her shirt to her skin.

At least it was quieter here. The wind and the rain sounded dull and far away, and the holly tree at the opening kept the wind from getting in and throwing more rain at her. Even the thunder sounded quieter. It would be nice, though, to get even farther from the wind. That would serve it right. Except that, of course, it was just wind and wasn't really trying to get at her.

She peered deeper into the cave. It went back deeper than she could see even with the lightning that lit up the cave in flashes, so she got out her phone again.

The ceiling wasn't quite high enough for Crystal to stand upright, especially with the cross beams that held the ceiling every few steps, so she went bent over. The cave got narrower and started to slope down, and it was getting colder instead of warmer, and she couldn't see the end. With the supports every few feet, it was just like a mine in a movie. But nobody had mines around here, did they? What would anybody dig out of a mine around here?

Who cared? It wasn't any use to go wandering around underground. She'd go back and find a spot where the wind couldn't get her and stay there until morning. She was just about to turn around when her light flashed over a pile of rags and grey-white sticks. What would sticks be doing way down in a cave? But maybe she could make a fire. She aimed the light and let out a squeak. The sticks weren't firewood. They were bones, a little heap of hand or paw bones and the long bones of a front leg. She jumped back and was about to run squealing like a little rabbit when she remembered the wind and the lightning, and even if she had imagined the rain-goblin thing, it was still scarier than a skeleton.

She thought about leaving the skeleton there and going back up to the cave itself, but then she pictured the skeleton laying here behind her where she couldn't see it and maybe moving… Stupid. Skeletons didn't move.

They just laid there. Still, it would be less scary to see than to imagine. Maybe a bear had come in here to find a place to sleep and just died. That wouldn't be scary at all.

She shuffled toward the arm or leg…she liked to think of it as the leg of a bear. The light exposed more and more—the paw, the arm, then a tangle of rags that definitely wasn't fur, then something round with strands of long black hair trailing from it. Crystal caught her breath. Well, she wasn't that surprised, was she?

She squatted and duck-walked closer. The head wasn't clean and white like a plastic toy in a store. It was more grey and brown with strings of dry gristle around the wide-open jaw. The bony face gave her the creeps until she realized it was just because with the empty eye-holes like wide-open eyes, the open mouth made it look like it was screaming. She clicked her tongue in disgust. Being stupid again, Crystal.

The skeleton had on the dark rags of a shirt with a plaid pattern, but the rest of the body just kind-of faded into the dark, and she wasn't about to get close enough to check out what it was wearing like some kind of skeleton fashion show.

Her feet were only a few steps away from the hand where it lay on the rock floor. Crystal dropped her eyes from the skull, whose empty eye holes seemed to be staring at the wall, and saw something she had missed when she first saw the hand from yards away. The bones lay over the hilt of a knife. Crystal didn't know anything about knives, but this one was big and long, longer than her hand with a slightly curved blade about two fingers wide with a saw edge on the back. Beside the knife, a word had been scratched in the surface of the rock. Dirt had blown over it and caked on the letters, so Crystal had to twist her head and squint to read what the skeleton man had scratched in the floor before he died.

Below.

Crystal squealed and bolted for the opening of the cave. Just as she reached the mouth, a triple fork of lightning crossed the sky, and a moment later, a single spear hit so close her hair rose, and something exploded somewhere down the slope in front of her. She jumped back and scuttled for the nearest thing to a corner she could find, a thick beam against the wall. She pressed her back into the angle and squeezed herself into a ball, afraid of the lightning and the rain, afraid of the dead man and the word he had written before he died, afraid to move in any direction.

She stayed huddled in her corner for a while, panting and rocking and whimpering until she started to calm down a little and realize that nothing was coming to get her. The lightning still lit up the cave every once in a while, and there was still the boom of thunder, but it couldn't hurt her where she was. And the word by the skeleton was just a word. Below. What did that even mean?

She'd jerked her hand loose from the makeshift bandage she'd made out of the hem of her shirt when she panicked. Now it hurt again. She bit her lips and tried to wrap the end of her shirt back around it, but she couldn't find a dry, unbloody spot she could reach. She needed something to cut with. She wondered if she could somehow tear the thin, knit cotton with her teeth. Then she realized there was something just a few yards away that could cut the thin cloth.

She uncurled a little and peered into the dark at the back of the cave. Somewhere back there, the skeleton's hand was lying on the handle of the knife. How much did she really want it? Bad enough to go near the skeleton again? Her hand really hurt, and she felt blood running wet and sticky down her wrist.

She got up and crept toward the back of the cave where it narrowed into the tunnel. Her light showed the grey bones of the hand and arm and the dull-colored blade of the knife. She crouched and reached for the knife, ready to jump back at any moment. Not that she expected the skeleton to move. She really didn't. It was just that it was better to be careful, wasn't it? She pinched the sharp tip of the blade between two fingers and began to pull it toward her.

The fingers and wrist were stiff with dried gristle and didn't want to move, but the hand was only lying on the knife, not closed around it. She pulled it toward her with a weird, guilty feeling as if she were stealing from a grave.

She chuckled at a thought. She ought to give something back, shouldn't she? Like a trade. Or a payment. Leaving the knife on the floor at her feet, she struggled and squirmed to get her backpack off her shoulders. When she could finally pull it around in front of her, she unzipped the top and felt inside until she found the two big plastic baggies with the zipper tops.

Scootching closer to the ancient, bony hand, she laid the two baggies beside it, covering the strange word, Below. Then she slid the tip of the knife under the longest finger and carefully lifted it up. The hand and arm didn't want to bend at stiff joints, but Crystal wasn't about to touch the bones with her bare hand, so she would just have to work at it until she got it.

The hand slipped off the point of her knife twice before she could lift it and move it over far enough to lay it back down on top of the bags. There. If that didn't make the old miner or whatever he was happy, she didn't know what would.

Holding the hilt of her new knife, she scuttled back to her corner.

Giving away the drugs had raised her spirits, which was just as well considering that her hand was still hurting and bleeding, and even with the knife, she had a hard time cutting enough cloth out of her shirt and coat to make a good bandage. She had to pull the cloth taut with her teeth or pin it between her knee and elbow before she could cut, and every motion hurt her sore hand. In the end, she got a lot of sticky blood from her shirt onto the knife, but she managed to cut out some of the inner lining and the cotton insulation of her coat and tied it in a thick pad over her palm with a wide strip of unbloodied fabric from her shirt.

With pressure on the cut again, she felt good enough to lean back against the support post and pull her backpack into her lap. The baggies hadn't been very heavy, but without them, the backpack felt a lot lighter. There was only the bundle of money and her little blue leatherette purse that she'd chucked in as she was running out of the house. She'd been in too much of a hurry to stop and count the money.

She propped up her phone on her chest for light and began to count and sort. One...two...three...ten... Ten one-hundred dollar bills was a thousand dollars, wasn't it? She checked her math. That was right. She tucked the first thousand dollars into the zipper pocket of her purse and started counting the next bundle. Ten more hundred-dollar bills. That was two thousand. That was more than two months pay at any job Crystal had ever had. And there was still more money. A lot more.

When she'd counted and folded and secured the last bill into her purse, she had eight-thousand dollars. It was too much money to imagine. What could you even do with eight-thousand dollars? You couldn't just piddle it away on rent and food and stuff. It was the kind of money you had to spend on something important. On the other hand, you couldn't buy a new car or a house with it, either. So something in between.

Where had Bryson got it from? If he'd been selling drugs for as long as Crystal had known him—and now that she thought about it, she was pretty stupid not to have figured that out—he could have saved up a lot of money, couldn't he? Crystal snorted. Bryson couldn't save a nickle for a day. Someone might have loaned it to him, but again, he'd have already spent it. So he had to be holding it for someone, right? The baby-head guy she'd seen him fighting with at the meth house? Man, Bryson was going to be in so much trouble if he didn't get it back.

Which meant that Crystal might be in a little trouble herself. Bryson would want it back, but she wasn't too worried about Bryson. Baby-head, though, could maybe be a problem if Bryson told him Crystal had all the stuff. She chewed her lip. No way she was giving it back—not the money, which was hers now, and not the drugs, which were Mr. Skeleton Man's, and anyway she wasn't going to do anything that might help Bryson. It served him right if Baby-head beat him up or something. She touched the scabbed bruise beside her right eye. Anyway, she'd figure something out. Bryson wouldn't tell Baby-head right away. He'd want to see if he could get back the money and drugs himself first.

Crystal zipped and buckled the backpack and pulled it back over her shoulders. She squirmed around into the most comfortable position she could find against the post, pulled her sleeves down over her hands and propped her head on the post beside her, which was going to make her neck hurt, but she wasn't going to lie down in this cave even if the floor hadn't been icy cold rock. Not with the storm outside and Mr. Skeleton Man back there in the tunnel.

Clutching her knife in her unhurt hand, she let her eyelids droop almost shut, watching the cave mouth.

She should have been too scared to sleep no matter how tired she was, but she woke with a little gasp and jerk the way you did sometimes when you dreamed you were falling. The storm hadn't ended. In fact, it sounded closer and bigger. The scariest thing was that when she'd fallen asleep, she'd dropped the knife. She felt around under her hip and found the point first—she only pricked the tip of her index finger—and felt her way down the back of the blade to the hilt. She felt a lot better once she had it back in her hand.

She couldn't remember what had woken her up, whether it was a flash of lightning or an especially loud thunderclap. She listened, cocking her head and slitting her eyes to concentrate, but she heard nothing above the roar of rain and wind, muffled a little by the stonewalls of the cave. She settled back into the corner, determined not to sleep again but reasonably sure nothing could get to her here.

Something rattled behind her, and she squeaked. Something hard had rattled on rock. Not outside the cave but behind her in the tunnel. The sound of her jumping had almost drowned out the rain, and she tried to breathe as slowly and silently as possible for fear her own breathing would prevent her from hearing anything that might be moving deep in the tunnel.

Not that it was. Moving. It was true she hadn't looked very far down the tunnel, but what would be down there below? She whimpered.

The sound didn't come again, but that didn't make her feel any better as long as she could imagine something in the dark behind her. She had to make sure. Maybe it was just a rock that fell? Maybe it was one of Mr. Skeleton's fingers falling off and hitting the floor. That could happen, couldn't it? She might have loosened it when she moved the hand. She tried to convince herself that was definitely what it was—a rock or a loose bone. Only she kept imagining other things. She couldn't help it. Mainly, she kept thinking of Mr. Skeleton. What if he was mad about losing his knife? Now she thought about it, back when he'd died, nobody had ever heard of meth. He wouldn't know how much it was worth. Of course, he couldn't sell it, so it wasn't any use to him. But neither was the knife, and if he wanted that back, that was just tough.

She wasn't going to sit here like a baby and scare herself imagining stupid things. Tucking the knife between her knees for a moment, she worked her cell phone under a fold of bandage on her left hand, leaving as much of the screen clear as she could while still keeping it secure. She could close her hand just enough to press the power button whenever the screen timed out and went dark. She could even close her hand enough to hold it a little more securely in case the bandage wasn't quite tight enough.

Taking the knife in her other hand, she scooched out of her little corner and crept toward the back of the cave, keeping close to the floor, ready to scramble to safety, afraid to stand up and expose herself to whatever was in the tunnel. Not in the tunnel, she reminded herself firmly. She was just imagining, and she wasn't going to let her own imagination scare her.

She held the phone up. It wasn't as bright as it would be if the whole screen were showing, but she could still see a little way ahead. In a few feet, she saw the pink bags with the skeleton hand still on them right where she had put it. She huffed a sigh of relief. See, she'd been imagining things. No need to go any further.

She had started to inch backward when she thought she saw something move in the dark. She started and fell back on her sore butt. Whatever it was moved again. Then she figured out what she had seen and made a little sound of disgust with herself. It hadn't been something moving in the dark, it was the dark. When she'd moved, she'd taken her phone with her, and the dark had seemed to jump forward where the edge of the light didn't reach. She tried to laugh.

Then the dark made a leap right at her, and this time she hadn't moved. She had a momentary thought that her phone screen might have dimmed, but she was already scrambling backward, trying not to either break the phone or stab herself with the knife, and she didn't care if it was just a shadow or a trick of the light. The darkness seemed to ooze toward her, a hungry, reaching shape, and then it pounced.

Crystal squealed and slashed at the air. The knife point caught for a moment on something hard, and she almost lost her grip, then the dark retreated, and she was jerked forward two whole steps before the knife came loose. She tottered, caught her balance, and just as she was about to turn back toward the mouth of the cave, the dark surged up like a wave and crashed over her.

She couldn't scream, couldn't breathe. She thought she was running, but her legs dragged like she was asleep. She waved the knife wildly, slashing at anything she could reach. Tendrils of blackness tugged at the blade like seaweed, dragging for a moment, then parting where she cut them.

She hacked her way forward against the pull of cold streamers, clawing with her left hand, feeling the darkness curl clammy and almost solid around her fingers. She tripped on something, fell hard on her knees and remembered to curl her hand around the phone and hold the knife away from her body, then she rolled, still slashing, and staggered up. Only now she'd lost her direction. Which way was the mouth of the cave? No, that was easy. It was the way opposite to where the thing in the dark was pulling her.

She plowed forward, almost swimming against the drag of a tide. Her knife bit into something heavier than the thick air. It felt like a body, but it jerked away before she felt any more than that. What would it have done to her if she hadn't had the knife?

A wall of clammy, clinging dark folded over her, sliding over her cheeks and neck and down her back under her coat. She slashed the knife down across the thickest tangle, and they snapped like rubber bands. Crystal shot out of the cave into a wall of rain and wind and rocketed right across the clearing onto the overgrown road.

She was relieved for just a second, then looking back to make sure the dark hadn't followed her, she saw the rain twist around and turn into a rain-goblin that bent forward and stretched toward her, reaching out like the dark had done.

She squealed like a rabbit. A ragged fork of lightning showed her a leaning tree just in time for her to duck. She fell twice, keeping only enough sense to avoid falling on the knife, then scrambling up and going on without slowing down.

She burst into the clearing where the cabin was and barely saw the pillar of congealed rain that rushed at her. She hacked at the air with her knife, and the vague man-shape fell apart as she ran straight through it.

The road was circling the mountain now, spiraling down around the side of the slope, the high bank on one side. Crystal bashed her head twice on overhanging branches, almost tripped more times than she could count, but she didn't slow down, and in moments of clarity, she heard herself still squealing like an animal.

A crash, a flash, and a white-hot line cracked the air. Her vision went white with a black bolt of lightning imprinted on her retina. Unable to see in front of her, Crystal shot straight ahead. Then her feet left the ground, or else the ground left her feet, and she flailed, her arms and legs churning like a cartoon coyote until she hit and skidded down a slope, clinging to the knife and the phone like they were a lifeline. Bushes and branches scraped her cheeks. She covered her eyes with her left arm. Then the ground went out from under her again, and she shot out like a waterslide, tumbled over and fell face first onto something hard.

She bashed her chin so hard her head swam, and she wondered if maybe she had broken her neck and would lie here wherever she was until the dark found her. The thought scared her all over again, and she pulled her knees under her. She'd kept hold of her knife and her phone, and she hadn't stabbed herself, so that, she vaguely thought, was on the plus side. She levered herself up enough to look around, blinking to focus her eyes, which wanted to swim and waver like old glass.

She'd fallen over the sheer bank and onto a log at the top of the beach. The sand ran flat and smooth right down to the water, and the tide had gone out even though the waves still crashed and crawled up the beach like they were trying to claw their way back up to where they had been when the tide was high.

Crystal wanted to get up and run again. She did manage to roll upright on the log, but her body wouldn't do anything but sit drooping no matter how many times she told it to move. The boat was here somewhere. She hadn't come out at the same place where she'd first left the beach when she got to the island, but if she could just get up and walk along the beach, she'd find it. She couldn't even lift her hand to wipe the rain off her face.

Lightning flickered across the water, followed by a rolling boom that went on and changed pitch until Crystal realized the sound was coming from behind her, and it was still going on and getting louder.

Without another thought, she sprang up and scrambled over logs and driftwood and darted toward the water until she could turn around and see in the intermittent lightning flares, the trees on the slope being shattered and thrown aside by something charging straight down the mountain toward her. It must be huge to tear up grown trees, bigger than an elephant, but Crystal couldn't see anything but more darkness and rain.

She didn't have strength to spare for screaming. She turned and bolted down the beach. She only had to find the boat. She could get out on the water and away from the island where it was safe, and it didn't matter that a few hours ago, she'd been terrified of the water and so, so grateful to get to land.

Her knees wobbled with every step, and twice, she hit a dip in the ground, and her knee just gave out under her and she staggered to catch her pace. Her side had stitched tight, slowing her down almost to a walk, but the crashing thing on the slope above her just kept on coming, curving its path to follow her, and she didn't dare stop and couldn't have stopped anyway, she was so scared.

The crasher kept closing in, getting closer and closer to the water, and Crystal was ready to turn and run straight into the waves. She'd rather try to swim and drown than be caught by whatever was after her. She'd almost made up her mind to do it, then a lightning flash lit up a line of posts running out into the water and, up on the beach, her boat.

The invisible giant had almost reached the bottom of the hill. Crystal half-fell across the side of the boat and clawed at the rope holding it to the piling, but her fingers were too cold and stiff and tired to loosen the knot. She sawed with the knife until the rope parted.

But the tide had gone way down. The boat was light. It had been easy enough when she was rested to pull it up a few feet from the water's edge, but now she was exhausted, and the water was fifty feet away. She felt so tired, she didn't think she could run any more even if the dark and the rain-goblin came down on her at once.

She wasn't going to get caught here. No matter what. Crystal dropped the knife in the boat, shoved the phone in her coat pocket, grabbed the back of the boat with both hands on one side of the motor and threw all her weight into pulling it.

It slid almost a foot over the gravel.

Crystal pulled in frantic jerks. The gravel turned to hard-parked sand. The slope was with her, and she'd pulled the boat two yards toward the surf when the crashing monster reached the bottom of the hill where the crumbled jetty had once met the road, and a squall of rain formed a shape at the edge of the beach.

She refused to look right at it. She'd keep pulling until it came too close, then she'd run into the water and try to swim.

But the rain-goblin didn't pounce. It stayed bending and weaving on the edge of the trees like it couldn't come any further. Maybe it was watching her, laughing at her before it got bored and started chasing her again. The wind howled like a giant blowing across a bottle, and rain slapped her in a sheet first on one side then the other like a cat batting a mouse, but the rain-goblin didn't leap out on her.

Of course not. The monster had lived in a cave, hadn't it. Below. It had turned back into the rain-goblin when she got out of the cave, then it had crashed its way through the trees after her, but if it came out in the open, the wind couldn't twist around the way it did in the trees. It would probably just blow away.

It was raining so hard she didn't feel the first wave that washed over her ankles until it went out again, pulling the sand out from under her feet so she thought for a second she was in quicksand. Another wave soaked her to her knees and raised the boat so it scooted toward her, almost knocking her under and scaring her so badly, she scrambled over the side and in before she knew what she was doing.

She sat up, holding to the sides to steady the rocking, and squinted back up the beach through the rain, but even in the strobe light effect of the lightning, the island was just a big, black bulk in front of her.

In front of her. Would the waves push her toward the shore? What about the tide? Was it still going out, and if it was going in, wouldn't that push her right back to the island? She fumbled with the motor, tipping its propeller into the water and yanking on the cord. It made a wet, spattering noise. She yanked again as hard as she could. It didn't even sputter this time. She whimpered. It was a tiny little motor, and she hadn't put any gas in before she left the dock that afternoon. She didn't have time to put up the little sail even if she'd been sure she could do it or that she would know how to use it anyway. The paddle. There was an emergency paddle in the bottom.

Crystal dropped to her knees in the bottom of the boat and felt around. On one side, she felt the smooth length of a handle and worked her way down to the curve of a paddle. She yanked and pried while the boat drifted back toward the sand until finally, she found the clasps that held it in place and released them.

She sat up. The boat was turned sideways to the beach and tipping a little every time a wave hit it. She leaned over and pushed the paddle into the sand so the front of the boat pointed out toward open water. Then, even though she hated to turn her back to whatever was back there on the land, Crystal dipped the paddle into the water and pulled as hard as she could.

It was easier than she'd thought. All that running and walking hadn't tired out her arms like it had her legs. She bent her head into the sheets of rain and paddled hard on one side, then hitched herself over to the other side and paddled over there until that arm got tired, then she switched again, trying to keep herself going in a straight line. It was hard to get her cut hand to hang onto the paddle. It was too cold and stiff to hurt, but that meant it was too numb to grip unless she really concentrated. She passed a broken piling. That was good. That meant she was moving away from the island. There was another post a few yards away. If she could just get that far, maybe she'd be be safe from the island. She bent and strained, counting out loud and spraying rain from her lips with every stroke she made with the paddle.

It didn't feel like she was moving, and when she passed another post, she thought for a second she hadn't gone anywhere at all, but this post was higher than the other one, wasn't it? She could maybe even tie up her boat to the post and rest. But she could barely see another piling up ahead. She could paddle that far, couldn't she? Hitching a breath, she took a tighter grip on her paddle. She passed two more posts, and the rain seemed like it wasn't so heavy. She decided she could get to the next one, and the lightning wasn't coming so fast, but she could see the next post in line even without it and realized it was getting lighter. It must be almost morning finally.

Meanwhile the paddle was getting heavier. She started to worry she should have stopped at the last piling. Her fingers were so numb, she was afraid she might drop the paddle, and her arms felt like they were going to turn to stone. The rain drizzled to a stop just as she reached the next post in line, which was hardly more than a stump sticking out of the water. She used her last little bit of energy to push herself close enough to lean over the side of the boat and grab on.

She braced her knees and pulled herself and the boat up to the piling and wrapped her arms around it. She tried to lay her cheek down on its top, but a splinter jabbed her right on the side of her eye where Bryson had hit her and she jerked up again. She was so tired, she'd never be able to hold her head up. If she didn't do something, she'd probably fall asleep and fall right into the water and drown her stupid self right when she was finally safe from the island. Blinking around her, she saw the rope with one end still tied to a ring on the front of the boat and the rest dragging in the water. She'd dropped it when she cut the boat loose from the post on the beach.

Had she left enough rope to tie around the post? She couldn't remember. She'd been too scared to hardly even know what she was doing. Well, she couldn't exactly think of anything else to try. Digging her fingers into the splintery top of the piling, she used her numb, swollen hand to scrape at the rope where the last few inches came out of the water and lay across the deck. She wasn't going to be able to reach. It was almost a foot away. Maybe she could let go of the post? No way. She strained harder, and the boat moved under her. She fell forward with a squeal of surprise, losing her grip on the piling just as her other hand came down on the rope. She tried to make her hand close on it, but she couldn't even feel whether she had grabbed it or not because she was flailing with her other hand and grabbed the piling just in time to stop herself drifting away.

She looked at her hand, and there was the rope laying there on her palm with her fingers curled kind of around it. She couldn't pull it up with just her cut hand. Her fingers kept wanting to let go. She hooked her elbow over the top of the post so she could hold the rope with her stronger hand and pull with the other one. Two pulls, and she had a few feet. That would be enough to get around the post, wouldn't it? Then another pull, and a knot came out of the water right in the middle of the rope.

Crystal laughed. She'd cut the rope against the post, not between the post and the boat. With the knot in the middle, she had plenty. She looped it around the post, tied it, making sure the first knot was tight and wouldn't come apart, then she sank down in the bottom of the boat. Now that she was safe from the island and safe from drifting away, Crystal felt so limp she couldn't move.

After a while, she started to shiver. She was already wet, and the wind out here on the water, even if it wasn't as scary as the wind on the island, was cold and sucking all the heat out of her, but she couldn't get herself to move. What could she do anyway? She couldn't paddle the boat any more. She'd put up the sail in a minute and try to sail back to land. She just had to rest a minute. Then she thought of something she'd heard once. Couldn't you die from cold? She'd heard about people who fell asleep in a blizzard and never woke up.

She sat straight up with a gasp and a jerk. No way was that was happening to her. She started to paw at the sail and mast folded against the side. She'd seen Bryson set it up, even if she hadn't really paid much attention, and it hadn't looked hard. There was a screw on the bottom of the mast. You screwed it right into the bottom of the boat. Then the sail went right up like a flag. She just had to get her hands to hold the mast without dropping it overboard.

A long blast from a horn made Crystal scream and jump. She whirled around and blinked into the sunrise. The horn blew again. It sounded closer. That must be a boat coming right toward her. She had to get them to stop. She fumbled for the paddle in the bottom of the boat, dropped it twice, then she got a grip and raised it up over her head to wave like a flag to get the attention of the people on the boat. She only waved it once before it slipped out of her hands and landed in the water.

There wasn't any time to fish it out. Crystal braced her feet and stood up slowly and carefully. The last thing she needed was to fall out of the boat right when she finally found someone to help her. She waved her arms over her head and screamed as loud as she could. Then she had to stop and cough because her throat was raw and dry, then she got out another scream before the boat hooted back at her.

A voiced boomed across the water. "Sit down. We're coming."

Crystal collapsed into the boat and clutched the sides to slow its rocking. She started to giggle, then clamped both hands over her mouth to keep from sounding like a crazy person. She was crying now, which was so stupid just when she was being saved, and the tears were making her cheeks colder. She bent over her knees, trying to squeeze herself together before she fell apart.

The knife lay by her feet. She'd never seen it in clear light. The handle was wrapped in leather, stained almost black by age and people's hands rubbing and sweating on it. The blade was dark grey with a hook at the base, and blood stained the handle and the blade where she'd dripped on it with her cut hand. It was about the ugliest knife she had ever seen. She should drop it right over the side where nobody would ever find it again.

She twisted around so she could pull the strap of the backpack off her shoulders. When she had it between her feet, she unzipped it and dropped the knife inside. She'd probably fall backward on it and stab herself, but she'd paid for the knife with the two bags of pink crystals, and it had her blood on it. It was hers now, and she wasn't letting it go.

The boat started to turn, and Crystal almost panicked until she heard its engine slow down, and saw it was turning to come between her and the wind. The loudspeaker on the boat said, "Sit tight. We're coming to you."

So she put the backpack back on while the big red and white boat let a little red inflatable boat over the side, and two men climbed into it and turned the little boat toward her. In about three minutes, the little boat pulled up beside her. The men inside had on blue uniforms, and Crystal wondered if they were in the army. But that was green uniforms. Who wore blue uniforms? Unless it was the police and they'd found out about the crystals. She thought of the money and the knife in her pack. Would that be enough to get her in trouble if they were looking for the drugs? "Are you from the police?"

The younger man laughed. "No ma'am, we're the Coast Guard. Are you Crystal Swanson?" He held out his arms, and Crystal let him practically lift her into the rubber boat without her having to do anything.

"How'd you know?"

He set her in the middle of the boat. "We got a call that you were out here somewhere in the middle of the storm."

"Mom called you?" At least that meant they wouldn't be looking for drugs.

"She was about scared to death." He had a nice face with curly blond hair and a short red-gold beard that didn't hide the shape of his face. His cheeks were red from wind where the beard didn't cover, and his blue eyes crinkled when he smiled at her.

"All aboard?" the other man said.

Crystal nodded. He was nice-looking too but more Crystal's mom's age than hers. He had some grey hair in the brown, but not much.

"Get her boat secured, would you?" the older man said.

"Leave it." Crystal glowered at the little sailboat that had been almost as much to blame for her being here as Bryson. "My ex boyfriend can come get it if he wants it." She touched the scabbed bruise by her eye.

The younger man's smile disappeared and his eyes changed from friendly to angry. He turned to the other man. "What do you think? Leave it here?"

His partner thought about it a second. "We shouldn't."

Crystal looked between them. "He'll come get it today, I promise

The nice young man said, "We can always swing by tomorrow and impound it if the owner hasn't claimed it."

The other man shrugged. "Guess so."

By the time they got back to the main boat, Crystal knew the nice young man was Fabian, which was Swedish and would she please not laugh, and the older one was Evan, and neither one had a wedding ring.

Another man with a thick black mustache pulled Crystal onto the main boat while Fabian lifted her from behind. It was embarrassing, but she was too tired to even think about climbing up herself, and anyway, Fabian didn't seem to mind, did he? He left the other two men to get the rubber boat back on board while he got her a blanket and a cup of hot coffee with cream and a nasty, chocolate flavored energy bar, which she wolfed down, holding one hand over her mouth and looking guiltily at Fabian for being so unladylike, but he wasn't looking. He was unwrapping her hurt hand.

He winced when he saw the cut. Crystal took one look and looked away again, feeling queasy and lightheaded. The bandage had gotten wet, and her palm was white and pruney around the slack lips of the wound.

"That's nasty. You'll need stitches. And a palm reader will have a heck of a time figuring out the scar." He started putting some kind of ointment on it. "This hurt?"

"Sort of." Her hand was still too cold to feel much. "Are you taking me to the hospital?"

"There's an ambulance meeting us on the mainland. Your mother knows we found you. You can phone her when you know what hospital they're taking you to."

To keep from thinking about her hand, she said, "Was there ever any mining around here?"

"Mining?" He forgot about her hand for a second and stared at her.

"I slept in a cave that looked like it used to be a mine." She didn't see any reason he had to know about Mr. Skeleton.

He looked relieved like maybe he'd thought she had gone crazy. "I think there were gold and coal mined around Seattle. I don't know what sense it would make to try mining anything on that little island."

"You must have to know stuff like that for your job, don't you."

"Nah. Geology 101 at the U."

"You went to college?" She felt a little let down. He couldn't possibly be interested in her. "I'm starting classes. In the spring."

"Good for you. What are you going to study?"

She hadn't thought that far ahead yet. "I don't know. Whatever they teach."

He laughed. She thought he was laughing at her, but he said, "Good for you. I didn't know I was into marine geology until I took Rocks for Jocks. Anyway, whoever was using your cave was probably doing a little bootlegging back in the day."

"Oh yeah." Crystal supposed maybe somebody had found the cave and thought it would be a good place to hide whatever it was bootleggers did. Something illegal. With booze, she thought. Probably Mr. Skeleton would have known just what to do with all that meth after all. He and Bryson would have probably been best friends."

He had finished re-wrapping her hand, but he held onto it for a second, scowling at her so that she wondered what she had done wrong.

"This ex…" he made "ex" sound like a swear word, "…boyfriend of yours. Is he going to be a problem?"

She thought about it a second. A smile curled the corner of her mouth. "He's not going to bother me." She didn't think Bryson was going to be able to bother anybody.

"Good. Because guys like that don't get better."

She leaned forward. "Want to know what he was mad about?"

He looked away.

"No, it's super funny. I made tuna casserole for dinner. It's his favorite. But I thought it would be nicer if I put in frozen peas and baby onions." She clapped her hand over her mouth to choke back that sneaky giggle that wanted to scream and laugh at the same time.

He waited a second. "That's it? Peas and onions? That's funny?"

She raised her hand just far enough so she could say, "So I flushed all his underwear down the toilet," and clamp it back down again. She took a steady breath and added. "It's all leopard print." Then she had to clench her eyes and mouth shut and bend over her knees. She was crying, she thought, but it was hard to tell because the laugh was still trying to get out, and if she didn't keep it locked in, it would come out screaming.

After a minute, he said, "You want a minute to yourself?"

She nodded violently with her hand still over her mouth.

He stood up. "I'll check back in a few minutes."

She grabbed his hand. She took a deep breath and looked up. "What's the name of that island?"

He shrugged and made a face like he didn't want to tell her.

She gave his hand a shake.

"Okay, but don't get upset. It's called Deadman's Island."

Well, that *would* be its name, wouldn't it. Crystal bit her lips hard, let go of his hand and bent over her knees with both hands clamped over her mouth. She stayed like that for a while, making herself think about breathing in and out.

She heard somebody up in the front of the boat saying, "…give her a sedative…"

When she thought she could stay calm for a minute, she sat up and pulled her cell phone out of her pocket. It had some water on the screen, but it lit right up when she pushed the power button. Only seven percent on the battery, but four bars. Plenty left to send a text. She found Bryson in her contacts and typed: *if you want your stuff back its up on the top of deadmans island in a big cave all the way at the very back.*

Send.

Melissa McCann has an MFA in Creative Writing from Eastern Washington University where she also taught composition. .She lives with her husband and five lapdogs called, collectively, Mummy's Unregenerate Little Curs.

Her current titles are:

Yetfurther, Symbiont, and King of Midwinter with a fantasy series, The Blackwood Curse, coming out December 2017.

THE BEST PEOPLE

By Uwanna Thomas

The Notorious Derrenasty D was gonna be a spaceman. He was gonna fly off to a faraway planet where he'd throw some serious earthman lovin' down on those green-skinned alien babes.

Derren didn't actually think babes of any kind lived on Ark Island. As far as scientists could tell, the planet with the Earth-like atmosphere was uninhabited, a serious stroke of luck for the otherwise out of luck human race. Still, the Captain Kirk fantasy persisted, though in reality, he'd likely have to make due with whichever honeys some computer program somewhere had chosen to escape the destruction of the soon-to-be former planet earth, as it had chosen him.

The world would not end with a whimper after all. The earth would not creep toward its annihilation with melting polar ice caps that drowned continents bit by bit. Alternately, neither would the rising heat of greenhouse gasses dry rivers and lakes into dusty pockmarks on a scorched planet no longer able to support life.

Instead, a planet-killer sized asteroid was hurtling through space on a direct collision course toward Earth. They'd named it Azrael after the angel of death.

The last ship carrying humanity's hopes for survival was due to depart in three days, just one day ahead of the apocalypse.

So Derren would end one of his few remaining days on earth as the earth itself would end, with one final, colossal bang.

Pain ricocheted around in Derren's skull and throbbed to the thundering beat of music--his music, or the music of Derrenasty D as he was known worldwide--that blared from the high-priced sound system. He prised his eyes open and, with some effort, lifted his head and glanced around. He lay on a capacious couch at the epicenter of the bacchanalian detritus of his going away party.

The beer bottles and cocktail glasses, displaced furniture, abandoned clothing, and limp, multi-colored streamers looked almost pretty in the muted vision of his bleary eyes.

The only guest remaining seemed to be the mostly naked woman who lay sprawled across Derren's bare chest, her blonde hair splayed across her face like a droopy fan, hiding her features. Derren swallowed hard to stop himself gagging from the odor of stale sweat, perfume, and sex that enveloped the two of them.

He rolled her off of him, and her body made a soft *boff* sound as she landed on the plush Persian rug next to the couch.

He'd have to have Otis check the rest of the house and roust any stray houseguest who might be passed out in one of the bedrooms or the game room or out near the pool. Then he remembered that Otis, who had worked as his *Man Friday* hadn't been there in weeks. He and most of the other left behinds had chosen to huddle with family or in churches to await the end. Some were living large driving the luxury cars and living in houses abandoned by the rich and powerful who had already shipped off to Ark Island, as the new planet had been dubbed.

Derren levered himself upright on the couch, the motion making him sway with a sensation of high and low tide. He reached across the large glass coffee table littered with marijuana blunts and the remnants of several lines of coke and punched a button on the remote killing the music.

The woman, whose name he now recalled was Hollis . . . No, Holly . . . Honey? . . . turned onto her side and started to snore. Derren rose gingerly to his feet and, stepping around Honey . . . Helen? . . .whatever, tried to remember where was the closest of the mansion's six bathrooms. He wanted to wash his face and rinse the nasty taste from his mouth. Actually, he thought he'd like to pop out his tongue completely and give it a good scrubbing. He wobbled toward the kitchen instead, passing by an assortment of bras and stumbling over a man's shoe (not his).

He steadied himself against a maroon-painted wall hung with a framed painting of some minor artist that his decorator had touted as a rising star. She had convinced Derren to pay a small fortune for the art piece, saying it would add a special touch of class to the décor. Someone had scrawled the word *please* over and over in bright pink lipstick all over the wall, including the painting. It didn't much matter. In four days, this room, this house, this entire earth would be nothing more than a wistful pang in the memories of the survivors.

Derren was one of the lucky ones. He had been chosen to be among those who would be whisked away to populate the new planet. He should have been happy. Hell, he *was* happy. Who wouldn't be happy to be spared from the apocalypse? Inside that happiness, however, was a hard kernel of

77

ire that the world had decided to end just when he was standing on top of it.

On Ark Island, he wouldn't be world-renowned rapper extraordinaire, The Notorious Derrenasty D, but he'd be alive. Besides, everyone on the new planet was from this one. Surely, he could parlay his big-time fame on this world into something just as big on the next.

He looked down at his wrist for the departure watch that would buzz, disclosing to him the secret location of his ship and how much time he would have before departure to get to the launch site.

He frowned, unbelieving, at his bare right wrist, then thinking there must be some mistake, checked the left, to discover it as bare as the first. Derren's head fell back, and he sputtered a relieved breath. He'd taken the watch off and put in in his pants pocket.

During the party, he'd wanted to show off the watch, to flaunt his good fortune. But before long, the attention it garnered began to make him feel anxious. After all, back in the hood where he'd come from, it hadn't been too uncommon to get jacked for a regular watch, much less a watch that would save you from being annihilated along with the rest of the world.

His rap fame had inured him to displays of envy, hatred, or rage that seethed just beneath the skin, making the most genial grins look more like feral animals baring their teeth. And those whose eyes flashed cold contempt for what they perceived as his underserved success only made throwing it in their faces that much sweeter. What had caused him to pocket the watch out of sight were the haunted, fever-bright eyes of the desperate.

Derren slapped his pockets and pulled out the hard lump. What he removed wasn't the watch but the tightly-rolled hundred-dollar bill he'd used to inhale the lines of cocaine. He tossed the money aside and gripped his front pockets, squeezing and kneading them as if they were breasts.

Derren's whole body flushed, and he was suddenly chilled and drenched with sweat. He felt wide awake now, the adrenaline killing his buzz. *It's got to be here. It's got to be here.* The chant repeated over and over and over in his head like a stuck LP, crowding out every other thought. *It's got to be here.* But it wasn't. His headache rebounded in force, and he lurched over and retched. *Nooooo. It's got to be here. The Notorious Derrenasty D is gonna be a spaceman.*

Derren dropped to the floor and scuffled around on hands and knees, tossing away dirty dishes, spilled food and discarded condoms in search of the watch. Breathing hard, he rose and began toppling the already tousled furniture. He pushed over settees, upended end tables, and threw a chair that went sailing through the open sliding door and out into the pool.

He jumped at sounds coming from the living room. In an instant, panic and dread coalesced into a calculating rage. He sidled over to a small, heavy black and gold table standing next to the glass slider. It had somehow escaped molestation. He slid open one of the ornate drawers and quietly drew out the gun, a custom .45 Bob Marvel Nighthawk. He checked the clip and flipped off the safety. He was going to get his watch back and then blow that thieving son-of-a-bitch away.

The blonde woman, Haley, shambled around the room assembling an outfit from the various discards at her disposal. She'd already donned a pink t-shirt that looked several sizes too big and seemed to be sizing up the potential of a leopard print mini skirt when she noticed Derren.

"Big D," she said, with a suggestive smile and a toss of her golden hair. "Hey, you haven't seen my . . ." When she spotted the gun, her eyes stretched saucer wide and a high-pitched squawk like that of a startled chicken broke from her throat.

Derren trained the gun on the woman, holding it palm side down like a proper gangsta.

"Where my motherfuckin' watch, bitch?"

Haley tilted her head in an attitude of incomprehension, and her jaw worked up and down as if hinged like a ventriloquist's dummy.

Derren rushed her, grabbing her by the hair and pushing the gun barrel into the hollow of her throat. He was breathing hard again, and his voice was a harsh whisper. "I said, where is my watch?"

Haley squeezed her eyes shut and sagged in Derren's grip. "I swear . . . I swear I don't . . . don't know," she stammered.

Derren loosed her hair and with his free hand frisked Haley, outside and then inside her t-shirt. Not finding the watch, he pushed her away hard enough that she fell, landing on her butt and elbows.

He re-trained the gun on Haley. "You better find it."

Wet sooty streaks stained Haley's cheeks where her tears had caused her cheap mascara to run. "If you're going to do it, do it. We'll all be dead soon anyway," she said.

We'll all be dead soon. The words hit Derren like a wrecking ball. Angry tears burned in his eyes and his voice wavered and cracked with stifled sobs. "Not me. I'm one of the chosen. The best people . . ." His sobs broke free and he collapsed to his knees, his slack arms grinding the gun into the carpet.

Sensing her chance, Haley rolled over and bolted for the front door.

Derren shouted after her. "It doesn't matter. We'll all be dead soon." He raised the gun and fired. "I'm one of the chosen. I ain't goin' out like that."

The shot aimed at Haley went way wide, the bullet lodging itself in the wall a foot or more to the right of the doorframe. Derren tumbled down onto the litter-strewn carpet, allowing himself to ride the wave of adrenaline that coursed through his body. His breathing slowed, his mind cleared, and by the time Derren finally pulled himself together, he had a plan.

Derren searched the house from top to bottom before he committed to going to see Clayton. He even scoured the rooms he'd rarely set foot into. He wanted to be sure he hadn't hidden the damned watch from himself as some kind of ass-backward security measure. But after searching every possible place the watch could be and more than a few impossible ones, he had to concede that going to Clayton was his only option.

He and Clayton had been homies back in the day before their life paths had diverged so completely. Clayton, Derren and his old girl Tamika had been inseparable. The unholy trinity, his mother used to call them. Now both Clayton and Tamika were doomed to die. They hadn't been chosen. His pointless search for the watch had been to forestall what was likely to be an awkward meeting. A part of him didn't want to admit that he'd been stalling. An even bigger part of him didn't give a damn. It's not as if he had any power to change things. He had been chosen and they had not. Now he'd do whatever it took to preserve his rightful place on that last ship. Clayton was in the position to make that happen. He was a computer programmer working for the only remaining authority on Earth. If that meant Derren having to pick at his survivor's guilt like a scab, then so be it.

Derren hadn't called to find out if Clayton would be in his office. Knowing Clayton as he did, he'd just assumed, it being a workday, that Clayton would be at work, diligent in his devotion to 'the man' to the very last.

The soft soles of Derren's shoes made a hollow echo as he trod through the cavernous room. The dozens of cubicles, most of them empty now, gave the space a look something like a deserted maze that tested the ability of human-sized rats to find the hidden cheese at its center.

A light shone from the single, occupied cubicle, and as Derren made his way toward it, he heard people talking in hushed voices. One of the speakers was definitely Clayton. "We agreed it was for the best," he was saying.

Derren rounded the partition. Tamika, his ex, leaned with her backside against the edge of a sleek, modern metal desk, her arms folded over her chest and her long brown legs crossed at the ankles. Clayton pivoted back and forth in his swivel chair regarding her levelly.

Both their heads snapped back in surprise at seeing him, and Clayton hurriedly cleared whatever had been on his computer screen. That, plus their unnatural stillness and darting eyes, gave Derren the impression he had intruded on something important, or at least private.

"Well, look at this. My two favorite people. 'Sup, Clay-man. Hey Tamika."

Clayton slid his black-rimmed glasses farther up on his nose with an index finger and blinked up at Derren. "Hey," he said. "It's been a while."

Clayton rose, and he and Derren slapped hands and exchanged what, for men, often passes for hugs--lots of back slapping and little warmth.

Derren put the bag he'd been holding down on the desk and gave Clayton the once-over, noticing his well-muscled arms. "Look at you. You got some guns." He slapped the back of his hand against Clayton's hard midsection. "I would have thought all that time sitting behind a desk would have . . ."

"Nah, man. That pudgy little 'four-eyes' that everybody picked on is long gone," said Clayton.

"Hey, nobody picked on you when I was around." He turned his attention to the woman. "And Tamika, you lookin' fine, girl."

Tamika still held herself stiffly and avoided looking him in the eyes. "What do you want, Derren?"

"So, it's like that?" asked Derren, taken aback by her mildly hostile tone. It had been years since their breakup. Was she still feeling burned over the way he'd ended things? He hadn't expected to see Tamika, but he wasn't about to let her ruin his reunion with his boy Clayton.

Derren smiled at his friends. It was his show smile, the smile that beckoned, 'come join the party,' from promotional photographs. It was the smile of a hustler. The smile that always got him what he wanted, part threat, part tease. And the part that never failed with the groupies--the wild thing wanting to be tamed. It was the smile that came most naturally to him now.

He reached into the paper bag and pulled out a bottle of single malt scotch. He'd bought the four-thousand-dollar bottle of liquor at Herrod's department store when he'd played London during a concert tour. He didn't usually drink scotch, but he'd bought it simply because it was expensive and because he could.

"I came to have one last drink with my home-boy."

"Yeah," said Tamika. "And it only took an impending global holocaust to make it happen."

Another time, Derren might have slapped back at the sarcastic comment, but he decided to let it slide. He could afford to be generous. After all, by the time his ship landed on Ark Island, she would have long since been turned into so much space dust. Too bad, too. She was one fine-looking woman.

Clayton left the cubicle and returned with three coffee cups, which he handed around.

Derren unsealed the cap on the scotch and poured everyone a drink. He raised his cup in a toast. "To the unholy trinity, back together again." He took a swig and smacked his lips. "Ahh, that's some good shit."

"I should hope so," said Tamika after a couple of sips.

A few beats of awkward silence passed before Derren said, "I see you still got that old picture," indicating the photo on Clayton's desk.

The photo showed the three of them together, clowning for the camera. It had been taken at a party shortly after high school graduation. They'd all had reason to celebrate. Academic scholarship had earned full rides to Caltech for both Tamika and Clayton, while Derren's YouTube videos had attracted the attention of some major players in the rap world, and his career was on the verge of blowing up. It had only been ten years, but the people smiling out from the photo might have been their duplicates in a parallel universe.

"Those were some good times," said Clayton, wistfully.

Derren fingered the photo frame. "Look, Clay-man, you know I'm supposed go on that last ship to Ark Island."

There it was again, he thought, noticing the uncomfortable look that passed between Tamika and Clayton, like they were experiencing a shared bout of gas.

"Yeah, your mom told me you'd made the cut," said Clayton.

"I helped you out a lot back in the day," said Derren. "I'm hoping you can do me a solid. See, my departure watch turned up missing, and I need you to get me another one."

Tamika laughed. The tinkling girly laugh he'd always found so sexy now rankled his nerves, and he had to rein in the impulse to slap the crap out of her.

As if sensing his struggle, Clayton stood up and removed his glasses, setting them aside on his desk. He was still shorter than Derren, but his clear eyes, muscled arms and hard abs were testaments to clean living, or at least moderation. Derren's youth had kept his years of debauchery from taking any outward toll on his body, but while he looked toned and fit, he doubted he could take Clayton in a fight. Good thing he'd brought the gun.

Clayton rubbed the spot where his glasses sat heavy on the bridge of his nose and relaxed back onto his chair. "What makes you think I can do that? You think we have those things sitting around here in a drawer somewhere?"

"C'mon man. Do that geeky computer hack-y thing you do and just make the computer issue me another one."

"Not possible. Once the system was up and running, it was closed to all external interface. It's un-hackable."

"You told me once that no computer was un-hackable."

There was that look again.

"Besides," Clayton continued, "the departure watches were made at the same secret site where the ships are built. One was manufactured for each name on the list of those chosen for resettlement. They didn't make any spares that I'm aware of."

Derren felt his stomach drop into a pit that had yawed open inside him.

82

He poured himself another drink to steady his nerves.

"Maybe it's for the best," said Tamika. She reached out to touch his shoulder, but he jerked away.

He glared at her. "Now that you think I'm gonna stay here and die like the rest of you, we all good? Fuck that shit."

A different look passed between the Tamika and Clayton this time, like they were making a decision. Clayton gave Tamika a small nod.

"Clayton detected some biases written into the computer's algorithms," she said. "It removed some of the randomness and skewed the computer's decision matrices when determining who would be saved and who would not."

Derren stared at her as if she was speaking in Farsi.

Clayton said, "She's trying to tell you . . ."

"I'm not stupid, Clayton. She's telling me the system is rigged. No shit. I'm a black man in America. You think I don't know that every which way I step is a trip hazard, a stumbling block, or an uphill battle? But every now and then, even 'the man' fucks up. No reason I shouldn't take advantage of it."

Tamika blew out a frustrated breath. "What we're trying to tell you is that the fuck up might be bigger than you imagine. I discovered something unusual about this asteroid. The destruction might not be as devastating as was first thought."

"So, because you *think* it might not be so bad, I should just hang tight, pray and take my chances? You two are trippin."

"We just think your being on the resettlement list and getting one of those watches might have been a mistake," said Clayton.

Derren rounded on Clayton, his fists clenched. "Just because you weren't chosen, you think it was a mistake that I was?"

"That's not what he meant," said Tamika.

"Oh no?" asked Derren. Now it was his turn to laugh. "Look at you two big-shot college grads with your big-time jobs." He turned an icy glare on Tamika. "You detected the asteroid that's gonna destroy the planet and then found a brand-new planet to move to." Turning to Clayton, he said, "And you helped program the computer that says who gets to go to the promised land, but you're slaving away in an office with two and a half walls. Neither one of you had enough clout to get yourselves on that list. Instead, you're sitting here trying to convince yourselves that it's all copacetic. You're still the same pathetic, weak-assed, four-eyes you always were."

Derren turned and stalked from the cubicle.

"Wait," Tamika called after him.

"Let him go, Tamika," said Clayton. "Maybe it's not a mistake. Maybe he really does belong on the list."

***

That night Derren churned restlessly in bed. The ticks and chimes of various clocks around the house served as constant reminders that his time was running out. He chided himself for wasting time with Clayton and Tamika. He should have known they wouldn't be able to help. They couldn't even help themselves. Losers.

Meanwhile, the clocks ticked relentlessly on, bringing his doom closer with every maddening swish of a second hand or ping of a digital oscillator. Derren clenched his teeth and pulled the pillows tight around his ears, but the sounds only seemed to magnify, filling the room with malevolent aural specters.

Tossing the pillows aside, he got up and ran to the walk-in closet adjacent to the bathroom. He drew out a baseball bat from behind the door, and returning to the bedroom, brought the bat down on the clock that sat on his bedside table, pulverizing it into shards of glass and plastic.

More clock sounds moved in to fill the void. A musical wall clock in the living room chimed the Jackson Five tune, *Never Can Say Goodbye*, then struck the four o'clock hour.

Derren rushed into the room, batted the clock to the floor and pounded it to pieces, its inner workings spilling out like guts.

In the kitchen, Darren attacked another wall clock, this time a blocky metal number that gave as good as it got, pitting the bat and gouging out big splinters. But when Derren finished, even this stalwart clock had ceased to tick. He also bashed in the clock on the oven and blotted out the time glowing from the microwave.

Derren charged down hallways and stormed from room to room, smashing clocks with his worn wooden club until finally he could hear nothing but his own rough, exhausted breaths.

Back in his bedroom, he flung the bat into a corner across the room and face-planted down onto the bed. His breathing calmed, and he was about to settle in to the quiet, when he heard the tick-tick, tick-tick, tick-tick of his own heart.

A few hours later, Derren gave up any attempts at sleep. It was just as well. He'd promised to pick up his mother and go with her to church today.

He got up, went into the bathroom, turned on the shower and stepped under the streams of hot water. The stinging spray purged the sluggishness of his troubled night from his senses.

Only three more days until the world ended. Two more until the last ship departed for Ark Island. Not much time left to find another departure watch. As he dressed, Derren ran through his mind a list of his music contacts who weren't already long gone and basking in the rays of Ark Island's twin suns. Tamika had said that the system was rigged. He must still know somebody with enough power and money to pull the strings. No matter what Clayton said, there were always people like that. He just needed to find one.

Derren jumped into his car and headed for his mother's house in the old neighborhood. He had wanted to buy her a house like his, in Bel Air or Manhattan Beach, but she had declined, preferring to stay close to old friends and most especially to her church. So, he'd had the old place renovated and a state of the art security system installed.

Derren's mother Joyce was watching from her living room window as her son pulled up to the curb in front of the house. She opened the front door and waved. "I'll be out in a sec." She straightened her wide-brimmed, navy-blue hat, grabbed her handbag from a nearby chair and padded down the walk to meet the car. At the curb, she stood next to the car door and waited.

Derren lowered the window and yelled out, "Get in, Ma. Let's get going."

Joyce crossed her arms and leaned into the window. She quirked her lips and fixed her son with one of her *who-do-you-think-you're-talking-to* looks. Derren sighed and got out of the car, went around to the passenger side, and opened the door for his mother.

"That's more like it," she said smiling pleasantly. "You can call yourself all that D-nasty stuff, if you want to, but we both know I taught you better than that. Now give your Ma some sugar."

They hugged, and he kissed her cheek.

When they were finally on their way, Joyce said, "It should be a good service today. I'm so glad you could make it."

"Huh?" said Derren, his mind elsewhere.

Joyce frowned at Derren's wrist, noticing the diamond studded Rolex where her son usually wore his departure watch. "Where's your watch, son?" She whispered the words in an almost reverential tone, leaving no doubt as to which watch she meant.

Derren stared ahead at the road. "I left it locked up at home in the safe. It's too dangerous to be wearing it around all the time. It might make people desperate."

"I guess you're right." She stretched her legs. Every time she rode in the strange little sports car with the doors that opened up like wings, its comfort surprised her.

She leaned back, closed her eyes and smiled. She was overjoyed that the Almighty in His wisdom had chosen to spare her son from the apocalypse. The new Rapture, some religious leaders had called it, where the righteous would be saved, rocketing into the heavens on ships bound for a new Eden. Her son would be among the righteous, though if she was being honest, from outward appearances, she would be hard pressed to justify God's choice. Then a line of scripture came to mind: . . . *for God sees not as man sees, for man looks at the outward appearance, but the LORD looks at the heart.* Who was she to question or seek to justify God's choices?

Joyce looked out the window and watched the passing streets, the bedraggled palm trees, and yards overflowing with flowering bougainvillea. The sidewalks, usually empty at this hour on a Sunday morning, seemed especially desolate. A man and his dog emerged from an apartment building for a walk as if it was just another Sunday, as if they had many more sunny Sunday mornings in their future. Joyce closed her eyes, and a tear ran down her cheek.

"You okay, Ma?" asked Derren.

Joyce shook her head. The rest of the way to church, she hummed, "What a Friend We Have in Jesus." Unlike Jesus, her son would be saved.

The specter of the last ship leaving without him loomed large in Derren's thoughts, and his spirits spiraled lower with each mile of the drive. He had expected his problems to be over after visiting Clayton. He'd expected to be wearing his new departure watch instead of lying to his mother about the old one. By the time they'd arrived at The Church of the Living Waters, he was downright pissed at the world.

As it had been since news of the asteroid went public, inside the church was standing room only. Extra seating had been set up on the lawn and speakers installed so that those who couldn't get in could still follow the sermon.

Joyce and Derren waded through the throng of worshipers gathered outside, some neighbors and as many strangers.

He trudged behind his mother making no attempt to hide how put out he felt as she stopped every so often to ask how this one was holding up or to fawn over that one's new baby.

All around them, excited whispers circulated through the crowd. The Notorious Derrenasty D was in the house.

Derren ignored the gawks and smiles aimed at him and shunned the girls who openly flirted. He absently hand-slapped or fist-bumped a few of the guys. Others he left hanging. He resented their attention, their attempts to bask, even tangentially, in the awe his fame inspired, awe that persisted even now. Didn't these morons get that all of this would be meaningless in just a couple of days?

Inside, the air was already stifling from heat radiating off too many bodies. The greenhouse effect from sun shining through the stained-glass windows amplified the impact.

Darren followed Joyce to a pew reserved for founding members like his mother. By the time they were settled, Derren felt as if he was roasting inside his suit. Sweat beaded his brow and ran down his back, making him itch, and he fought the urge to squirm like he had when he was a kid, bored and trapped.

The service began with the choir singing "I'll Fly Away."

Derren scanned the rapt faces, the bodies swaying. No one seemed the least bothered by the perverse song choice.

Pastor Joe Jenkins, aka Reverend Joe, preached a sermon about, big surprise, the end of the world.

We all knew this day was coming," he said, his booming voice as sonorous as any church organ. "The Bible foretold that this day was coming. Jesus told us this day was coming, and He wanted us to be ready. So, I'm asking you today, with the hour almost upon us, are you ready?"

The tepid response from his audience incited the reverend to pump up the volume.

"I said, are you ready? Cause I'm ready. Are you ready?" he thundered at the congregation.

The churchgoers caught the spirit, and shouts of "Yes, Lord" and "Yes, Jesus," rose above the general babble of assent.

"That's right," said the reverend. "That's what I'm talking about. We're ready. We don't need spaceships for our salvation. Christ is our salvation. Can I get a amen?"

"Amen." The word gushed forth in a chorus. "Amen."

"We don't need no spaceship. Jesus is our ship. Are you ready?" the reverend shouted. "Cause I'm ready."

The church organ player struck a few dramatic chords, and Reverend Joe glared down from the pulpit, his eyes boring into his flock. "We don't need Ark Island. We don't need a new planet where man's depravity, his savagery, his wickedness, and his corruption will surely follow." Reverend Joe pounded the pulpit with each statement of man's transgressions. "Heaven is our new planet, where God has chosen only the righteous there to dwell. But only if we're ready. Are you ready? Cause I'm ready."

His flock responded with shouts of, "Amen" and "I'm ready" and "We'll be there with you, Reverend Joe."

Derren sat with his arms crossed, unmoved, wondering at the stupidity of these people. Reverend Joe seemed to think Christ would return in the form of Azrael, the planet killing asteroid, and that the righteous would be spared from its wrath. Even if it was true, the pastor couldn't possibly believe that he'd be among the saved. Derren stole a sideways glance at his mother, at her enraptured face, her eyes brimming with tears. Was she really buying this load of horse shit? He was willing to bet his three Grammys that every member of the assembled flock would trade their Christ-ship bound for heaven for a seat on a spaceship bound for Ark Island in a New York minute.

Reverend Joe trudged from behind the pulpit. His shoulders drooped, and he shook his head, looking beaten and sad. "I don't think y'all ready," he said, his voice raw with emotion.

Worried rumblings and protestations issued from the congregation.

Sweat popped from Reverend Joe's forehead and the bald dome of his receding hairline like water sputtering in a pan of hot oil. "I need to know that y'all ready, that my brothers and sisters will be there with me when I'm lifted up to everlasting life. But that's only gonna happen if you're ready." He screwed up his face and jumped up and down like a toddler in a fit. "Are. You. Ready."

"We're ready. We're ready," shouted the congregation.

"That's right, brothers and sisters. We're not rocketing off to some unknown planet in the cold darkness of space. The arms of the Lord will lift us up into the warm light of glory. 'Cause we're ready."

The congregation exploded into a crescendo of hallelujahs, amens, and yes, Lords. The rich round sound of the organ rippled the sentiment throughout the church, through the windows and doors, out onto the lawn.

During the pastor's arm-flapping histrionics, the slick black face of a departure watch caught the light for a fraction of a second and winked at Derren from just inside the reverend's sleeve. Derren's spine stiffened to attention as adrenaline fired in his brain. His eyes locked on Reverend Joe's left arm. Had he seen what he thought he'd seen? Maybe not. Maybe the reverend was wearing one of those fitness trackers. Nah, he couldn't see that fat fart working out. And two days before the end of the world? So, he's a hypocrite, too. Big surprise. Derren's lip curled in disgust.

Throughout the rest of the sermon, Derren hawked the reverend's movements like prey, trying to get another glimpse of the watch, but he never got a clear view.

Filing out of the church, Derren tried to think of an excuse to talk to Reverend Joe alone in his office. Ironic, he thought. He'd made it a point never to be alone with the good reverend ever since the pastor had put his hand down Derren's pants when he was eight years old. We'll see who's a victim this time. He made his way down the line of parishioners waiting to have a few parting words with their pastor. Derren was a long way down in the queue when he felt a tug on his sleeve. He turned and frowned into a smiling grill full of gold teeth belonging to Sean 'Gangsta GrrRhymes' Grimes.

Derren and Sean had always been rivals, battling each other in rap wars on the street corners, back in the day. They'd eventually both broken into the big-time, signed with the same record label and ended up working with the same producer. Sean's success had burned brightly, at first, but flamed out prematurely, while Derren's star had continued to rise.

Sean whispered in Derren's ear. "I heard about your problem. I can help you with that."

Derren stepped out of line and followed Sean to stand under the shade of a maple bordering the church lawn.

"What problem?" Derren asked.

"You don't need to be frontin,' man." He pulled a departure watch partway out of his pocket. "Your problem." He slipped the watch back out of sight. "I might be able to help you out."

"I'm not the one frontin," said Derren. Everyone knew Sean was broke, but he was living large as if he was still pulling down serious cash. Now he made his living playing has-been gigs at some of the smaller casinos or a low-rent club every now and then.

"Look, man," Sean said. "I know a guy. He can hook you up. Know what I mean?"

Derren leaned against the tree, trying not to look too interested. "Where'd he get it?"

"Huh?" said Sean, distracted by a couple of the church honeys who paraded past arm in arm. Sean smiled, flashing his gaudy grill. The girls giggled and continued on. Sean followed them with his eyes. "Uh, uh, uh. I hope there are some like that on Ark Island."

"The guy with the watch," said Derren, refocusing Sean's attention. "Where'd he get it? I heard they only made as many watches as there were people on the list. So, where'd he get it?

Sean turned his head toward the people still visiting in the churchyard and cut Derren a sideways glance. "You know how it is. Don't ask, don't tell. Know what I'm sayin'?"

"Why would you want to help me?"

"Man, why you think? I've got a seat on the last transport ship to Ark Island, and I plan to arrive loaded."

The thought crossed Derren's mind that this asshole might be trying to sell him back his own stolen watch. Derren drew himself up, stepped up in Sean's face and spoke through clenched teeth. "What's to keep me from jacking your ass and taking the one in your pocket?"

Sean lifted his shirt revealing the grip of a gun sticking out from his waistband. "My buddies, Smith and Wesson."

Derren deflated into a less threatening stance. "How much?" he asked.

"I would think something that makes sure you escape certain death is worth a lot."

"How much?"

"I heard you're worth a couple hundred mil," said Sean. "So, why don't we make it half. Let's say one hundred million."

"You heard wrong, Bro. Who you think I am, Jay-Z? No way I got that much green."

Sean shook his head as if he'd known such an ask was a longshot. "Okay . . . Ah . . . Thirty million. And no paper. I ain't tryin' to fool with no dead presidents. I want gold, platinum, diamonds. You feel me?"

If Derren had counted on Sean being the fool he'd always taken him for, he was disappointed. Like most people, even Sean knew that the value of cash fluctuated daily. A hundred million yesterday was two million today. No one knew what paper money would be worth on Ark Island, if anything at all.

Derren had stashed over a hundred million dollars in his bags, ready to travel, just in case. He'd liquidated most of his assets when the financial markets started to tank in response to the news about the destruction of the planet. But by the time he'd gotten around to trading his cash in for something of stable value, every gold coin or precious gemstone had been scarfed up by others savvy enough to have read the signs.

Fortunately, he'd been good to himself over the past decade, so in addition to the cash, he'd accumulated in the neighborhood of ten million dollars worth of personal jewelry, but he wasn't about to give it all away to this asshole. He, too, intended to start life on Ark Island loaded. "Tell you what? I'll pay you five million for it."

Sean scoffed at the insult. "Are you kiddin' me right now? Shit." He pointed a finger around the churchyard at the dispersing congregation. "Any one of these people would pay double what I'm asking."

"Yeah, but you also know none of them can afford half of what I'm offering. Five million."

Sean grimaced as if someone had twisted a knife in his gut. "Can't do it, man. My partner won't let that watch go for less than twenty million."

Derren's palms itched with the prospect of a new departure watch slipping through his fingers. "I can give you ten. I swear that's all I got." He pulled at his collar. "In a couple of days, that watch'll be worthless."

"Yeah, it will. Twenty million. Final offer," said Sean.

Derren looked up at the sound of his mother calling his name. She stood in the harsh sunlight with her arm around the girl with the baby, waving him over.

Sean smirked. "You're a good son, huh, D? Your moms be rocking some serious bling." He flicked his earlobe with an index finger.

Derren noticed that his mom was wearing the diamond and ruby earrings he'd given her last year on her birthday.

From the time he'd started making serious bank, he'd been even more generous with his mother than he had himself, at least in the jewelry department. She hadn't let him buy her the house, so Derren had lavished his mother with expensive jewelry. He'd bought her a platinum bracelet set with 30 carats in diamonds for Mother's Day, and for Christmas, a gold necklace in the shape of a coiled snake, studded with black diamonds for spots and emerald eyes. The amount of jewelry he'd given his mother over the past decade had to amount to twenty million dollars, easy.

Joyce made her way across the grass, the girl with the baby in her arms tagging behind.

"It's not like she's gonna need 'em," said Sean, his voice sibilant.

Before his mother got too close, Derren called back. "Coming, Ma." He turned to Sean. "Deal," he said, and strode off to intercept his mother.

Joyce had Derren drop the mother and child off at their place before driving her home. All the way, Derren contemplated how he might get his mother to part with her jewels. He could come clean. Tell her about the stolen watch and how, with her help, he had a chance to buy another one. Wouldn't she willingly give them up in such a case? Hadn't she said many times how happy she was that her baby boy would escape the doom that awaited the rest of the world?

When they parked at the curb in front of her house, Joyce sat in the car while Derren came around to her side and opened the door.

"Why don't you come on in," Joyce said, exiting the car. "I made a real Sunday supper. All your favorites, fried chicken, corn on the cob, potato salad, fried pecan okra, cornbread."

"Sounds great, Ma," Derren said, following her up the walk and into the house.

The house where Derren had grown up was both foreign and achingly familiar. The dingy rooms crammed with cheap mismatched furniture were now decked out in crisp whites and accented with silver and Caribbean blue. The house that had seemed so cramped as a child, now had an airy, cottage feel.

It was the smells that brought him home. The fresh paint and new carpets and designer furniture, even his ma's Sunday supper couldn't totally obliterate the smells, the barely perceptible hints that his olfactory sense interpreted as home.

Joyce went directly to her bedroom to change out of her church clothes and into something more comfortable. "Pour yourself a glass of iced tea," she called. "I'll be out in a few. You can start setting the food out on the table."

"Okay."

Derren was heading for the kitchen when his phone lit off. He eased it from his pocket and stared down at the screen. Sean had texted him the time and location of the meeting with the watch guy. He had an hour. That didn't give him much time to be persuasive.

"Ah, I can't stay, Ma. I've got . . . ah . . . business."

"What did you say, son?"

Derren made an about face and hurried to the small storage/laundry room at the back of the house. He pushed an area of paneled wall that sprang open revealing the wall safe he'd had installed along with the other security measures. Derren opened the safe, sighing with relief at the bounty of small boxes that filled it. He opened the first couple of boxes to ensure himself of their contents. He grabbed a linen laundry bag and dropped them in. His hands shook with the wrong of it all, and his head shook no, no, no, even as he hurriedly ransacked each box and dropped the contents into the bag.

He recited a litany of rationalizations for his treachery, "She's not going to need them. She won't miss them. Won't even know they're gone."

Derren checked his watch. Just enough time to drive across town. With this haul, at least he wouldn't need to swing by his house for the balance of the payment. This would be more than enough.

Joyce emerged from her bedroom and ambled into the kitchen chuckling under her breath. "You probably couldn't find the napkins. I moved them to . . ." She stopped to scan the empty room. "Derren?" she called, thinking he might be washing up in the guest bathroom. She backed out of the kitchen and walked to the living room. "Derren?" She said, looking around. Maybe he'd left something in his car and had gone out to get it. Walking to the window, she pulled aside the drape and looked out. Derren's weird little sports car was gone.

Joyce sighed and clutched at a sharp pain in her chest. Breathing heavily, she made her way back into the kitchen and slumped into a chair at the table. A folded sheet of paper stood propped between the salt and pepper shakers. She pulled the paper toward her and unfolded it, and read the note Derren had scrawled.

Ma,

Sorry I didn't have time for a last meal or a proper goodbye. We always knew I might get the call to meet my ship at any moment. The moment's come. I'm going to be a spaceman, Ma.

You know I'm not much of a believer, but I hope your pastor is right and that your Jesus-ship will come to save you.

I'll miss you and think of you a lot, (Especially your fried pecan okra.) Here he'd drawn a lopsided smiley face.

Luv U, Derren

Derren felt as if he'd been holding his breath since he left his mother's house. He'd met Sean and his business partner, Roofie, clearly the brains of the operation, in the front room of one of the abandoned mansions in Beverly Hills. He'd handed over the laundry bag full of his mother's jewelry. Roofie had examined each piece, appraised its value and decided it would suffice. He nodded to Sean, who disappeared into another room and came back holding the watch, which he'd tossed over to Derren.

Derren examined the watch. Its smooth black surface and narrow, shiny blank face looked identical to the one he'd lost. *The Notorious Derrenasty D was gonna be a spaceman.* Finally, he could breathe.

Sean winked at Derren. "See you on the flip side."

Strolling back to his car and feeling lighter than he had in days, Derren shoved his new departure watch deep into his pants pocket. He wouldn't make the same mistake twice. After he returned to the security of his house, he'd strap the watch to his wrist and take it off only after he'd boarded the ship. Maybe not even then. Better to wait until the ship had blasted off and there was no turning back.

Derren sped towards home. One up-side to the population load on the planet having lessened by over 800 million, traffic was light. Noticing that the car was running low on gas, he kept an eye out for gas stations along his route, but almost every one he saw bore a sign reading 'No Gas' or 'Closed.'

He finally spotted a station that looked, not exactly promising, but he was running out of options. At least there was no sign warning up front that there was no gas to be had.

In the face of the planet's imminent destruction, many of the employees had simply abandoned their posts. Many employers had walked away, neglecting even to turn off the lights. The place might still have electricity. If so, the pumps would still be working.

As if anticipating the actual event, the gas station had adopted an apocalyptic mien, its cadaverous convenience store and gas pumps coated with white dust, standing like ghostly sentinels.

He slid his car in next to the pumps, popped open the gas cap cover, and got out. The heat hit him like a furnace after the cool comfort of the car's air conditioning. His forehead immediately dampened and he wiped the sweat on his sleeve.

He unhooked the pump nozzle, pushed the button underneath it, inserted the nozzle into the opening of his gas tank and squeezed the trigger to start the fill. The trigger clicked like an empty gun. He squeezed a couple more times. Click. Click.

"Shit." He frowned back at the pump and noticed a sign that said, 'Pay Inside.' "Seriously?" he asked, annoyance overtaking relief. His desire to get home had taken on the urgency of an itch.

A bell jangled as Derren entered the store. A tight beam of sunlight shone through a small window illuminating rows of empty snack food shelves in the center of the room. Derren walked over to a high counter behind which a man stood mostly in shadow.

"I need a fill-up. Pump number . . . I don't know. It's the one there on the end."

"You think we got one?" came a voice from behind Derren. He turned and watched a solid bruiser of a man cross in and out of his field of view as he skirted the rows of shelves. The man planted himself squarely in front of the door, blocking the exit, a gun in his hand, pointed at the floor.

The hairs on Derren's arms and the back of his neck spiked. He thought of his gun, stashed away in a drawer at home, useless to him now. With slow, cautious movements and keeping his hands in full view, he turned back to face the guy behind the counter, who had shifted slightly so that a sliver of light cut a diagonal across his body.

"Empty your pockets, please," he said, one eye on Derren, the other on what looked like a gaming console with an antenna sticking out from its center. He pushed a combination of buttons, and the contraption crackled and popped like a Geiger counter. He slid his glasses up on his nose with an index finger. The gesture reminded him of Clayton, but that's where any similarity ended. This man's small beady eyes, whiskery pointed chin, and pronounced overbite gave his face a rat-like effect.

Derren hesitated. Was he about to lose his watch again? *Oh, hell no.* He had ransomed his mother's jewelry for this watch. They'd have to kill him. He scouted the room for anything that might suggest an escape route or give him an edge in a fight. Nothing immediately presented itself.

"Mr. Forbes asked you nicely. Do what he said," growled the guy with the gun.

Derren countered. "Hey, man. That car out there. It's worth two-million-dollars. Let me walk out of here, it's yours."

"You hear that, Gord," said the rat-faced Mr. Forbes. "We can joy ride til the asteroid hits."

"Empty your pockets," said Gord.

Derren placed his wallet, keys, a small baggy of marijuana, and a package of rolling papers on the counter.

Gord frowned. He abandoned his station by the door and moved in close behind Derren.

Derren felt the barrel of the gun poke his spine through his thin suit jacket.

"Search him," said Gord.

Mr. Forbes came from behind the counter and patted Derren down, then reached inside Derren's pants pocket and pulled out the watch. "Here it is."

Derren's heart pounded in his chest, his fists clenched. Rage and panic rang in his ears.

Forbes pushed his glasses again, this time with a knuckle, and ran his contraption over the watch. It emitted a constant static-y chitter. "Something's wrong with it though."

"What?" Gord and Derren's voices collided over the same word.

Gord moved back a couple of steps but kept the gun trained on Derren. "I thought your detection thingy was foolproof."

"I can pick up the broadband signal but not the decryption code. I don't understand," said Forbes. "Unless . . ." He went back behind the counter and brought out a tiny jeweler's pick. His dark pink tongue stuck out at the corner of his thin gray lips as he worked the point of the pick into a hole Derren had never noticed before. Then he picked up the console and ran it over the watch again.

"Yeah, thought so. It's counterfeit," Forbes announced.

Gord prodded Derren's back with the gun barrel. "You scamming asshole. Are you trying to sell fake departure watches to dumb fucks?"

"Nah, man. Look at his face. He *is* the dumb fuck.

The men broke into riotous laughter.

Derren had turned as ashen as a corpse. He snatched the watch from Forbes and laughed, feeling hysteria rise in his throat. "That's bullshit," he said, clinging desperately to that conviction. "You stupid motherfuckers and your stupid little toy . . . trying to tell me . . ."

Between snickers, Forbes said, "Dude, that watch ain't gonna tell you where to find the spaceship. I don't even think that thing can tell time."

Forbes and Gord doubled over with fresh peals of laughter.

Derren's sunken eyes looked glassy as if he'd been suddenly struck with fever. "You don't know what you're talking about," he screamed. Fisting the watch, he sucker-punched Gord, wrenched the gun from the man's hand and fired off a round, clipping Forbes in the shoulder. The rat-faced man yelped.

"Y'all keep laughing, motherfuckers," Derren shouted. He adjusted his grip on the gun, nearly choking on his desire to smoke these two ass wipes. But the memory of Sean's wink, his gaudy gold smile, his "See you on the flip side," reared up in front of him like a three-headed cobra. The departure watch was worthless.

Derren grabbed his belongings from the countertop, shoved them into his pockets and fled the store. He didn't know how many bullets were left in the gun, but he'd resolved to save every last one for Sean and Roofie.

Derren cranked the car around and sped back up the freeway toward Beverly Hills. He jerked the car into park in the driveway of the house he'd left only about an hour before. He felt the reassuring weight of Gord's gun in his pocket as he pounded toward the front door. His blood boiled, he panted like a thirsty dog, and murder surged in his ears. He would kill them. He'd take both their watches and give one to his mother. They would go to Ark Island together. But first Sean and Roofie were going to pay.

As soon as he burst through the door, the emptiness of the house, its mournful and obvious abandonment crashed down on Derren like a weight. He stood in the center of the room where he'd handed over all his mother's wealth for the counterfeit watch. The cotton laundry bag lay discarded at his feet. He ran through the house, cursing and trashing the sparsely-furnished rooms, substitutions for the disappeared Sean and

Roofie. With each fresh reminder of his loss, he kicked in drywall, smashed windows and furniture, and shot holes in upholstery. The stuffing spewed into the air where it swirled about the rooms like snowflakes.

Derren emerged back in the main room spent, dragging, and dripping sweat. His bottom lip trembled. Sinking to his knees, he grabbed up the laundry bag and crushed it to his chest. Something hard dug into his palm. Searching the bag, he unearthed a single item Sean and Roofie had overlooked among their glut of bounty. A delicate gold cross dangled from a length of fine chain. Suddenly, he remembered Reverend Joe. Derren rubbed a sweaty hand over the gun in his pocket. Reverend Joe had a departure watch and he was gonna give it up.

Reverend Joe liked the church best when it was empty, occupied by no one except himself and the spirits. He'd divested himself of his robes and sat in his office at the back of the church with his feet propped up on his desk, musing and getting quietly drunk. He'd preached his final sermon, on this planet anyway.

He'd assumed the computer would select all the best people to begin a new society. He'd had the shock of his life when he found himself among them. Knowing his own sins was probably his sole virtue.

Although his shock at having been chosen had worn off months ago, it had given way to a new and startling revelation. Something was deeply wrong with the list, with a system that would choose him for salvation, something deeply wrong with a god who would save a man like him. None of that would stop him from getting on that ship, of course. He gulped another glass of bourbon and reached for the bottle to refill.

Reverend Joe had just tipped the fifth glass of bourbon onto his lips when he spotted Derren raging toward him over the rim of the glass. He straightened in the chair, tried to stand up, but the boy was on him before he could take his feet from the desk, clouting him on the side of the head with the butt of a gun, knocking him to the floor.

"Give me the watch," Derren said.

The pastor's fall had sent the drink flying. The liquor sloshed over his gray suit and stained his tie. The sharp odor burned his nose in contrast to the mellow taste that still lingered on his tongue. He stared up in wide-eyed confusion.

Reverend Joe had seen Joyce's son Derren only rarely over the years when he'd attended the odd service from time to time with his mother. He'd attended this morning's service appearing smug and distracted. Now he looked rumpled and rabid, a dangerous liquid fever brightening his eyes.

"Now look son, you don't know what you're doing," Reverend Joe said, using a hand over hand maneuver on the desk to haul himself up off the floor. He stared down the barrel of the gun, trying to think, fear not having as sobering an effect as he'd hoped. The next words he spoke surprised him. "Are you an instrument of God?"

Derren was shaking, but his voice came out smooth and hard as worked metal. "Don't give me another excuse to kill you, old man. Just hand over the watch."

Reverend Joe regarded the watch, nodded, then lunged forward.

Derren fired the gun, squeezing off rounds until the clip was empty and the slide ratcheted back.

He knelt beside Reverend Joe's bullet-ravaged body, snatched the departure watch from his wrist and strapped it onto his own. He felt a buzz vibrate his bones, from wrist to elbow. A bright green digital alphabet lit the screen and scrolled up the watch face spelling out the rendezvous point for the spaceship, GPS directions, and pertinent timetables. A small window counted down to blast off.

Derren stood open-mouthed, mesmerized by the display. "Hot damn."

Tamika and Clayton lounged on one of the rocks jutting out of the sand on El Matador Beach, watching the red-orange glow of sunset over the water.

"The last of them will be gone soon," said Tamika.

"As many as we could find and stuff into those ships, anyway," said Clayton.

They'd brought along Derren's expensive scotch, and Tamika took a sip from her glass. It really was good stuff.

"Derren's going to be pissed," she said.

"Pissed that Azrael didn't pulverize the planet?"

"We should have let him in on it from the beginning, is all."

The beginning. It hadn't started out as a lie. Azrael's trajectory put it on an unalterable collision course with Earth. The world's nations soon realized humanity's survival depended on finding a new home. Tamika had discovered ARK-I5, a lonely island of a planet in a system otherwise consisting of two suns and three mini-moons.

Clayton's team had been tasked with programming and monitoring the computers that would sort and evaluate humanity. When the computer had begun to spit out the list of those to be relocated, he'd gone to his supervisor to report what he'd first thought was an unintentional glitch in the programming. It seemed people of color were culled with surgical meticulousness, dropping through the computer's algorithms like corrupted code.

His supervisor had assured him that the computer was incapable of bias.

"It'll all work out in the wash," his supervisor had said.

It had not. After a couple of weeks, he'd taken his concerns up the chain of command, meeting with various results, from patronizing to hostile.

97

One had asked, "Why do you people always see racism everywhere you look?"

Clayton had declined to dignify the question, the answer being self-evident.

He was smoldering with barely suppressed rage when he'd gone to see Tamika, still at work in her cluttered office at 2 am. He'd picked up pizza and a bottle of merlot, intending them as offerings to make up for her listening to him rant.

When he walked in the door, she grabbed him and peppered his face with excited kisses. He'd struggled to hold on to the pizza and wine while she waltzed him around the room. He'd be the first to hear her incredible news. Azrael was gigantic but hollow. Earth's atmosphere was going to pop it like a balloon and burn what was left to cinders.

She'd checked her calculations six times. She was certain. She needed to wake her bosses, call the president, spread the good news.

"I can tell them we're all saved," she'd said, her eyes brimming with emotion.

Clayton's story had dampened her enthusiasm for sharing. He told her how the computer had been programmed to cheat and about how his company seemed to be in on the fix.

They'd sat for a long while, each in their own thoughts.

Finally, Tamika had said, "This is an opportunity."

They'd talked all night before deciding on a course of action. Clayton would insert a few surreptitious tweaks to the computers' programming, piggy-backing on the already rigged system. The computers would now target a different, very select group. The entire basket of deplorables would be emptied out onto a far-away island planet. The meek might finally inherit the Earth.

"Derren will be grateful that he dodged that bullet," said Clayton. "Especially when we tell him who he'd have been stuck with on Ark Island. White supremacists and Nazis, corrupt politicians, dictators, warlords, drug lords, climate change deniers, corporate raiders and robber barons, terrorists . . ."

Tamika shivered with disgust. "He'll see losing that watch as a blessing."

Clayton twiddled the watch between his fingers as he gazed out at the horizon. "We did it. Tomorrow we can start building a better world."

Tamika refilled their glasses and held hers up for a toast. "To new beginnings."

The enormity of the spaceship gave Derren vertigo, like looking down into the Grand Canyon. The Notorious Derrenasty D grinned and hummed a tune as he jostled past his glowering shipmates, toward his assigned seat in the far rear of the cabin, toward his destiny.

Uwanna Thomas is an African American writer and avid fantasy and science fiction reader. Noticing a dearth of characters of color and non-European magickal systems represented in the genres, she decided to create some of her own.

Uwanna writes urban fantasy, magic realism and sci-fi. She is a member of the Pacific Northwest Writers Association and Rainforest Writer's Village.

Her other published works have appeared in Rosebud literary magazine and The Herb Companion.

She is a world traveler, quilter, jewelry artist, Master Gardener and a witch with particular interest in plant and Earth magicks.

She lives on Maury Island with her husband and three spoiled felines.

ISLAND MAGIC TALES

By Jane Valencia

Dear Islander,

Yes, I am writing to you. Whether you live in the mountains or the desert, the city or suburbs, or in the deep heart of a continent, you are an Islander living on Island Earth. The stillness within you knows the waves meeting the land and the mist speaking with trees. It knows that people grow from the roots of a small place like the big old trees that used to march across the continent, but which remain expansive and wise in our imaginations and in our bones. It knows about bird song and kelp, wood smoke, and cougar and deer.

Everything is connected on an island: you can't help but meet and remeet your neighbors, to gather blackberries abundant in yards and along roadways, and to deepen with one another into village. The island murmurs of the "thin places" where we can cross into new understandings about one another. Whether you consider yourself a citizen of Vashon Island, Turtle Island, or of another water-encircled land, each one of us is a member of the first island, the blue planet we call Earth.

Here is a bundle of island tales to ferry you into the true magic of the world.

Love,

Your Island

A note from Jane: These stories are ones I tell to families, adults, and to young children. Sometimes I perform them with song and harp, and sometimes I tell them outside to groups adventuring in the forest. Some of these stories feature heroes and tricksters from myth. A few involve characters – Shell, Govan, and Annie – from my children's fantasy novel, Because of the Red Fox, which is set on an island much like Vashon.

Enjoy!

1. Raven in Bird Land – a retelling of a native tale from the Puget Sound

Once upon a time, at the very beginning of things, Raven lived in the Land of Spirits, a place called Bird Land – and, heaven knows, that's just what this land was.

Goodness and gracious, for a place that is nowhere, birds are everywhere! And their entire chatter and song is total nonsense.

"Good morning, how are you? Aren't I pretty?"

"Hello, are you there?"

"Yeah, I'm here, are you there?"

"Hungry, hungry!" – and so on.

The conversation – or lack of it – is driving Raven crazy! Ugh, he can't stand this time before time and all the racket of the birds.

After an eternity of exasperation, or maybe in a moment that has no end, he senses something different below him. After a peck, prod, and jab here and there, Raven discovers that he's in the company of … a Stone. In Bird Land Raven hasn't had any opportunity to be surprised, but now he is.

"I'm Raven," Raven says, inspired to be polite and to introduce himself. He ruffles his feathers, proud to have thought of this thing: manners.

The Stone says nothing.

"You don't have much to say, do you," Raven says.

The Stone says nothing.

"Why are you so quiet?" Raven asks.

But the silence of the Stone only deepens.

Raven grunts. As he regards the Stone, an idea emerges.

"Ugh, and haw," says Raven. "Let's find our way out of here!"

Grasping the Stone with his talons, Raven plunges through nothing, and just like that – he is out of Bird Land. He finds himself in a place of endless salty waters. Startled by the sight – after all, he's never really seen anything before, and this experience is so very new – he drops the Stone.

And the Stone falls! A whistling arises as Air moves past Stone. Stone gives a little hum, and begins to grow. It splashes into the water, and sinks, but continues to grow, larger and larger.. Raven finds himself soaring over the Stone who now stretches in all directions. Stone has become land, and this land has become Earth. Earth speaks of possibility, of many more conversations than have ever been heard in Bird Land, and of space for silence too. Raven circles the Stone that is now Earth, and sees that the salty waters remain, encircling it.

Raven drops down to explore something new.

2. Birch Secrets

More than a thousand years ago, a boy and his family sailed away forever from their home country to settle on an island in the distant north and west. The island was a young land, with volcanoes that spewed lava and ash, and hot springs and geysers. Mosses, lichens, and other plants coated the land, turning the volcanic rock into soil. Other plants grew too, as did some trees. The trees were low-growing and twisted, not tall and far-reaching like those in his home country, but the boy's family and the other newcomers to the land found these stunted trees to be useful all the same.

And so it was that the boy had the task of heading into the land to find more trees. Like the other landholders in this place, the boy's family set out to clear the land of birch forest to make way for the sheep they had brought along from their home country. They used the downed trees to make tools, and to provide timber and charcoal for their fires. So the boy set out into the land, wondering if he might find a new stand of birch, for much of it had been cut and cleared already on the farmstead, as it had been on many neighboring farms.

The boy held in his mind and heart the scent, texture, and being of Birch, just as his mother had taught him. His mother had been Irish, and the Irish had a way with trees. And sure enough, he felt a quickening in his heart, and it was as if a silver strand connected him to something else. He followed this silver strand – which wasn't so much a thread he could see with his eyes as a sensation he could feel in his bones, in the very inner places of his being. Sure enough, he came upon a grove of Birch trees.

Well, the Birch we know here on Vashon are the same as those with which this boy's mother had grown up with in Ireland, and which much of Europe knew: the Silver Birch, tall, graceful trees that actually often grow from a single tree, and which might lean and curve as if they are walking or dancing. The Birch we know live to be as old as a human, and have deep furrowed bark with a white papery coating, and with a purple-red lace of twigs from which the leaves and catkins dangle. The Birch in this new land were more curved and squat, as I mentioned before. But they had a rosy furrowed bark, and the boy couldn't help but reach out and place his hand upon it ….

No.

The word was more feeling than sound. It rolled with the force of an ocean wave.

The boy snatched his hand away. "What?" Surely he hadn't heard the tree speak to him!

But … his mother spoke often of the trees. She said the fairies lived in some, and that the trees had minds and hearts of their own anyway, being the people of the plants.

No.

Again, that trembling, enveloping sense.

The boy moved backward, slowly rubbing his palms against his pants.

You will not tell your people about us.

"Won't I then?" The words left his lips before he could think whether he meant them.

No.

The boy took a few stumbling steps to the side, puzzling over the words of Birch. How could he not tell his people about these trees? They needed these trees! This folk knew of no other way to survive here!

You need us, yes.

The words and the sense of them slammed the boy to his knees. In a moment he felt himself to be a fallen catkin beneath a grandparent's foot. The earth hollowed beneath him, and the Birch before him seemed to unfurl and straighten. It grew and grew, extending dancing limbs, and then twisting and curling again. Could it be true? The boy felt the roots of the tree reaching far and wide below the earth, and the whole of the tree reaching deep and wide, spreading everywhere, the branches reaching huge and high above, into the heavens.

The boy had often heard stories and poems at the hearthfire of home and neighbors, and at least one of the tales spoken of the World Tree that held the realms of the upper and lower earths, as being a Birch tree. And of course his folk burned Birch twigs in their saunas to purify their bodies and spirits, and his mother spoke of making medicine with Birch back in Ireland …

Now he looked down, and it was as if the hollow that cradled him was a polished bowl, and that before him was a puddle or a well, covered with strips of birch bark. He pushed aside the Birch bark, and before him was indeed a well. The liquid within was clear and so sweet-smelling as to be intoxicating. And he knew the well from the tales: Mimir's Well, which, legend said, holds the waters of wisdom, inspiration, deep life. And certainly the vapor above the well was like the bees around honey that he'd known in his home country across the sea.

Beside Mimir's Well lay a wooden spoon carved with the sun and moon.

If you promise to protect us, you may drink of these waters.

The boy was dazzled, and of course he had to agree. "I'll protect you. I'll do whatever I can!"

Leaves like green-gold coins shivered in the breeze.

The boy dipped the ladle into the waters, but as he brought it to his lips,

103

eager to sip from the well of the world, he blinked. And in that instant, he fell over, tumbling into darkness.

He awoke in the Birch grove and there was no huge World Tree. Just the curving, low-growing trees with their white bark.

But in the birch-ringed hollow, he felt as if an ancient noble family stood in circle, observing him.

With a nod, he put down the twig in his hand (no ladle after all), and headed home.

The boy never spoke of the Birch grove. And indeed, he never was sure he could find it again.

But he thought often of the grove. And when he saw other trees, he treated them with the utmost respect, even when he cut them down and cleared them from the land as his folk told him to do. As he must do, because he knew no other way.

In time other trees grew on the land, Rowan and Alder. And other plants as well: Angelica and Yarrow. They grew on the family's land, even when in other farmsteads few plants grew, and no trees. In his family's farmstead: such an abundance! The place seemed a little grove itself. The boy became a man, and his family cared for the plants and trees and were kind to them, even when cutting the trees for wood, or harvesting the plants for food and medicine. Each winter, the family went out to a different part of the land, and gave milk to the ground – a humble gift to the World Tree Birch grove that … might still be there. And for generations the family prospered.

3. Coyote and the Gifts of the Animals – a continuation of a native tale

Perhaps you know of the epic tale, Coyote Steals Fire. If so, you recall how Coyote found the animal people shivering with the cold, and hungry because all they had was raw food to eat, and how they thought they must die if their situation didn't change.

And you recall how Coyote climbed a high snow-covered mountain, and watched the three fiercesome sister creatures called the skookums who jealously guarded the fire.

And how when Coyote needed to come up with a plan, he got one from the three huckleberry sisters who live in his stomach. He told that plan to the animals, and they agreed to help.They all positioned themselves up the mountain, and when Coyote stole the fire and the skookums chased him, he passed the fire from one animal who passed it to the next and the next, until finally Frog, in her escape, spat fire into Wood. There Wood held onto Fire until Coyote used two sticks to free Fire.

Well, Coyote's gift of fire to the animal people changed life in so many ways for them! Not only were they able to be warm and cook their food, but having fire meant having other good changes. They had light to see by at night, they figured out how make certain objects using fire – like burned bowls and spoons – and how to make beautiful things, like designs on wood.

And, ah! the beauty of fire – the way fire moves and changes. Fire, they discovered, tells stories! Or inspires others to do so. Fire awakens brightness and warmth in the heart. Because of fire, the animals began to explore. It was so much easier to venture away from camp, because the animals knew that not only would they have a warm fire and welcome to which to return, they'd have friends and family eager to hear all about their adventures and discoveries.

Around the fire, listening,to one another, the animals found that they could be kind to each other in ways they'd never considered before.

Can you imagine what in your life you enjoy because of fire? Imagine how much more so it was for the animal people!

One night, a long time later, on an island like this one, near the water and a hill and a forest, and around the fire, the animals told the story again about how Coyote Stole Fire, and of their part in the tale. Cougar was proud of the way he'd bounded from branch to branch through the high trees, Fox about how he'd moved invisibly through leafy underbrush, Antelope – how she'd sprung and changed course with impressive speed and agility, Squirrel, leaping branch to branch, Frog plunging into water … All the animals, not just Coyote, had done their best, each in their special way, and had kept the skookums from getting the fire back. The animals celebrated their abilities! All of their gifts had helped bring fire to the animal people. They had worked together, and they had used their gifts to do this thing that had helped all the animal people, everywhere.

And though Coyote causes trouble sometimes – his mayhem is legendary – the animals were hugely grateful to Coyote. He had heard their plea and seen their pain. He'd gone up the mountain. He'd made the plan –

"No," a Dragonfly interjected. "His three sisters in the form of huckleberries did."

Well, then, all the animals were grateful to Coyote and his three huckleberry sisters! What would be a good way to express their gratitude?

Suggestions pelted round.

"We can yell: 'hey, Coyote – thank you!'"

A nice idea, but maybe not enough.

"Let's make a pleasing potion for Coyote to drink – to give to the sisters in his stomach!"

Nice. But .. well, wouldn't it be great to give Coyote and his sisters something that was more directly inspired by what Coyote had done? Maybe the gift could involve all the animals in some way?

Maybe the gift could help Coyote in some way that he might especially need?

The animals pondered this last thought. Then Rough-Skinned Newt had an idea.

"Back before fire, we were too cold and miserable to enjoy the world, much less notice anything good about it. Why don't we each go out, find something special that we'd never have noticed before fire, and bring it back for Coyote?"

This notion seemed just right! Clapping their paws and claws, the animals cheered.

So, the animals divided into four groups, and spread out to the four directions, heading up hill, along beach, through marsh, and into forest. They sought treasures that spoke to their hearts, and found some: a moon snail shell, a beautiful piece of Madrona wood, lichen that had fallen to the ground ...

Raccoon came upon a rock. He held it up. He sat with it. The rock seemed to be listening to him. Raccoon whispered a secret. The rock quietly held it. A Listening Rock! Who didn't need a Listening Rock? Coyote had his three huckleberry sisters to listen to him, but sometimes you need something or someone who is not your immediate family to truly hear you.

When the animals returned to the fire, many were excited, and several were thoughtful. Fox had placed a basket near the fire. One by one, the animals dropped their treasures into it. Soon it was Raccoon's turn. Raccoon was about to drop his treasure into the basket – but then he couldn't.

"Oh, this Listening Rock is so special," he said."I don't know ... I'm not sure if I can just give it away like this."

The animals got into an uproar. "You mean you don't want to give Coyote a gift after all?"

"No, no." said Raccoon, confused. He wasn't sure what he meant. But then he turned to the rock. The rock seemed to listen to his heart. As the rock listened, a thought dropped into Raccoon's mind.

"No. It's just that this is a Listening Rock. I want you all to know about it. If you all know what I love about this rock, then we'll all hold the story of it. I won't forget the rock, even though I'm giving it away."

The animals discussed this, wondering what to do. The Listening Rock listened. A plan dropped into hearts.

This is what they did.

Raccoon held the rock and told the animals about what he found so special about it. When he was done, he passed the Listening Rock to the next animal, and that animal passed it to the next. When the rock reached Antelope, Antelope placed it in the basket.

Then Squirrel held up a beautiful hazelnut. Squirrel told about finding the hazelnut and how she knew it is one of the most delicious ever. She passed the hazelnut around the circle. Raccoon put it in the basket.

And so on. Each animal shared a few words about the treasure they'd found, and passed it around. In time the animals had put all their gifts into the basket.

Bear then swam the basket across the water to the mainland. He made the long trek through the mountains to the drylands beyond, to where Coyote had gone. It took some time to track down Coyote, and that journey is worthy of the telling at another time. In any case, one crisp cold night under a milky scatter of stars, Bear found Coyote.

"What's this?" Coyote snapped, stirred from some far away place in which he'd been dreaming.

"We animal people want to thank you for bringing fire to us," Bear said, "and for helping us learn how to use it. Because of your gift, we now have the strength to explore and find wonderful things all around us, and we have curiosity. We've brought you gifts from the four directions in which we travel. We wanted to share our discoveries with you, with thanks."

Coyote eyed the basket. He thrust his paw into the treasures. One by one, he held them up. He peered at the shining sunset-glowy hazel nut, the mysterious moon snail shell speaking of endless motion of the sea, and so many other treasures.

The gifts remind Coyote of the beauty of the land he had left. Feeling a deep yearning and churning, he realized he missed the land around which he'd found fire. "I want to go back," he thought. An ocean of joy opened within him.

He hadn't needed the gifts, Coyote realized, but something new had opened in him like a flower because he been given them.

Coyote held up the Listening Rock. The Listening Rock listened to Coyote's heart.

Coyote thought of the skookums, so afraid to share, atop the distant snow-covered mountain. They had been afraid that sharing fire would make them weak and powerless. But fire had helped the animal people find their own strength. It had been a good thing. And the good thing had spread to Coyote.

"Thank you," he said to Bear.

Coyote and Bear journeyed back to the west. But before they reached the island, Coyote parted company with Bear to make a separate journey. He whispered his plan to the three huckleberry sisters who live in his stomach. They nodded in agreement.

107

With the treasure basket Coyote climbed a tall snow-covered mountain. Yes, the very mountain where the skookums lived, the skookums who knew nothing of desert, ocean, island, or anything else but their mountain top.

Coyote was excited and curious to share the gifts with the skookum.

4. Lia and the Old Woman

Some of you may have heard the story about a wood elf named Lia Starglimmer and how her village sent her out to live in the woods for a week all by herself. She's been out there, managing well enough with a shelter she's built for herself and foraging for plants and mushroom. But at this point, she's feeling pretty hungry. The food she's gathered just isn't enough. So Lia begins some very hard work on gathering materials and making some tools. She fashions some traps and other tools for hunting, feeling painfully hungry all the while, and sad too that she'll need to eat an animal.

With her sadness beginning to overtake her feeling of hunger, Lia sits down by her shelter. She thinks about all the plants and animals and things she's eaten all her life. She thanks those plants and animals, taking a lot of time with that. And she takes time away from working on her tools to make an honoring for all the life that has sustained her until now.

Then Lia goes back to her tool making, finishes a trap and sets it up. She whispers a thank you into the air, and that's for the next animal she will eat. Maybe it will be today, maybe tomorrow.

And amazingly enough, when Lia goes out with her throwing stick, she spies a squirrel on a branch. Faster than thought, she hurls that stick … and … hits that squirrel, killing it.

Lia sits with the squirrel. "Thank you, Squirrel. Thank you for your life. Thank you for feeding mine."

Then she sets about making it into food – I won't go into the detail about that right now. Suffice it to say that, sitting at her fire later that night, she felt well-nourished indeed. And again, she thanks that squirrel for giving its life to help her.

Satisfied, Lia sits back and gazes out into the night. She notices a glimmer of light in a very different direction than the wood elf village. And … maybe … she hears a little music. Some singing, a drum. It's very faint … but … maybe.

The next morning, Lia wakes up hungry. She checks her trap, but nothing's there, so she heads out. Something about what she heard and saw last night makes her turn in that direction to seek it out. And in time she discovers the source of the light and the music.

It's a human camp. Some poles with skins on them are set up like little tents, and a fire is still smoldering. By that fire is an old woman. Wrapped in a heavy blanket, the old woman is asleep. She has a sad look on her face. No one is around.

That seems strange to Lia, that the human people would leave such an old elder alone like that. But Lia knew that sometimes humans have different ways than the wood elves in that regard, and they didn't always think about the way they cared for people.

The humans must feel that the old woman will be just fine. And, in fact, Lia can almost hear that old woman talking to the people that morning, "Go on now, I'll be fine." Sometimes old people are very proud. Still, in Lia's village, when an old person says, "Go on, I'll be fine," an elf will usually secretly come around to check on them, or even stay hidden nearby.

Hidden in the shrubs, Lia sneaks around the human camp. It doesn't seem that any of the humans have done that, stayed hidden away while the rest of the group hunted or gathered or did whatever they'd set out to do. Lia turns to go too … but …

Lia finds that she can't quite return to her hunting. She can't leave that woman alone! And anyway … it looks like the old woman's fire needs building up.

So, as quiet as a cloud, Lia searches the area for twigs and larger pieces of wood and she quietly approaches the old woman, and quietly builds up the fire.

Then Lia notices that the old woman has a mug, but only about a mouthful of water is within it. So Lia quietly reaches for the cup goes off to a nearby spring and refills the mug and quietly brings it back and places it by the sleeping woman.

Then Lia thinks that the woman might be hungry when she wakes, so, whispering thanks to the plants, she gathers new nettles and salmonberry leaves and miner's lettuce, and other good stuff just coming up, and sets them in a neat pile beside the woman. As a last thought, she tucks some of her precious squirrel meat into the leaves.

Now Lia moves to a place where she can see all around. And she stays there, through the afternoon. She looks out for this old woman and tends the fire from time to time. A little dandelion is pushing up through the leaves, and Lia thinks about eating it—she's so hungry again, and dandelions are so delicious, but it seems like the dandelion is looking too, watching out for the old woman.

As the sun begins to set, the junco makes its smacking noise, and some birds dart up in the trees, calling out. Lia hears people coming, loud in talk and laughter, birds alarming all along the way.

The dandelion speaks quickly into Lia's heart.

"Ok! Then! Thank you!". Lia plucks the dandelion, and, quietly as a cloud, she slips between the shrubs over to the old woman. She places the dandelion ... gently ... on the old woman's lap.

As stealthy as a fox, Lia returns to the forest. No bird darts away. Chewing its cud, a deer glances her way but remains where it is.

Back in the camp, the old woman wakes to the sunlight yellow of the dandelion flower. Her heart, she realizes, is cheered, and, what do you know–she's hungry. Ah, here's why! A lovely new spring salad is by her side, and–is that squirrel meat? The old woman enjoys the food and the fire as her people return.

Out through the forest, Lia heads back to her own shelter, feeling satisfied.

5. Annie and the Secrets of Nettle

Once upon a time a girl named Annie goes to stay with her Aunt Elinn in a pointy house in the forest. Her aunt runs a business where she sews dolls and quilts, but she also makes medicine and foods from herbs, and this she provides for the forest folk. It's springtime, just like now, and Aunt Elinn has a lot of people eager for the dolls and dragons she makes, so she's asked Annie to help her harvest the new spring plants while she focuses on sewing.

Yesterday, Annie harvested big leaf maple flowers and dandelion flowers to make fritters, which are like pancakes. But today Aunt Elinn has a big mission for her.

"I want you to harvest Nettles," she says. "I need a lot of them." And she holds up a big basket. "Another day I'll have you harvest Nettle to make medicine, but today you'll go out and find Nettles to make into food. We'll be preparing teas and salad dressing and a big pot of soup today, and to have on hand for infusions. So the purpose is food, Annie. Food and nourishment."

Aunt Elinn sighs, closing her eyes. "Ah, there's nothing like Nettles at this time of year. When I drink my Nettle infusions, it's like a green river of life energizes my whole body. Nettle, ah! So very wonderful for our bodies and spirits. Especially in the spring, when everything is new again."

Annie nods as Aunt Elinn talks. Aunt Elinn is very particular about giving and receiving when it comes to gathering plants for food or medicine or for anything else. Picking up the basket, Annie grabs a pair of scissors. She reaches for her gardening gloves ... but then stops.

Truth be told, Annie is a little nervous about getting stung by Nettles. She's been stung before, and the feeling is a tingly and a little jabby and fiery

... but it goes away, and of course she's learned how to soothe and cool those Nettle stings. Sometimes she uses the plantain salve she made with her aunt. Other times she uses the juice of a sword fern, yellow dock, or even of Nettle herself.

Aunt Elinn doesn't mind Nettle stings at all. In fact, she picks Nettle with her bare hands not even trying to avoid being stung. She even gets a fiery glee when she gets stung, as if she enjoys the feel of it!

But Annie is more careful than that. She knows that the hairs containing the formic acid that causes the sting are on the undersides of the leaves and on the stems. Harvesting works the same way too. Grasp from the top, and use your scissors – snip! And drop the Nettle tops into your basket. She could use gloves, or a tea towel to grasp the Nettle, but in that moment she is "stung" with a wild idea. Annie decides to leave those things behind and just use her hands and those scissors.

So, Annie heads out of Aunt Elinn's pointy house, through the garden, and out along a trail. She finally arrives near a huge Nettle patch. It's positively green with health and new growth.

"Hello, Nettle," she calls. And just like her Aunt Elinn always does with the plants, she finds one that seems to the largest and most vibrant of the group: the grandparent plant. She settles down beside that one to talk with it.

First, she gives Nettle a sprinkle of dried lavender and corn meal. A little gift.

"Hello, Grandmother Nettle. I'm Annie. How are you today?" She chats with the Nettle for a bit. Then, says: "I'm here to harvest a basket of Nettle for food and drink for the forest folk. May I harvest some here?"

Annie listens then. For a feeling, to the forest sounds, to the quality of quiet. As she feels a yes, a second wild idea drops in.

Something about Nettle reminds her of a cat. Annie recalls how Aunt Elinn's cat, Mischief, will gently or firmly let Annie know when she is too rough or when he's had enough attention. And if Annie is particularly carried away, Mischief will nip her or spring away. What if Nettle is like a cat?

Annie leans over to sniff Nettle – ow! Her nose. Maybe she was too pushy or big for Nettle in some way.

Leaning back on her heels, Annie considers. What might be 'quiet' enough to be just right with Nettle? Annie looks around the forest and into the sky. Hm ... ah, cloud! The clouds are like ghosts today. Annie wonders, What might happen if I imagine myself as a cloud?

Annie takes time to turn herself into a cloud (in her imagination, anyway!). She is cool vapor, full of space and stillness, yet moving. Filled with cloudness, Annie drifts into the Nettle. This time, oh so gently, she touches the tops of the leaves. No stings. Now, Annie touches the undersides, and the stalks ...

Really, no stings! Annie goes from one Nettle to the next, petting them oh so gently. She recalls Aunt Elinn saying, "Nettle teaches you to pay attention."

Oh, how magical when one does!

Now Annie is softly touching a whole patch of Nettles.

Ha! Emboldened, she breaks a leaf off with her bare hands. "Ouch!"

Fine, then. Not with her hands. Annie reaches for the Nettle top, and with her scissors, snips the stalk. The Nettle drops into her basket. She continues on, harvesting in this way.

Soon Annie finishes, but she doesn't feel ready to leave. So, like a cat, she moves carefully between the Nettles. And carefully she lays down on the ground, nestled in their midst.

Birch trees slant overhead. Nuthatches beep companionably. Nettles wave gently close around her but do not sting her.

After a long green dream or two, Annie gets up and carefully makes her way out of the Nettle patch. She wants to give a gift, a thank you to Nettle but what? It would be fun to sing a song to Nettle, but no song she knows comes to mind. Instead, a melody wakes up, and she hums it. Maybe, if you listen carefully, you can hear it right now.

With a wave to Nettle, Annie heads back to Abracadabra House. Humming her Nettle melody, Annie is filled as if with a river of the magic and kindness of Nettle that she'll be sharing with the forest folk.

And now you too know how to give and receive Nettle magic and kindness.

6. Finn and The Salmon Of Wisdom – a retelling of an Irish myth

Right now is the time that the salmon return home from their many years in the ocean. Up streams and rivers they swim and leap and lunge, inhaling deeply of the waters along the way, taking in the scent of this turn of the bank, that eddy, this mix of plants on that part of the river – smells that reach into their beginnings and urge them forward, tugging them onward, leading them to their home stream and up it, back to the place of their birth. They make a long and dangerous journey to birth a new generation of salmon and, in doing so, to die.

This is a story about one particular salmon, a large, and very old salmon. This Salmon has made its way hundreds of miles from out in the ocean to return to this river, a particularly sacred river. And this story is about an

112

elder man and about a boy, and about the intertwining of their destinies.

Well, the legends say that this particular Salmon is none other than the oldest of all animals. It was born in the pool at the head of the river back in the beginning of the world. And this Salmon, being the oldest, is said to hold the memories of the land since the beginning of time. And it is said that this Salmon, having lived thousands of years out in the ocean, holds all the wisdom as well of the sea.

The old ones and the old tales all agree: one day the Salmon's life will end. Someone named Finn will catch that fish and kill it and eat it. And in the eating of it, Finn will gain all of the Salmon's memories and wisdom.

Well, Finn in this land is a common enough name. It's a word that means "fair one" – one who is pleasing to look at, or one who has a quality about him that makes you look twice. You might be given the name at birth, but you might also receive it later, as the result of some deed, or because someone admires you for another reason.

One of the many people of the land named "Finn" is a poet and wise man named "Finneces", which means Finn-Seeker. And certainly, Finneces is a seeker. When he learns that the Salmon of Wisdom has made its way up the River Boyne to the pool of the head of the river, he make his way up there too. As a poet it is his greatest dream to be the one to receive all of the wisdom from this ancient salmon. Imagine the poetry he would compose! Imagine the noble folk – kings and queens, druids, and priests – who will journey to consult with him on important matters.

Finneces indeed discovers a pool at the head of the river, a pool surrounded by nine hazel trees. And as those hazel trees drop nuts into the water, Finneces watches, open mouthed, as the ancient Salmon of Wisdom rises up from the depths of the pool. This Salmon is battered, lumpy, aged, and large, like an old-growth tree. Swishing fins and tail, as if offering a bit of gratitude to the trees above, the Salmon eats the hazelnuts that have fallen into the water. But the Salmon leaves some of the hazelnuts as well, and the hazelnuts get caught in the currents and begin to float out of the pool. Finneces snatches the hazelnuts out of the water, and in a few moments he's cracked those nuts and eaten the meats of them. At Finneces' action, the Salmon turns on its side, one eye upon him, then slips away to some hidden place in the water.

Seven years pass. Finneces has tried catching that Salmon by any way you can think – line, nets, weir – but the Salmon evades him, remaining mostly hidden in the murky depths of the pool. The Salmon arises only to eat an occasional hazelnut that drops into the water.

"Ah, some day," sighs Finneces, as he adjusts the nets in the water, and settles under the trees, a manuscript in his lap in which he writes poetic verse as it occurs to him. As he reflects on the beauty around him, it seems that a breeze moves through the woods like a salmon, and that the trees themselves begin to murmur like water ...

And now another sound layers into the wind. The sound of laughter, a youthful cry – close at hand!

Finneces scrambles to his feet.

A boy, maybe twelve years old, bursts up from the bushes beside Finneces. The boy laughs.

"You didn't hear me, did you, or see me! You were so intent on your thinking – I just wondered .... and so I snuck ... But I hope you're not offended. My grandmother sent me to you – she's a lady of the forest, and she said I'd be safe with you if I became your apprentice. My dad's enemies will try to kill me someday, but a poet's body is sacred. So I'm safe if I'm your apprentice – that's true isn't it?"

Finneces is feels himself dazed and dazzled. This boy seems to have appeared out of nowhere, and where once were the quiet forest sounds, now ... all this talk! And, indeed, something seems to be ... dazzling about this boy.

"Yes," says Finneces, coming to his senses. "Yes, you'd be safe as my apprentice. Do you ... do you want to be wise, lad?"

The boy laughs – such an infectious laugh. "Yeah, sure," he says.

And at that moment, water bursts like a geyser from the pool. From its center the great Salmon of Wisdom himself flings forward in a wave of water. Rolling onto its side, the Salmon peers with one eye at the youth.

"Amazing!" Finneces says. "I've never seen the salmon take much note of a person, why I – "

In that moment, the Salmon thrusts itself into Finneces' nets. The fish begins to thrash.

"Boy," Finneces yelps. "Help me!"

As Finneces lunges for the net, the boy springs for the other end. With a strength that takes Finneces further by surprise, the boy hauls the Salmon out of the pool.

Finneces pulls out his knife – his hand is shaking. This is it! This is the moment he's awaited for seven long years. In an eternity that lasts an instant, Finneces stares at this huge creature, battered by many long years, many long journeys. As the Salmon returns the gaze, Finneces understands clearly that the Salmon has decided to give his life.

"Thank you, ancient one. Thank you, lord of the ocean, of the river, keeper of the memories of the land." Finneces plunges into prayer. His knife fumbles from his fingers..

The boy retrieves the knife.

"Go ahead then, boy," Finneces says.

And the boy first lays one hand on the great creature. He looks into the Salmon's eye, and seems to know too that the Salmon is giving itself. With a deep breath the boy accepts the gift and takes the life.

The boy and Finneces rest in that shining stillness that opens when a soul leaves a body. And for a time that stillness lasts.

Then the sounds of the forest return.

"Fine then," Finneces says. "Boy, I'm – my hands – I'm too worked up. Prepare the fish – you know how to do that, don't you?"

"Yes," the boy says. "Of course."

"Fine," Finneces says. "I'll get the fire going."

And Finneces does. The boy himself works carefully, cutting the fish into fillets, placing them on sticks around the fire once it's burned down to coals.

Finneces cannot feel settled. "I – you cook the fish, please. I'll gather more wood, yes – that will help me focus. Just don't eat any of the fish."

And he races off into the woods.

As soon as Finneces leaves, the salmon begins to cook. The boy tends the fire, talking with it, sensing just what to do to keep it alive in just the right way. He hears Finneces returning up the hill. And at that moment, the fat on the fish bursts and three scalding drops fall upon the boy's thumb.

"Ouch!" The boy thrusts his thumb into his mouth.

As he tastes the fat, all the memories of the land ... all the wisdom of the ocean ... flow into him.

He draws his thumb away, just as Finneces returns bearing the wood. "Boy—are you all right?"

"Fine," the boy says. "I just ... fat from the fish fell on my thumb, and..."

But something in the boy's eye tells a story to Finneces. Finneces chuckles. "Boy, it's all right. What's your name then, lad?"

"Fionn. Fionn macCumhaill."

"Finn. Son of the mighty warrior Cumhaill." Finneces chuckles again. "Oh, yes. I see clearly now. The prophecy was meant for you. All that wisdom, all that inspiration contained in only the first taste of the Salmon. Well, then. It's all yours. Let's continue with our task of enjoying this Salmon.

And so they prepared a plate of Salmon for the Ancestors, as well as for themselves. And they set out Salmon for the animals that had begun to gather at the edges. And the Gulls ate, as did Raven and Wolf. Bear dragged the carcass out to the trees, so that not only did Bear eat, but so did the forest. All were nourished by the Salmon.

They fed Salmon to the waters and to the earth. And the two finns, Finneces and Fionn mac Cumhaill, savored the flesh of this incredible salmon, in awe of the tremendous gift that Salmon brings to all of us.

We may not experience the wisdom of the ocean and memories of the land in quite the burst that Fionn mac Cumhaill experienced, but something of it enters our cells and nourishes our flesh and bone, and we are changed, just as Fionn was, by the awesome, generous gift of Salmon. Next when you eat Salmon, you may want to take time to not only give thanks to this mighty creature that braves so much to return to its birthplace and give of itself, but to savor the secrets that are meant just for you.

7. Shell and Govan and the Little Sun

This is a story about a brother and a sister on an island very much like this one, during a time of magic. Shell and her brother Govan are very comfortable in the woods. They both wear leather tunics and leggings dyed green and leather boots of a pale deerskin that they have fashioned for themselves. When they move through the forest, they walk absolutely silently. Sometimes it seems like they are trees moving through the woods, they blend in so well. Their mother lives in Abracadabra House, a pointy house like a witch's hat, and their father lives in a green house that once was a church. Now that magic is back in the world in a way that is easy for everyone to experience, their family lives in a single house that changes. Sometimes the house chooses to be Abracadabra House, and sometimes it appears as a little place called the Green Church.

On the morning of the shortest day after the longest night, Shell wakes before sunrise and slips outside. A dream has awakened her, a shiver of a dream, so she heads outside to see if she can find it. In the clearing just outside Abracadabra house she indeed discovers that shiver of a dream. It's lying on the ground — a small silver star. In wonder, she picks it up and slips it into her pocket.

Now, I hope you all know that winter is a time when our dreams are wide awake. So, take a look at the surface under your feet (or hooves or paws) right now, and imagine that you see a little star lying on the ground. Do you see it? Right in front of you? Let's all take a moment to scoop up our little stars. You can hold your star in your lap, or you can tuck that star into your sleeve – whatever you like. Just keep it nearby for now.

So, Shell has tucked her little star into her pocket. She takes a moment, listening like a deer and with open heart, then continues on her way, following where the land calls her.

Up through the trees, she sees the flicker of flame and a glow. She steps between the trees and...stops short. Her brother Govan is there, tending a fire. He frowns as he tends it. Then Shell realizes ... he isn't actually working with the fire after all, not in the way we might with a camp or cooking fire. The fire is tending itself.

As Shell watches in wonder, she notices how very different this fire is from any other she's ever seen. You know how fires seem to talk and gesture? This fire is alive like that but even more so. This fire has flames that leap and spring about, that open and close like petals. If you've ever seen a sunflower, maybe the smaller ones with all the longer petals—the rays, and the tiny flowers within the head—you might think that this fire resembles a flower like that.

"What did you find?" she asks.

Govan gives an unhappy sigh. "I think it fell out of the sky."

"What fell out of the sky?"

With his stick, he points up at the sun's arc. With a jolt Shell realizes that the sun isn't in the sky where she would expect it to be − even early in the morning, even on the shortest day of the year.

"This is the sun? But ... it's so small!"

Govan shrugs. "The sun gets older all year, until it's the very oldest it can get, as it was yesterday. Then it becomes young again, a baby. But ... like a baby − say, a baby robin − I ... I think the sun fell out of its nest."

"The sun doesn't have a nest up in the sky, does it?"

Govan shrugs. "Maybe and maybe not. Anyway, I think the sun dropped out of where it's supposed to be right now."

They both gaze at the sky, and then at the little sun.

Shell sighs. "Little sun, can we help you ride the wind back into the sky? Somehow?" she asks.

The sun doesn't speak in words, but it sings in color and warmth and in the flicker of its flames. Sun language.

Govan shakes his head. "It keeps talking like that. I just don't understand."

They watch for another minute.

"Wait," Shell says. "I found something when I got up this morning. Maybe it can help."

She pulls the star from her pocket. It sparkles and shines, silver and a little bit bright blue. Without thinking she places it in the fire − and the sunfire flares up, mingling with the star.

The sun lifts just a little bit off the ground, and Govan and Shell jump up, excited. But − the Sun pauses. It just can't seem to drift any higher.

"Oh, we have to help it," Shell says. "What can we do to help it return to the sky?"

Clenching his hands, Govan shakes his head. "Oh, I don't know!" Suddenly he turns to—you, me, to all of us readers and listeners of this tale. "Do you have any ideas?"

"How have folk helped the sun return to the sky during this time of year?" Shell asks. "I know we've all done this before!"

Around this tale, one thought sparks, and then another. The people of earth have always helped the sun return. Maybe you have helped it yourself. Now, many thoughts and suggestions fly. Do you hear them. Do you offer some yourself?

"Yes, yes!" Govan and Shell say in excitement. "Gathering with family and friends, giving gifts, feasting, singing, dancing – yes, people have all done these things to help celebrate the sun back into the sky. We've all done this."

Springing to her feet, Shell turns to all of us (and I don't know about you, but I feel mighty surprised that a character in a story can see me!)

"Were you here when I put that dream-star into the sunfire," asks Shell. "Did you see the sun rise up just a little bit? Each of you has a star too – a star from your dreams and wishes. In fact – even though I put my star into the sunfire, I think I have it right here again." She pats her chest. "Come on, everyone: let's gather your stars into your hands. Blow them into the fire. … Yes, like that! Now with the magic of our stars let's wish the sun back into the sky. We can let our fingers be the breeze to send it on its way!"

And there it goes! The little sun sails up into the sky. We are all helping to get it there!

"And you know?" Shell says, turning to Govan and to all of us. "I bet we can help the sun keep growing bigger and stronger. I bet that's what celebrating with families and friends, giving gifts, and sharing fun does – it helps the sun grow big and strong!"

Well, that may or may not be what happens in our everyday world. But in our imagination and dreams it can. Certainly when we celebrate, and share gifts and fun, it feels like the sun is that much stronger and brighter.

And that is the end of the Shell and Govan's tale, but … it's only the beginning of ours.

8. Flame and Nest

Once upon a time, a small Flame was looking for a home. The Flame was invisible and had no heat. It was just an idea of Fire. It wanted to find a home on earth so that it could actually be born, and do what it was meant to do. This little Flame yearned to give warmth and light to the human people, and to help them gather together to tell stories, get to know each other, care about each other, and to discover each others' dreams. This Flame wanted to help inspire those dreams . The kinds of dreams that could be born from the stories and from kindness, and from listening around this Fire would be beautiful and strong, and help all of nature to thrive – the animals, the trees, and the insects, the waters, and the people, and Mother Earth herself. That's the dream that lived in this Flame that had yet to be born.

But Flame had to be born.

Flame wandered, looking for just the right place, time, and opportunity to emerge as a spark.

Flame noticed some kids playing hide-and-seek in a park, but when she arrived there, she realized that though fun was being had, something wasn't really there for her to show up in the way she was meant to be, so she moved on.

Flame entered a library, but though there were a lot of stories there – shelves of them! – and there were humans of all ages, big ones, little ones, all gathered around seeking stories and even looking a little into their dreams – that wasn't a place either for a fire to burn or for people to gather round.

Flame went into the woods. She found all kinds of life intertwined – the bacteria in the soil, the insects, trees, mice, animals, and so on, all of them busy with the things they needed to do as winter came to an end and spring was a much nearer promise. She even came upon a child or two from the hide-and-seek game in these woods – hiding among the shrubs, or hugging a tree, or gazing at a mushroom in their hiding place. But she didn't really find the right place and opportunity to be born.

Flame was discouraged. Leaving the forest, she hovered at the edges, wondering what to do, trying to sense where to go. She began to be afraid … afraid that there was no place on this earth for her to be born. No place on earth for her special magic.

Finally, she gave a deep sigh, as only an unborn flame can do. And she closed her flame eyes, as only a flame can do. She settled into a quiet darkness and just released herself into it. The quiet, strangely enough, began to feel comforting. And it began to suggest some things to her.

Open your Deer Ears, it whispered. Don't try to find anything. Just listen.

So Flame cupped her flame hands to her ears so that she had ears like the Deer she had just seen in the forest, and she listened. Bird sounds came into her awareness.

Open your Owl Eyes, the Quiet whispered. Don't try to see. Just notice.

So Flame put out her flame hands and imagined she had the wide vision of an Owl, and she just noticed.

Tune deeper into your heart, the Quiet said. Just settle into it as if it were a cozy nest.

So Flame took a deep breath, and nestled into her heart, as if it were the most cozy, comforting nest ever. Just right for her.

And indeed that nest felt just right.

As Flame lay in the nest of her heart, with her Owl Eyes open to movement, color, and anything else all around her, and her Deer Ears listening in all directions – to the nearest sound, the farthest … the softest, the loudest — she noticed again the bird sounds. And she noticed a bit of movement.

Something within her sparked awake.

A pair of robins flew to and fro to a shrub. Each time they flew to the shrub, they carried a bit of dry grass, or dry moss, or little shreddy things to that place. They busied themselves, then flew off, only to return with more dry grass, tiny twigs, fluff, or shreddy things.

Flame listened to her heart, and to what her Owl Eyes and Deer Ears noticed, and wandered over to where the Robins were so busy.

She saw this: The Robins were building a nest of dried grasses and soft things — a cozy little bundle of this and that. She looked at that nest, that she knew it to be for an egg the mother would soon lay. The nest would become a home for a baby bird, and for the whole bird family.

"Oh, how cozy something like that would be for me too!" the Flame thought with longing. "How can I have my own nest? Who could be mother and father birds to me?" — because although some flames have a parent fire, Flame knew she wasn't that kind.

Flame wondered for one quick moment if the Robins could become her parents. What if she could snuggle into their nest and they would feed her special things (she somehow knew that that's what birds did for their young)? She might even call out to them "beep, beep!" — crying out for food. Next moment she shook her flame self. If she was born in that nest, Flame somehow knew that she'd eat it all up — and no baby birds could born there!

Who, then, could be her parents? Who could build her a nest?

Flame settled back into her Deer Ears, Owl Eyes, and into the nest of her heart. After all, that's where she'd noticed that something like a nest might be a good idea.

At that moment, Flame heard shouts and laughter. The playing children! And she heard low, kind voices. The grown-ups gathering stories in the library were now outside with the children! She hurried over to the humans. A whole bunch of humans of all ages, young to medium to old, gathered at the edge of the woods in the park. They were gathering! In just the way that she'd dreamed!

"This is a great place for our picnic," an old man said, settling on a bench.

"Oh, yes," said a woman. "It could be just the right place to tell stories, if only we had a fire."

"Oh, that would be so fun," a girl said.

"How could we do that?" asked the boy playing hide-and-seek. "We don't have any of those charcoal briquet things."

"Hmm," muttered the woman.

"I know, I know!" thought Flame, and at that she dropped into the boy's heart.

"Oh," said the boy, his eyes widening. "I have an idea." He quickly told the other children. And immediately they were out in the woods, gathering dried grasses, and fluff, and tiny woody bits, and thin twigs that snapped, and quickly they wove a nest, just like the birds had.

They brought the nest back to the picnic area. Some teenagers had gathered a bundle of wood from the woods – twigs and branches of different sizes, all of them dry and snappy. The boy laid the nest in the fire pit, and the woman brought out a box of matches. Flame was so astonished and excited. She hovered above the nest, and when the woman struck the match she burst forth at the end of it. The woman lowered Flame gently into the nest.

And, what do you know! The nest was a cozy and comfortable as Flame had dreamed. Now that she was born, she was hungry, and she began nibbling on her delicious nest.

The woman laid twigs around Flame's nest, and fed her with twigs. She laid larger and larger sticks around. Oh, what a beautiful home for Flame! And she was being fed, just like those Robins would feed a baby bird! And just like a baby bird, she was also being fed on song. All the children and teens and grownups gathered round sang to her as she came more and more into life. Soon she was a full grown fire, strong, and alive. The people celebrated with food and drink, and stories sparked and burned and grew. And when day turned to night, the people began sharing their dreams – their hopes and visions for what they longed to bring alive in the world.

Flame gathered all those stories, songs, dreams, and visions, and shone them to the sky!

And the community wove together like a nest around her.

Jane Valencia is a bardic harper, storyteller, author and illustrator who enchants young and old alike with her magical tales, wise village ways, beautiful music and whimsical art. An instructor with the Vashon Wilderness Program and with Heartstone School, she shares her love of the natural world with youth, adults, and families, telling stories each week to her students, and listening to their stories in turn. Jane is the author of Because of the Red Fox, a children's fantasy novel set on an island much like Vashon.

Visit Jane at Foresthalls.org.

WATCHING FROM HEAVEN

By Torena O'Rorke

A pale young woman stood on the beach, gazing warily at the glassy water, perhaps lost in sorrowful thought or contemplating a dangerous plunge. The Puget Sound would be deep and cold, allowing the average swimmer just minutes in its crystal depths before the icy grip of hyperthermia set in. Christian observed the beachcomber from her deck., wondering at the reason for the girl's obvious apprehension. For a moment, Christian considered whether she were imagining the girl. Her ability to occasionally see visions might have resurrected itself, though it had been some time since she'd had a psychic experience. As she stared at the girl, Christian knew that she was strangely familiar. Years of working in Eastern Washington as a criminal investigator had left her with many familiar faces, though not always welcome ones. Christian had come to Vashon for other purposes, however. She'd fled the Tri-Cities to heal her mind and heart as well as to disappear from some living monsters who had made her former life unbearable.

To do that, she'd had to leave two very important people behind. Her precious child would soon join her, but her husband was another story. She missed Daniel terribly, but he had refused to move to Western Washington immediately. Her beloved husband had said that he would soon follow, but from her history with people whom she'd loved, that wasn't always the case. Sophia would spend the summer with her father before joining Christian on Vashon for the school year. She was ten now and already entering middle school. Fortunately, Sophia was tall like her mother, so she was able to fend for herself. Learning karate hadn't hurt either. Christian's little girl could even take her daddy down when he wasn't prepared. Luckily, a new private school for gifted children had opened on Vashon, so Sophia would receive a decent education.

Observation had been a requirement in Christian's career. Now she would leave that keen investigation of the human species to others. On Vashon, Christian would save observation for the world of nature. In the short time since her relocation, she'd experienced the pleasure of observing Barred Owls, shy deer and their newborn fawns, the nocturnal appearances of an incorrigible raccoon family, the alluring dance of a dolphin pod and the evening visits from a resident seal she called `Pup'. Soon, Christian would have to interact with humans again. But not today.

The warm, sunny day was perfect for visiting an old family haunt. Christian drove down to the Quartermaster boat dock. There, she found the rental shop and chose a boat. Climbing into the sliver of fiberglass, she paddled across the glittering water toward a waterfront property her uncle had once owned. Her destination, a century-old, low bank cabin, once sat on an acre of land. Stepping out of the boat, she was shocked to see the beachcomber standing on the porch of the deserted property. Christian thought the woman was an apparition until she got out of the kayak and started to approach her. "Why are you following me?" Christian asked sharply. The slender waif resembled a client who had been brutally murdered on Christian's watch the year before. The Leanne-look-a-like only smiled wistfully and walked into the woods. Christian tried to follow her, but when she entered the forest to find her, the ghost of a girl had left no trace.

Christian wandered around the property, reliving memories in a deluge of happy moments. When she had been a young child, her parents and sister had drowned while sailing off the coast of Washington, leaving her as the only survivor in a terrible winter storm. Growing up with her uncle and aunt and a bevy of cousins had healed her to some degree. Vashon's magic had also been a part of that healing.

Tears formed in her eyes as she peeked into the windows of her memory, reliving the evenings around the kitchen table, playing cards and eating homemade chicken pot pies while rain had drummed rhythmically on the metal roof. Her older cousin had painted on the kitchen wall when she'd been ten years old. It was a scene out of the movie, *Heidi*. With a backdrop of the Swiss Alps, giggling girls in dirndls and prancing boys in lederhosen along with snorting goats and comical alpine horns, the scene was a throwback to days gone by. Her mother's family had been from Bavaria, hence the painting's traditional German theme. With a lingering gaze, Christian turned towards home.

That night, Christian dreamed that she had become friends with a mysterious woman who taught her how to fly. Awaking at midnight, full of giddy recall, she walked out to her deck. There in the yard below her stood an animal. The creature looked straight at her for a long moment. Soon she realized she was staring into the face of a cougar. Years ago, her shaman--

Daniel's grandmother Maria--had given her the cougar as a totem. The great cat had once kept her safe during a raid on a farmhouse full of neo-Nazis. This cougar paced back and forth on the lawn, looking up at her with curiosity. Unable to climb up to the high deck, he eventually gave up and found his way back to the woods.

The next three days passed without a dull moment. Christian picked wild blackberries and made compote, walked the beach every day for miles and appreciated the wildlife. She dropped a crab pot off her dock and cooked up meals of the tasty shellfish, which she washed down with some treasured wines. Despite the distractions, Christian mourned the man whom she'd loved and lost. Her heart ached for Daniel, the proverbial love of her life.

Finally, Christian could no longer avoid the human race. She had run out of several necessities, including coffee. She rolled into the village of Vashon after lunch that afternoon. By then, the apprehensive beachcomber had revisited again, staring up at Christian from the beach earlier that morning as if she had something to say. But as soon as Christian had walked down to talk to her, the girl was gone. Despite the beachcomber's frequent appearances, Christian had decided it was futile to seek her out. Better to just ignore the mystical for now.

Once in town, Christian arrived at Thriftway in search of coffee. She was browsing the coffee aisle when a bearded man dressed in a long black robe and a large crucifix pendant passed her. She guessed he was a priest from the island's Greek Orthodox Monastery. She always felt comfortable around the clergy. His presence seemed to be a good omen.

After making her grocery purchases, Christian stopped at 'Rock It,' the consignment clothing shop across the street from the market. She was searching for a pair of beach shoes. The cashier at the counter greeted her cheerfully. As Christian looked at their shoe selection, another pretty woman came out of the back of the store, giving the younger cashier a loving hug. Christian chatted with them briefly about the 1950's polka dot, pin-up style dress she'd discovered. "It's an original," they said, murmuring the name of a once-famous actress from the Mad Men era. Christian tried the dress on, coming out of the dressing room to gaze in the large mirror nearby. She felt a sudden sense of feeling pretty for the first time in a long time. She remembered a time when she'd worn a similar dress. It was during one of her first dates with Daniel. He'd been taken by surprise, accustomed to seeing her in the nondescript clothing of a public servant. On a whim, Christian bought the dress, and on a whim, decided to wear it out of the store. Across the street from the dress shop was the metaphysical store called 'Mysteries'. Christian had studied with her Mexican shaman Maria for many years. Perhaps she'd find a Day of the Dead doll, something Maria would have given her in the days before her death. The cashier working there wore long dreadlocks and a mischievous grin. "Hello, my name is Jonas Bones," the strange little man said. "May I help you?"

"Just looking," she answered, eager to wander around the unusual shop. She studied the arcane items, including ancient maps of Atlantis, séance guidance tapes and out-of-print books from mystery schools. No dolls. Instead, she decided to buy an amethyst crystal pendant to wear when she was feeling low. Jonas Bones added as she was leaving, "Please come to our workshop on astral travel tomorrow if you can." Nodding, Christian took the flyer, promising to consider his invitation.

Tucking her packages away in her trunk, she felt eyes on her. Glancing up, she saw the beachcomber standing just a few yards away. The stranger gave a wave and disappeared into the alleyway before Christian could return the gesture, but a tingle of prescience stirred her, causing the hairs to rise on the back of her neck. What was going on?

On the tenth day since her arrival, Christian knew the time had arrived to do a big shopping spree. Her ice chest stash was at zero. Driving toward the village, she began looking more closely at the various establishments on the outskirts of the tiny town. She noticed another winery and marveled at the tiny Norwegian church no bigger than an elevator. There were billboards for women's retreats, island operas, a local book signing, a musical theater production and a series of concerts.

Glancing over at a thrift store aptly called 'Granny's Attic', she parked next door at the small market to stock up on water, canned goods, fresh vegetables and bread as well as coffee and milk. Walking into the store, she picked up a shopping basket and stopped short. a man who looked like Daniel stood behind the checkstand, running groceries over the scanner and chatting with a middle-aged woman with rainbow-colored hair. Ducking behind an aisle, she tried to keep the confusion and pain from rising to the surface like the blood welling up from a deep wound.

Though they had been together for over thirteen years and had a child together, Daniel hadn't moved to Vashon with her. His issue was his job as well as family concerns. His beloved grandmother had died, and the family was in deep mourning. At first, Christian had understood. She'd loved his shamanic grandmother very much, but her death during the previous winter was something of a relief in Christian's mind. She sensed her spiritual teacher had moved on to a better place, but Daniel and his family hadn't yet recovered. He didn't want to leave his mother until she, in particular, had processed her grief. Later, Christian had been too hurt and confused to understand his steadfast position. Their own immediate family should come first. But Daniel had stubbornly insisted that he couldn't come with her.

Christian wheeled around the store, throwing things in the cart. Her home was also devoid of cleaning supplies, so she was forced to take an additional detour to the far aisle. Believing she was one of only a few customers, she slowed down with the hope of avoiding the familiar cashier. She took her time until she felt a tap on her shoulder. Startled, Christian turned to stare into the face of the Daniel doppelganger. She froze, aware that she was imagining things. This man wasn't Daniel. He was simply a checker who asked, "May I help you find anything?"

With a shake of her head, she answered, "No." Grabbing some laundry detergent, Lysol, Comet and washing liquid from the shelves beside her, she looked around for the checkout line, making up her mind to avoid this store in the future. Then the man smiled warmly and said, "You remind me of an old friend."

Christian gazed at him for a long moment as tears welled in her eyes. "You remind me of someone, too."

He laughed. "I'm Jack." He put out his hand to shake hers.

Hesitantly, Christian took his warm, solid grip in hers. "Chrissie," she replied shyly.

He grinned. "Now we're new friends!"

She smiled. With a brief nod, she replied, "Sure."

By the time she'd loaded her car, Christian felt happier about her encounters that day. She decided to take a drive toward the Tahlequah ferry. Passing a cute hotel and restaurant called Lucy's, she came across a dilapidated building called "Minglement" where coffee was brewed. She pulled in for a hit of her only addiction.

She was surprised to pass a fair-sized crowd of customers chatting on the porch. She stepped through a screen door into a world of days gone by. Intrigued by the time warp, she gazed around at the large bean roaster that ground coffee beans like a cement truck, as well as the wall of mason jars filled with unusual herbs and teas, the high wood tables and low booths covered with piles of newspapers. Steering toward the back wall, she found the espresso barista and ordered a creamy cappuccino.

Continuing down Vashon Highway, she was delighted to see how much deeper the woods had become. Enormous Redwoods and Firs grew thick, creating a tunnel that only occasional rays of sunlight could pierce. Christian wondered who lived in the woods off the disappearing dirt roads with huge 'no trespassing' signs marking their territory. If there was crime on the island, she guessed it occurred in the hollows and valleys of the dense terrain.

Soon she arrived at the south end of the island. Locating the Southend ferry dock, no bigger than a tennis court, she found a turn-out and headed home.

As she approached town, she spotted a large nursery called 'Kathy's Corner'. She drove in, hoping to cash in on some evergreen flowering plants that were deer-proof. Climbing from her car, Christian entered the largest nursery she'd ever seen. She marveled at the breathtaking flowers and trees, realizing again that living in the desert for so many years had deprived her of such beauty. "And I can have these plants in my new yard," she said aloud.

"Indeed you can," a voice replied, causing Christian to nearly jump out of her skin for the second time that day. She turned to face a broad-hipped, grinning woman in her late sixties who was covered with dirt. Errant fuchsia blossoms adorned her shoulders, and she had several begonias stuck in her hair. "I know," she added to Christian, "I'm a mess at the moment. I've been planting hanging baskets. A bit of a challenge."

Returning her smile, Christian nodded. "Could you help me find my new yard?"

"Sure. I know this island like the back of my hand," the nursery owner replied with a wink. "Name is Kathy," she added. Before Christian could respond, she heard the sound of a dog barking. She shivered. The canine's voice was exactly like her deceased dog, Bear. Shuddering with emotion, she dropped her eyes to avoid tears. "You okay?" Kathy asked tenderly.

Christian shook her head. "Sorry, the dog sounds like my dog who died this spring. I'm still not over him."

Kathy raised a paw of a hand and stroked Christian's cheek, coating it with soil and sympathy. "So it's your lucky day. This lady of mine..." she paused as the Rottweiler mix with heavy teats bounded up and jumped up on the woman, licking her face furiously. Laughing, the woman pushed the dog down. "Enough loving' on me, Yogi."

"Her name is Yogi?" Christian laughed.

The old gardener nodded. "Yeah, like the cartoon bear. Anyway, I have one last pup from her litter." We named that little fellow 'Cub'. You can have him if you want."

Christian shook her head. "I don't know. I don't think any dog could replace my Bear."

"You don't know about Yogi and her pups then." The woman smiled even more broadly this time, showing some capped teeth. "The dog is bilingual. I've taught her Spanish, and now Cub is taking up the second language, too," she explained matter-of-factly.

That was too much for Christian. She began to laugh and then cry. Tears of both sadness and joy rolled down her cheeks, disabling her from speaking. Kathy looked on in surprise. "Didn't know teaching dogs new tricks was so funny. And so sad."

Christian got ahold of herself. "It's just that I taught my Rott, Bear, Spanish, too."

"Then it's a meant-to-be!"

"No, I can't..." Christian responded firmly.

Shrugging, Kathy replied, "It's up to you. I sold the rest of the litter for four hundred dollars a pop… or should I say 'pup'?" The gardener winked again. "You can have Cub for free. I'll keep him until you change your mind. Now, those evergreen bushes you want."

Christian ended her visit an hour later with her SUV laden with Star Hydrangea, Rhododendron, lavender, daisies, bamboo and a few plants whose names she couldn't pronounce. As she said goodbye, she thanked Kathy, adding, "Don't hold that pup for me, please. If someone else comes along…"

"Oh, someone has. A man said he once a dog just like Cub. See the puppy is a bit disabled. His right hind leg is messed up. But I told him 'no'. Didn't know if a fella knows how to take care of a disabled dog. But you, you seem different. You're a lovely girl. I'll hold out for you. You'll come back, I'm sure." She glanced at Christian's credit card. "Christian Vargas. Christian like the religion?"

"Yes…but no." She blushed. "I'm not a practicing Christian."

"Well, you don't look like a typical Christian with that big crystal hanging around your neck. I see you've visited Jonas."

"Yes. And I'm a bit of everything, I guess. But call me Chrissie."

"Okay, Chrissie. You are a bit of everything…curious, deeply sad, determined and beautiful in a complex way. You've been through a lot in your life, I can tell. And death has followed you. But here on Vashon, we're all about life."

Christian was confused. How could a mere nursery owner glean so much about her in such a short time? It was strange and yet reassuring to hear her words. Indeed, Christian was so intrigued by the woman's premonition that she climbed into her stuffed car in a complete daze. She'd taken Kathy's words to heart as she drove away. "Death be gone," she repeated like a mantra, naming all of her losses, including her first child.

*

Daniel and Sophia had made landfall the night before. They had chosen to stay at a hotel in the heart of Burton. Burton Inn was a retro hotel, adorned in Victorian lamps and oil paintings from the turn of the century. Sophia had murmured in quiet protest as he'd put her to bed. After his child was fully asleep, Daniel had pulled out all of the letters Christian had written to her daughter since her departure, once again looking for a clue to beloved wife's whereabouts. Christian was stubborn, as was he, and it seemed they were now living a standoff. He had finally found a new job with the Seattle Police Department as a specialist in cybercrime. He was ready to join Christian. Would she take him now, after their cold war had entered its second week? He loved his wife and knew her like the back of his own brown Hispanic hand. She had needed to flee, and he'd encouraged her, despite her anger that he wasn't immediately following her. They rarely fought, but this time, he had remained firm in his belief that she needed to revisit the island alone, at least to begin with. Still, Christian had suffered so much loss in her troubled life, she had jumped to conclusions, despite his many attempts to right the situation. Daniel hoped that he and Sophia would be the surprise that his wife might be waiting for. He prayed that she had released some of her demons, so their life together could have a new start.

That morning, father and daughter got dressed and had breakfast at the restaurant next door called Lucy's. Sophia was as excited as a ten-year-old at Disneyland. "When will we find Momma?"

"Honey, that's up to our investigating skills. But this island isn't too big, and she would have had to buy food at least, so I'm guessing..." he held out before adding, "Next year."

"Daaaddd!" Sophia whined. "Are you kidding?" Her round blue eyes were wide as she flipped her long dark hair over her shoulder.

Daniel winked. "What do you think? Shall we make a bet? We'll find her by tomorrow's end."

Sophia shook her head. "No, Dad. We'll find her today."

After their meal, they took off with Christian's photo in hand, but not before showing it to the restaurant staff. No one had seen the elusive woman.

They drove up the green island on its main two-lane highway, passing occasional farms and a gorgeous new performance art center. Soon they reached the center of the village where an old movie theater, cute boutiques and several restaurants lined the thoroughfare. "Shall we start at the grocery store?"

His daughter nodded eagerly, jumping out of the car and skipping into the large grocery. Following her inside, he passed a priest of some kind and nodded with deference. He had been raised a Catholic and knew to show respect to those who served the Lord. By then, Sophia had chatted up the Gelato sales girl and was apparently using her allowance to buy two cones. He smiled, mussing her hair when he reached her.

"Any luck?"

Sophia frowned. "No. "Let's ask a few more people here, then go to the consignment store up the street. Mom loves those places."

They wandered around the grocery store. Some of the people they asked thought they might have seen Christian, and everyone was friendly, but there was no real progress. Next, they went to the consignment store where they found a cute clerk who reminded him of the star of *The Sound of Music*. In seconds, Sophia was squealing in delight. The clerk had recognized Christian from the photo. "Yes," she said, smiling at his child. "She bought a 1950s dress, you know, the kind that has polka dots and a swirling skirt."

Daniel frowned. "Hmm. She wouldn't normally wear something like that. Maybe it was another customer you met. Did she pay with a credit card?"

"No. We only take cash or checks. I know I haven't deposited any checks for a few weeks. Let me ask my partner. "Meri, did you take any checks to the bank this month?"

Another woman appeared from a doorway. She was grinning. "Leli, you control the big bucks. No, I haven't. Who is this darling little girl?"

"My name is Sophia and I'm looking for my missing mother. See!" She pushed the photograph towards the second woman.

"Yes, I believe she bought a dress, but she was definitely hesitant. She said she wasn't used to feeling pretty. A shame, really, because she is pretty."

"So if she comes in again, call me," Daniel said, handing them a card. "It's very important."

The women nodded. "Well, I wouldn't normally..." they answered together.

The younger woman paused. "I think she asked about the metaphysical store in town. Perhaps she stopped there."

"Where is this store?"

The women pointed to across the street. "Just across and a bit north."

Sophia was already out the door and at the crosswalk. Daniel could hardly keep up with her as she ran down the street towards a store advertising metaphysical products. He caught up with his swift daughter as she opened the door. "Hi," she cried out. "I'm looking for my lost mother."

She walked up to a small man in a rainbow shirt and dreadlocked head with something tattooed onto his forehead between his eyes. Getting closer, Daniel saw it was the all-seeing eye. Indeed, Christian would have been drawn to this place. The man was staring at the photo. He slowly nodded. "Yes, she bought a crystal from me, I'm sure. But she didn't say her name or where she lived. I'm sorry."

Again, Daniel gave the man his phone number as his daughter moped away with big drops of tears in her eyes. As they walked to the car, Sophia began to cry in earnest. "We'll never find her," she moaned.

Daniel knelt and wrapped his daughter in his arms. "Sweetheart, this is what investigating is all about. It takes a lot of patience and a lot of courage. Your momma is the best investigator I know. You need to follow in her footsteps now. We'll find her, don't worry."

"I want to go to the beach," she announced.

"Ok, we can do that. Why don't we drive back to the hotel and get your swimsuit." Nodding, she compliantly climbed into the car. On the way back, Daniel made note to take her to a movie after dinner.

As they headed south, they passed a large nursery. Sophia suddenly shrieked, "Stop, Dad. There's a dog over there that looks like Bear."

Daniel slowed down. Bear had died earlier that spring. The loss still haunted all of them. Turning around, Daniel drove up to a woman and a dog. He had to admit, as they climbed from the car, that the female did resemble Bear. As Sophia dashed toward the dog, a puppy appeared. The child dropped to the ground to exchange slobbery kisses with the ecstatic creature.

The woman with the dog smiled down at the girl and the pup. "I see you're here now. I tried to give him away to a…" the grinning woman gazed down at Sophia. "Oh my, you must be Christian's daughter."

At that, Sophia flung her arms around the stout angel and cried, "You know my mommy?"

The next few minutes were a flurry of voices, barking dogs, a child's happy cries and Daniel conceding that in exchange for Christian's information, he would take the puppy. The puppy's name, Cub, only cemented the deal. As the woman laboriously searched for Christian's credit card information, Sophia was entertained by her new companion. The next twenty minutes seemed a lifetime, but finally they got an address and directions to Christian's house. They drove back into town, down the highway, passed a cute Norwegian church and a winery to a narrow gravel road leading to the water. When they reached the house, they searched the property, looking for Christian but there was no one at home.

"Pumpkin, we know where your mommy lives, and this is your new house, too. But I'm beat, and you want to go swimming. We'll come back afterwards."

Sophia furrowed her brow but eventually agreed. The dog's attentions certainly distracted the child. They drove again through town, noticing a great-looking burger joint and a climbing wall for kids.

Check, check, Daniel thought. *This seems a good place for raising kids.* They parked and decided to go up to the restaurant to order a lunch to-go. Daniel said, "Soph, go to the patio and wait for me. They allow dogs out there."

"Ok, but order something to go for Cub."

Daniel nodded. "Of course. Otherwise Yogi will come after me, like the big bad bear."

Sophia looked confused but went through the gate as Daniel proceeded to the restaurant. Suddenly, he heard a curdling scream that could only be his daughter's. Racing back out, he jumped the gate and saw the happiest sight he thought he had ever encountered. There was his wife on her knees in a 1950s polka dot pin-up dress, holding their daughter in her arms while Cub raced in circles around them.

*

Later that night, Christian tucked her daughter and Cub into bed and climbed into her own. Curling up against her husband with her head on his shoulder, she considered how Vashon had truly become a place of healing.

Most of her ghosts had already been vanquished. She felt clear for the first time in years and in love and at one with her man and child. Tomorrow she would take them back to the meadow where her Uncle's house had once stood. A meadow now, it was another island place where she could truly observe heaven.

Torena O'Rorke M.Ed. has practiced as a mental health therapist for over 30 years in Tri-cities, Wa. After several unsavory interactions with ruthless criminals, Torena and Her husband decided to escape to Vashon Island, where Torena considers running from hell to sweet heaven. An author of 7 published Novels and several curriculums and domestic violence preventative class as well as advocated for sex trafficking homeless teens...

MODERN LOVE

By Victor Evans

I hit the gas and tried to speed through the next stoplight. It was 7:45 p.m. The ferry was leaving in five minutes. The black truck in front of me suddenly came to a dead stop, forcing me to slam my brakes. Through the corner of my eye, I saw my bags and papers fly from the passenger seat onto the floor. The driver of the stalled truck had stopped for a car that was exiting the parking lot in front of him, but I couldn't have cared less. I hunkered down on my horn because just those few seconds forced us all to sit through yet another stoplight.

I tried to keep my composure, but my road rage started to swell up like lava in a volcano, and I felt like I could erupt at any second. I was scheduled to meet my friends on Vashon Island for dinner at 8 p.m., so there was already no way I was going to arrive on time, but if I missed this boat, I wouldn't even be fashionably late. I would just be late. Sadly, Mike and Margaret were very accustomed to my perpetual tardiness. I am pretty sure the entire time we were at Northwestern together, I never showed up on time to any class or school event.

I met Margaret on move-in day at the dorm. I was walking down the hallway when I heard The Smiths "How Soon is Now" blaring from one of the dorm rooms. I had to see who was playing it, so I rushed down the corridor and peered in the doorway. Margaret had her long blond hair tied in a scarf while she unpacked her belongings, singing along with the lyrics.

"I am the son
And the heir
Of a shyness that is criminally vulgar

I am the son and heir
Of nothing in particular."

I walked into the room and without missing a beat, she smiled and waved her hand in the air, gesturing me to join her. There was no way I could resist, so we crooned together.

"You shut your mouth
How can you say
I go about things the wrong way?
I am human and I need to be loved
Just like everybody else does"

I knew right then and there that we would become the best of friends. We soon learned we were both taking Italian language classes. That's where we both met Mike, who later became the love of her life. Margaret and I were inseparable, always going to concerts and speaking Italian to one another, especially when we were trash talking about classmates and didn't want them to understand what we were saying. In fact, Margaret was the first person I came out to during a Siouxsie and the Banshees concert. Her response was "OK" and we just continued singing "The Killing Jar."

The light finally turned green, and I shot ahead and cut off the car on my left, finding an opening in the traffic. I accelerated to 50 mph down Fauntleroy Way, heedless of children and small dogs that might dart out of the park, and finally turned into the Fauntleroy ferry terminal in West Seattle. The clock on the dash read exactly 7:50. As I reached the toll booth, I could see the ferry was still loading. Phew, I might be able to make it after all.

I didn't visit the island very often, despite Mike and Margaret's incessant invitations. As much as I loved to hang out with them, the ferry was such an annoyance. Unlike many of the other islands in the Seattle area, Vashon Island can only be reached via the ferry, so that meant you had to plan your trip carefully. Organization and meticulous planning were not my strengths.

An attractive ferry worker in shorts that showed off his muscled calves directed me onto the boat. His tight-fitting polo shirt barely contained his large biceps which bulged out just below his short sleeves. Maybe I should take the ferry more often. I decelerated and took my time admiring his brawny physique before I was funneled down a lane on the far-left side of the boat. I debated going upstairs to the main cabin, but I looked out the driver's side window at the pristine view of the water and decided to stay put. I figured the 20-minute ferry ride would be a good chance to catch up on email. I released my seatbelt so I could stretch across the seat and feel around on the floor for my phone. I finally grabbed it and resettled into the driver's seat.

I could faintly hear the radio, so I turned it up and recognized the song as The Cure's "Pictures of You." How perfect that I would hear that song on my way to see Margaret. We played that CD constantly throughout our sophomore and junior years when we lived in an apartment together. There was no way that I couldn't sing along with The Cure.

"If only I'd thought of the right words
I could have held on to your heart
If only I'd thought of the right words
I wouldn't be breaking apart
All my pictures of you"

I was probably singing at the top of my lungs, but all my windows were up, so my tone-deaf rendition wouldn't disturb anyone. I closed my eyes. This was my favorite part. *"Du du du-du-du du… "*

CLACK, CLACK! I opened my eyes to see the cute ferry worker I had been lusting after earlier staring at me through the driver's side window. Had I been singing that loud? I wanted to melt into the seat and disappear. Now that he had my attention, Mr. Cutie made a twisting gesture with his hand. I had no idea what he was talking about. He could see the blank look on my face, and he pointed to the hood of my car and then made the wrist motion again. The light bulb finally went off in my head. I had forgotten to turn my engine off. I didn't ride the ferry enough to remember all the protocols.

I reached for my keys and quickly shut the engine off as I mouthed "sorry" to him. He just smiled and gave me a thumbs-up, giving me a chance to notice his bright green eyes. Hmmm… Maybe I should get in trouble on the ferry more often. He walked away toward the front of the boat, and I turned my attention to my phone.

I had planned to check email, but after all the commotion I needed some entertainment. So what better site to go to than Grindr? Most of the guys on there were all pretending to be something they weren't, so it was like watching a bunch of one-man shows. I clicked on the icon, and my phone was soon filled with pictures of all the guys on the site within proximity to me. I was sure most of them resided in West Seattle. I couldn't imagine there were many guys from Vashon Island on the site. Hell, I wouldn't even think there were very many gays and lesbians living on the island at all, but you never know. Wouldn't it be funny to meet the man of my dreams on an island? The commute alone would kill the relationship.

I checked to see if I had gotten any messages since I had last logged on at lunch. As I suspected, nothing out of the ordinary, just the usual webflies, using the same pick-up lines to try to start a conversation with me for the hundredth time. Get a hint. If I haven't responded by now, I'm probably not interested.

I continued scrolling down and I noticed a reply from NICEGUY34. I usually never respond to someone with such a generic screen name, but there was something about his big brown puppy dog eyes that drew me to him. Most guys with such an obvious screen name are the furthest things from nice guys, but he actually looked the part. We'd only been corresponding for the past two weeks, so I didn't know that much about him. His name was Jordan. He was an accountant at Amazon. He moved to Seattle two years ago from Atlanta. Most of our conversations were the typical "hi, how is your day going" fare, but I did want to know more.

In a previous chat session, I did ask if he was seeing anyone, and he said, "That is a longer conversation and will require drinks." That's a definite red-flag, but there was no harm in conversing. After all, this was just entertainment. I clicked on his message: *Scott, how is your Friday going? Are you ready for the weekend? HMB*

Yep, typical message. I typed back: *Hey Jordan, TGIF. I am meeting friends for dinner tonight. What about you? Do you have any big plans for the weekend?* I hit send.

I clicked off Grindr and was just about to check my email when I heard a voice over the loudspeaker. "Vashon Island."

I could see the boat entering the dock. Yay, finally here. *It's about time. I'm starving. I hope they have the food ready.*

I smiled and waved at Mr. Cutie as I rolled off the ferry. To my surprise, he smiled and waved back. Well, that was his job. I shouldn't read anything into it. I hadn't had a serious boyfriend in six years, nor had I even met any potential suitors that I had been remotely interested in, so I had to take my thrills wherever and however I could get them. Today, it was a smile and wave from Mr. Cutie.

Mike and Margaret only lived a mile and a half from the ferry. It was literally one left turn and then a quick right turn and I was there. Their being so close to the ferry added to my guilt for not visiting them as often as they would like, but even with that convenience, I still had to deal with the dreaded ferry.

Mike and Margaret were fortunate enough to have a home right on the water, thanks to Mike's being an Oscar-nominated screenwriter and having the salary that comes along with it. Their home was located on a small ridge just above the water in Vashon Heights.

Towering above all the others, their 3,000- square foot, three-story home looked remarkably majestic sitting at the top of the hill, especially with the rays of the setting sun shadowing it from behind, creating a stunningly dramatic halo effect. As I drove toward the house, I could see movement in the large over-sized windows on the second floor. I pulled into the extremely steep, narrow gravel driveway leading to the back-right side of the house. The uneven surface caused me to bounce up and down in my seat until I glimpsed the water down below. Parking here always made me nervous. I felt as if one false move and my car would end up in the Sound, but I had to admit this was a spectacular view. I could see all the way across the Sound, West Seattle to my right, Blake Island straight ahead and Southworth to my left. What I wouldn't give for a view like this..., but with my mid-level news producer salary, that would never happen, especially not in the Seattle area. If I wanted this, I would have to marry rich.

The clock read 8:20. I was only 20 minutes late. For me, that was practically early. I turned to look in the backseat for the bottle of wine I had brought for the occasion, and I heard a chime. I clutched my phone and saw I had a new message on Grindr. I quickly clicked the icon to see that Jordan had replied to my message: *Dinner sounds nice. I'm just meeting a friend later.*

That was my opening. *Oh really? Is it a date?*

As soon as I set the phone back down in the passenger seat, I heard another chime. Damn, he already responded. He must be online. *I wouldn't say that.*

What did that mean? I needed to know more. *So what would you say?*

I need to take care of something tonight that I should have done long ago.

Why was he being so cryptic? Although I really shouldn't have been surprised. That was typical behavior on Grindr. These guys created profiles to entice you to chat with them, and then when you took the bait, they acted like they couldn't be bothered. Attention-whores, the whole lot of them. So why did I keep getting onto this site? I had to keep telling myself it was just for entertainment.

The song on the radio abruptly caught my attention. I recognized the music but couldn't place the song until I heard the lyrics.

"I would like a place I can call my own
Have a conversation on my telephone
Wake up every day, that would be a start
I would not complain 'bout my wounded heart"

It was "Regret" by New Order. I closed my eyes and sang along until another chime jarred me back to the conversation.

Whens your dinner?

It started a 8. I am late. I just got here.

a=at. I hated making typos. Being a journalist, I prided myself on my grammar and punctuation. But sadly, thanks to texting, I was slowly losing that battle. My fingers just didn't text as fast as my brain.

You better go.

Ya I should. One of my fav songs just came on the radio, so just chillin for a sec.

Which song?

I decided to tell him even though I knew he would probably have no idea. His profile said he was 35. If that were true, he would have been in elementary school when the song first came out in 1993.

Regret by New Order

137

Great song!

You've heard it?

Uh yeah! That's my favorite song from that album, but "World" is a close second.

He really did know who they were. *Ya that's a great song too. I can't believe you know New Order.*

I listened to all that stuff in high school. I was kinda goth.

No way... I clicked off the chat window and pulled up his profile picture. He was dressed in a bright orange polo, a perfect complement to his light caramel-colored skin, and blue jeans, with his crinkled, curly dark hair deliberately mussed all over his head. He must have grown out of it. There were no remnants of anything remotely goth in that picture.

I am not getting that at all from your pic. I will need proof. ☐

I'll see what I can find. I can't believe you listen to New Order. I don't get that from your picture either.

I was a waver in high school so I listened to everything from Depeche Mode to the Thompson Twins.

Great bands. A waver? Now I totally must see a pic. Let's trade!

LOL. The clock flashed 8:30. I hated to cut the conversation short, but I had to go.

Deal! Now I'm really late. I gotta run. I'll be waiting for that pic. When I get yours, I will respond with mine. I just hoped I could find one. That was over 25 years ago. Maybe Margaret had one from our early college days.

Sounds good! Have fun!

TTYL

I closed the chat window, grabbed the bottle of wine from the back seat and gathered myself out of the car. As soon as I stepped onto the porch, the large-arched, Tuscan-style wooden front door opened.

"So nice of you to finally join us." Margaret stood in the doorway. She was wearing a long flowing red dress, a nice contrast to her pale skin, and it perfectly accentuated her hourglass figure. She only stood five feet, four inches tall, but she was blessed with curves in just the right places and that still hadn't changed. She smiled and held her arms out.

"Hey, Margie." I gave her a long, tight hug and a kiss on the cheek. As we scurried into the house, I handed her the bottle of wine. "I know, I'm late, but I am bearing gifts. Doesn't that count for something?"

"That always counts." We made our way into a large foyer just off the living room. The entire downstairs was an open floor plan, so I could see all the way from the living room into the kitchen and even over to the dining room on the far right, which contained enormous floor-to-ceiling windows, allowing diners to bask in the spectacular view of the Sound.

"What took you so long to get in here? I saw you park a few minutes ago."

"I was finishing up a chat with a friend, Miss Nosy."

"A friend?" Margaret stared me down and raised her eyebrows. "Please tell me you aren't on that silly website again. Remember how that turned out last time."

How well did I remember. I met my ex of six years on Grindr. It started out well enough, mostly physical, but the actual relating to one another outside the bedroom never really panned out. We could barely hold a conversation, and it wasn't because he was Colombian and his native language was Spanish. Long story short, just after we moved to Seattle together from Texas, he ran off with one of his co-workers, leaving me with a broken heart and over ten thousand dollars of debt. I don't know how I could have gotten through it without Margaret.

"Well, we all can't meet the man of our dreams in Italian class during our sophomore year of college."

Margaret rolled her eyes and stuck out her tongue. We heard a voice from the kitchen.

"He's right, you now. We're very lucky." We turned to see Mike in the living room, heading toward us with two glasses of wine. We each took a glass. Mike was average height, average build with brown hair, olive skin, and a large Roman nose. But there was nothing average about his gregarious sense of humor or his emerald eyes that always seemed to light up the room. Mike could make you laugh even when you didn't want to, which after some of the days I've had, I was so thankful for. His incessant sarcasm and nuanced inflections always cheered me up. I kept asking Margaret where was the gay version of Mike because if there was one, sign me up.

"I know. We're lucky. Here is to Scott being just as lucky. Who knows, maybe true love is just around the corner." Margaret raised her glass.

Cheers to that. I took a sip of wine. Their romance was a fairy tale. I met Mike first when we took Italian together our freshman year. I felt some gay vibes from him in the very beginning, so I was hoping to make a play for him myself. Unfortunately, my gaydar is only partially accurate, and in his case, I was definitely beating the wrong drum. I soon learned that Mike was dating a young woman in his dorm, but when I met her the first time, I was flabbergasted. Number one, I would have never pegged Mike to have an African-American girlfriend, which I must admit did give me some hope if he ever decided to bat for the other team. And number two, she was short, loud, obnoxious and thought her opinions were the only ones that mattered. That relationship didn't last long, and as soon as it ended, I began matchmaking.

I told Margaret about Mike, thinking they would really hit it off, but she was smitten with another boy at that time who, in my opinion, was totally wrong for her, so it wasn't until our sophomore year, when she changed Italian classes, that she finally met Mike. Sadly, my schedule had changed, so I was no longer in the class, but that didn't stop me from organizing events like bowling, movie-nights and frat-party outings, prompting them to hang out and get to know each other. By the end of our junior year, my tactics had worked and the two of them had fallen head over heels in love with one another.

Just after graduation, Mike wrote and illustrated a comic strip outlining their courtship that he submitted to a local morning show contest. He won, and to their astonishment, the prize was an all-expenses-paid wedding and reception, on ice. They were married with four other couples on the ice skating rink in Millennium Park in downtown Chicago. Margaret gave me one of the few tickets to the event, and while I know it was one of the happiest days of their lives, it was for me too because it was proof that true love does exist.

That was how I wanted my love life to play out, but that's the exact opposite of how things turned out for me.

"Uncle Scott." I looked up the stairs and saw Ben rushing towards me. He almost toppled over his four-year-old feet as he hit the bottom step and ran over to attach himself to my right leg.

"Well, hello there, Mr. Ben." He was the spitting image of Mike. Same brown hair, Roman nose and bright green eyes. He looked so cute in his Thomas the Train pajamas. "I see you are already in your PJs. I like them!"

"Ya, mom told me to put them on because she said by the time you finally get here and we eat, it'd be time for bedie-bye."

"Ben! What have I told you about repeating everything I say?" Margaret said with a half-serious grin.

We all chucked, including Ben, looking at everyone, as if he was not quite sure why he was laughing.

I scooped Ben up into my arms. "It's all good, Ben. Your mom is right. By the time we finish dinner, it will be bedtime. Speaking of dinner…"

"Yes, let's get some food in our bellies." Mike motioned for everyone to follow him into the dining room.

Margaret stood at the foot of the stairs. "Grace, it's dinner time. Get down here."

"Oh, did Uncle Scott finally show up?" a voice called out from upstairs.

"Yes, I am finally here, Grace," I yelled up. I looked back at Margaret. "Geez, does everyone know that I am notoriously late?" I placed Ben down on the lush green rug covering the light-brown bamboo floor.

She smiled back and I could see it in her eyes. I ran over to her, and we both sang.

"*No-no-notorious*

No-no-notorious"

Ben ran over to join us, waving his little fists in the air. Margaret and I both increased our volume, waving our hands in the air, playing off each other.

"You own the money, you control the witness
I hear you're lonely, don't monkey with my business
You pay the profits to justify the reasons
I heard your promise but I don't believe it
That's why I'll do it again
No-no-notorious"

"I should have known we wouldn't get through dinner without a sing-along," Mike shouted from the kitchen.

"Really, Dad? It's Uncle Scott. I'm surprised it took them this long." Grace was now at the foot of the staircase. Her long blond hair framed her round face as she peered at them with her light brown eyes. It was astounding how much she reminded me of Margaret when she was younger.

"Hey, we held out as long as we could. Nice to see you, Grace." She came over to give me a hug.

"OK, now can we please eat?" Mike called us all into the dining room.

Margaret darted into the kitchen while the rest of us took seats at the elegant glass dining table. "Why don't we start with some hors d'oeuvre?" Margaret placed a tray of scrumptious-looking bruschetta in the center of the table before sitting down.

"Oh wow, aren't we fancy tonight?" My stomach gurgled loud enough to make Ben jump. He pointed at me and smiled. I patted him on his little round head.

Mike laughed. "Nothing but the best for you buddy."

Mike was sitting at the head of the table, Margaret opposite him, Grace and I sat together on the right side of the table, which left Ben alone on the left side of the table next to an empty place setting. Wait a minute, Margaret was being unusually formal, and we had never had hors d'oeuvre before. She was up to something.

"Margie, what's going on?" I slitted my eyes at her.

She immediately looked away. "What do you mean?" Her voice squeaked up an octave higher.

"I mean, there is an extra place setting. Are you expecting someone else?"

"Well, you never know when someone might just stop by."

"Smooth Marge, real smooth." Mike looked down at the table, trying to contain his laughter.

Ben immediately perked up. "Who is it, Mommy? Is it the man you were talking to on the ferry today?"

"Margaret Ann Charles, please tell me you didn't." I took a sip of wine, trying to calm myself.

"Oh, she did!" Mike said shaking his head. He gulped his wine.

"C'mon, Uncle Scott, you know she did." Grace popped a piece of bruschetta into her mouth.

Grace was right. How could I have not expected this? Margaret was infamous for trying to set me up. She had done it all through college and even tried long-distance matchmaking when she and Mike lived in California. It was cute at first. After all, she was happy and in love and she wanted me to be as well. But the problem was that the only requirement Margaret had for the guys she fixed me up with were they were cute and gay. Oftentimes, I had nothing in common with any of them. I had tried explaining this to her:

"But he is so cute, he would be perfect for you."

"So, do you have a connection with every cute straight guy you meet?"

Her failed attempts included everyone from self-involved lawyers, narcissistic restaurant owners, arrogant film producers and holier-than-thou doctors. The last guy was a washed-up musician still trying to hang on to his glory days. After that, we both agreed that the matchmaking had to stop. It wasn't her fault she didn't have the gift, not like I did anyway.

I was just about to remind her of all this when the doorbell rang.

"I wonder who that could be?" Margaret said coyly as she got up and rushed toward the front door.

Oh no, I wasn't going to let her get away that easy. I jumped up from the table and followed behind her. She made it to the foyer just before I grabbed the back of her arm and stopped her from opening the door.

"Margaret, we have talked about this."

"Scott, trust me. I know what I am doing this time. You're going to thank me for this. I promise you." She gave me her classic "I have this totally under control" smile, which almost always meant she didn't, then she turned back toward the door, forcing me to release my grip. "Drink some wine. You'll be fine."

"Wait..."

Ignoring my protests, she opened the door. I cowered behind her-- which didn't help because I was at least a head taller than she was, and there stood Mr. Cutie, still dressed in his ferry uniform.

"Christopher, I'm so glad you were able to make it." Margaret beamed.

I stood speechless, following Margaret's lead as she moved aside to let him enter the foyer.

Mr. Cutie--apparently his name was Christopher--looked abashed. "I apologize for the way I'm dressed. I had to come straight from work. I hope that's OK."

"You're just fine. We're not at all formal around here." Margaret laughed.

Really, Margaret? I just rolled my eyes. She was too much.

"I want to introduce you to my good friend Scott. We go way back."

I finally found my voice. "Hi there, nice to meet you." I extended my hand.

"Wait a minute, I remember you." Recognition flashed in Christopher's eyes. "You're The Cure guy on the ferry with your engine running." He shook my hand with a fierce firm grip.

"That would be me." My face flushed.

Margaret erupted in laughter. "Oh yes, that would totally be him." Margaret waved her hand toward the living room. "We were just having some hors d'oeuvre so you're right on time."

Christopher led the way, followed by Margaret, who turned and whispered over her shoulder, "See, I told you to trust me."

I leaned in toward her ear. "The jury is still out."

We made our way into the dining room where Margaret made the introductions. "Christopher, this is my husband Mike, my son Ben and my daughter Grace." Mike went to stand up.

Christopher waved him down. "Oh please, don't get up. I apologize for interrupting. I'm sure everyone is starving."

That was the truth. I took another sip of wine as I sat down. I'd need a refill and soon.

"Christopher..." Margaret motioned to the seat next to Ben. "You can sit right there, just across from Scott. Help yourself to the bruschetta."

So subtle, Margaret. I glared at her. She grinned from ear to ear. Christopher double-fisted the last two pieces of bruschetta as he sat down.

"Mike, can you help me bring in the first course? Scott, Christopher told me earlier that he's really into hiking. Maybe you guys could go sometime?"

I winced. Mike, seeing my discomfort, stood up and led Margaret into the kitchen. "We'll be right back with the salads."

Grace started the conversation. "So where do you like to hike, Christopher?"

"I honestly don't care. I'll go wherever." He was still munching the bruschetta, his mouth full. "I just really do it to build my calf muscles. I've been working on building them up for a few years now." He popped the last gigantic bite of bruschetta in his mouth, wiped his hand off on the tablecloth before pulling his cell phone out of his back pocket and placing it on the table in front of him.

"Well, it has definitely paid off," I said without thinking it through.

"Thanks, man" There was a beep from his phone. He looked at it for a few seconds, then started texting.

After a few seconds, Ben broke the silence. "I like to go by the falling water."

I smiled. "You mean the waterfall... Snoqualmie Falls. I like going there too."

I looked at Christopher, but he was still engrossed in his texting.

Mike and Margaret reentered the dining room and began placing baby romaine wedges in front of everyone. I couldn't help but smirk. They were plated rather decoratively with an ample of amount of Caesar dressing drizzled over each one and topped with parmesan flakes. So much for being totally informal.

"This is a funny looking salad," Ben said, picking at it with his fork.

"Hey, buddy, why don't you let me help you with that?" Mike reached over to Ben's plate and cut the wedge into bite-size pieces. "There you go."

Christopher stopped texting long enough for Margaret to put the salad in front of him before she settled into her chair. "So, what did I miss? Did you guys find a time to go hiking together?"

"I wouldn't say that," Grace said in a low voice just loud enough for Margaret and me both to hear.

Margaret looked confused, but I shook my head, signaling her to leave it alone.

Christopher finally looked up and set the phone down next to his plate. "This looks delicious." He proceeded to dive right in, picking up the entire wedge with his fork and taking a bite, leaving dressing around the corners of his mouth.

"So, Babe, you never told me how you and Christopher met," Mike said, watching Christopher attack his salad.

"Oh, yes, I did. Remember I said I see him on the ferry every week when I go into town for my Costco runs, and one day we just struck up a conversation."

I couldn't imagine what about. His calves? I supposed I was going to have to engage in conversation. "So, Christopher, how long have you worked on the ferry?"

He set his fork down. He had already made it halfway through the wedge. "I just started three months ago. I'm just doing it while I beef up a little more and work toward my personal training certification."

"Nice, are you going to school for kinesiology?" I inquired.

"No, what's that? I am just going to do the online certification. That is all need to get hired on at LA Fitness." He picked his fork up and went back to work on the rest of the wedge.

"That works too." Mike winked at me. At least he saw the humor in the situation.

A loud beep resonated from Christopher's phone. "Oh, sorry, about that." He dropped his fork and grabbed his phone. With dressing still draped over the edge of his mouth, he looked at the screen, then began texting again.

This was getting to be too much. I downed the last bit of wine in my glass. "Margaret, I'm out of wine. Can you help me find another bottle in the kitchen?"

"Oh, boy," I heard Grace mumble under her breath.

"Sure, I think I have the perfect one for us to open." She gathered herself up, and I followed her.

Once in the kitchen, I headed straight for the wine cabinet. Once out of earshot, I started right in. "Really, Margaret?"

"Give him a chance. He has a lot of varied interests"

"Oh, really? So far it's all texting and bodybuilding." Margaret's face turned bright-red. I couldn't tell if she was abashed or if she was trying to stifle laughter, but once our eyes meet, we both failed miserably at controlling our snickering.

"That's your problem, you're too judgmental." She gave me a shove.

"And you're a bleeding heart." I grabbed a bottle of Malbec. "How about this one?"

"Yeah, that's fine."

"Do you know his last name?"

"I believe it's Colton."

"His name is Chris Colton? Does that sound like a porn star name or what? Hmm, he definitely has the body of a porn star."

"Stop it! Be nice." She shoved me again.

"Hey, don't make me spill the wine. This is the only way I'm getting through this night."

"Give me that, I'll open it and pour you some." She grabbed the bottle from my hand and scurried over to the sink.

Well, since Mr. Cutie was checking his phone, I might as well check mine too. I reached into my pocket and pulled out my phone. I unlocked my screen to see if I had a message waiting for me on Grindr. I clicked on the app and saw that Jordan had sent me a message. I opened it up to see a pic of him in full goth get-up. He was dressed in black from head to toe with his short-straightened hair spiked up and enough guyliner to make Johnny Depp's Captain Sparrow jealous. Although he still had the same beautiful brown eyes, proving it was really him. Below the pic was the message: *Now it's your turn.*

"Margie, that pic of us at the Siouxsie and the Banshees concert, do you still have it on your Facebook?"

"Yeah, it should be under my photos, why?" she said, digging the corkscrew into the top of the wine bottle.

"Just wondered." I didn't want her to know I was on Grindr. I launched my Facebook app and searched for Margaret's page. Her profile picture was a family pic. It must have been taken just before church because they were all dressed in their Sunday best. Ben was grinning so big it looked like his teeth were bursting out of his mouth. I went to her photos and found an album called "concerts." I clicked on it, and sure enough, after scrolling through what seemed like hundreds of pics, but was only about 20, I found it. There we were, wearing our concert tees and decked out in matching combat boots. I had three crucifixes around my neck, all different sizes because one was never enough. My hair was in a flat top, straightened and sticking up thanks to an entire can of hairspray. Cigarettes dangled between our index and middle fingers. That was back during our smoking days. Fortunately, that didn't last long. I had my share of guyliner on but not nearly as much as Jordan in his snapshot. Gosh, I looked so young. Where had the time gone?

I heard the pop of the cork as Margaret finally opened the bottle. She fumbled to remove the cork from the corkscrew. I quickly saved the pic. While I was on Facebook, I figured what would be the harm in checking out my new friend Chris Colton's page. I quickly searched for him and surprisingly only three names came up and only one lived in Washington State. His profile picture was him standing on top of a random mountain flexing his muscles. He did have some spectacular guns. I scrolled down his posts, and as I suspected everything related to bodybuilding, best nutritional tips for gaining body mass, protein shakes, etc. But as I scrolled back up to his "about" section, I found something very interesting. Under relationship status, it read "It's complicated."

"Margaret! This guy has a boyfriend or something." I barely kept my voice down. I walked over and held my phone in front of her nose.

She looked down at the sink. "Oh yeah, about that..." She threw the discarded cork into the sink.

"You've got to be kidding me," my voice rising.

"Shhh...." She put her finger up to her mouth. "That's what we talked about on the ferry. They're on the verge of breaking up. The guy sounds like a real tool."

"And you thought this was the best time for a blind date?"

"It's the perfect time." She placed her hands on my shoulders. "Don't you see, he's all upset and vulnerable as his relationship his ending, and then Waalaa... he meets you, you give him a shoulder to cry on, and before you know it, you two fall head over heels in love." She wriggled with excitement.

"Oh my, it is truly scary how your mind works." I patted on her the cheek and then walked back over to the wine cabinet. I wanted to send the picture to Jordan before I forgot. I clicked on Grindr and attached the pic with the message: *If this doesn't scare you away, I don't know what will LOL*

Margaret grabbed the bottle of wine and peered over my shoulder. "You better not be on that site." Margaret reached around and tried to grab my phone. "Especially when I have a real man right out there for you."

"That's debatable." I planted the phone back into my pocket before she could grasp it. Margaret stuck out her lip and folded her arms.

I reached out and gave her a hug. "Relax. I promise I'll be on my best behavior."

She gave me that knowing look. *"Relax..."* She crooned.

I followed up with, *"Don't do it"*

We flung our arms and gyrated our hips, singing in unison.

"When you want to go to it
Relax, don't do it
When you want to come
Relax don't do it"

We danced our way back into the dining room.

"So, creatine is great because...." Christopher, in mid-lecture, dropped his jaw, showing everyone in the room his mouth-full of salad as Margaret and I sang and danced our way back into the dining room.

"Hey, no singing at the table. That's what you always tell me." Ben raised his arms in protest. Margaret and I stopped our crooning as we sat back down.

"That's right, Ben. Mom and Uncle Scott don't always follow the rules," Grace said while twitching her nose.

"Well, that's not fair." Ben furrowed his little brows.

"No, it's not, Ben. I'm sorry." Margaret reached across the table and grabbed his hand. "Do you forgive me?"

"Can I get extra dessert?" He grinned.

"Well, we've got to get through the main course first, buddy." Mike laughed. "And you guys interrupted Christopher. He was telling us all about creatine."

"Oh darn, I'm sorry I missed that." I couldn't help myself. Margaret shot me a stern look.

"It's OK," Christopher said, totally missing the sarcasm. "What was that song you guys were singing?"

Now my jaw dropped. "You don't know 'Relax' by Frankie Goes to Hollywood."

"That's what it is," Christopher said like a light bulb had just gone on in his head. "I don't really listen to that kind of music, but my friend... uh... boyfriend... loves that stuff."

"Friend or boyfriend?" I repeated.

"Yeah, right now things are kinda..."

"Complicated." Once again, I couldn't help myself. Grace snickered.

Margaret stood in a clear attempt to change the conversation. "It looks like everyone is ready for the main course."

"Yes, let's get that going. And how is everyone doing on wine? I know I could use a recap." Mike reached for the Malbec in the center of the table and poured some into his glass.

I looked at my glass and realized I had already drunk half of the previous refill. "I could." I quickly stood up. "Margie, let me help you clear the table." I grabbed my and Grace's now empty dishes.

"No, you…" But before she could finish, I had rounded up Mike's and Christopher's plates and was hurriedly making my way into the kitchen.

"Scott," she snipped as she came around the table to follow behind me, but Mike stood blocking her path as he capped off my wine glass. Instead of sitting back down, Mike turned to enter the kitchen right on my heels followed by Margaret.

She stopped right at the door and turned back. "Christopher, can I get you anything else to drink?" He shook his head sideways, once again engrossed in vigorous texting. "Ok, we'll be right back."

"Well, this is just going swimmingly," Mike announced as we all three made our way into the kitchen.

"You're telling me. This is a disaster." I placed the dishes in the sink and rinsed them under the faucet as I turned to look over my shoulder at Margaret. "Now do you see why I say no matchmaking."

"Stop it, you two." Margaret lifted the lid and frantically stirred the sauce simmering on the stove. The sweet smells of fresh oregano and basil permeated the kitchen air. "I can't believe we left him out there all by himself with the kids." We all tried to control our laughter. "Poor guy." Margaret began pouring her signature spicy sausage sauce over the spaghetti.

She was known for her pasta dishes, but nothing could ever beat her spaghetti bolognese. That alone was worth making a trip over to the island. Mike handed her plates as she began placing piles of the heavenly aromatic mixture on each one.

I walked over to the wine bar and reached into my pocket. Once again, why should Christopher be the only one checking his messages? I touched my screen and immediately saw I had a message on Grindr. Jordan had responded. *Oh wow, you weren't kidding. You were a waver. I think you looked adorable. BTW, I don't scare easily.*

I smiled as I typed my response. *Good to know. Have you met your friend yet?*

As I was putting the phone back in my pocket, I heard a chime. He had responded already. He must be online. *We aren't meeting until later. I'm kinda dreading it. I hate giving people bad news.*

Sounds serious

Ya but it's the right thing to do for both of us.

So you said. I wanted to pry but forced myself to resist.

I was just listening to this and I thought of you.

I felt a sharp pain in my left forearm, causing me to almost drop the phone. "Are you on the stupid site again? What have I told you about that?" Margaret had given me one of her infamous pinches.

"Ouch." I jerked away from her. "Hey, fair is fair as Ben would say. Christopher's on his phone, so why can't I be on mine." I looked back at the screen and clicked on the link Jordan sent and it immediately opened YouTube. A video began playing. I recognized the music right away as did Margaret and Mike.

"Oh, here we go again," Mike said as he picked up a couple plates, steadying them on his arm.

I started us off this time. *"However far away."*

Margaret tilted her head and joined in. *"I will always love you
However long I Stay
I will always love you"*

"At this rate, we'll never eat. I'm going to start serving." Mike headed into the dining room.

I quickly texted Jordan. *You know me so well already.* Still bellowing, I deposited the phone back into my pocket, picked up a couple of plates heaped with pasta and handed them to Margaret before picking up my own overflowing plate, snatching another bottle of wine and prancing into the dining room.

*"Whatever words I say
I will always love you
I will always love you."*

Grace heard us coming. "Oh no, not *Lovesong* again." She shook her head and glanced down at the pasta now in front of her. Thanks to Margaret and me, she could have probably recited the song by heart. We had so many songs in our nostalgic repertoire, but there was rarely a get-together that didn't end with us singing *Lovesong*. *How Soon Is Now* by the Smiths was a close second, but that made sense considering that was the song that first brought us together.

Christopher was still frantically texting but looked up when we stormed into the room. Margaret placed a plate in front of him. He dropped his phone on the table, grabbed his fork and immediately stuffed his mouth with pasta. "I recognize that song too. That's another one he plays all the time," he said showing us all the food in his mouth.

I set a plate down in front of Grace before sitting down with mine. "Sounds like your friend-slash-boyfriend has good taste in music," I said and jammed a forkful of pasta into my face.

"Not really my taste. I am more a country kind of guy. I love Garth Brooks."

I almost spat the pasta out of my mouth. With my mouth full, I couldn't respond with, "Really? Out of all the country singers, you love Garth Brooks?" so I just curled my lip.

Mike sensed my disgust. "Scott, you could use some more wine. Why don't I fill that glass up for you?"

Margaret looked down at the table and took a deep breath, and I could see the corners of her mouth shaking, trying her best to stifle laughter.

When she finally gained her composure, she leaned forward in her chair. "So, Christopher, you do a lot of cycling, don't you?"

Christopher, who had been shoveling the pasta in his mouth faster than an undernourished child in one of those TV commercials, finally took a breath and looked up. "Ya, at least two or three times a week," he mumbled with pasta flying around in his mouth. A few random food particles flew from his mouth and landed in the middle of the table, causing Ben to giggle.

Margaret shot Ben a look. He quickly fell silent and began wiggling his fork in the pasta. Margaret turned her attention to me. "Scott, do you still do those spin classes? You go two or three times a week, right?"

You're not slick, Margaret. I knew exactly what she was doing. The hiking ploy didn't work, so she decided to use another tactic. I narrowed my eyes and looked at her.

Ignoring my warning, she continued. "Scott, maybe you can get out of that boring gym and go enjoy nature by biking with Christopher."

"I actually love my spin classes. My one instructor plays all kinds of 80s new wave. It keeps me pumped."

"Yeah, but you listen to that stuff all the time. I'm sure some fresh air and nice scenery will do you good." She was not giving up.

"Well, babe, we all know how much Scott loves his music." Mike came to my aid.

Christopher stopped scooping food into his mouth long enough to say, "I actually don't bike anywhere fun. I just go up and down my neighborhood. I just do it to strengthen my hamstrings and glutes." He started right back in on the pasta.

"Well, it definitely seems to be working for you." I smiled. I remembered his glutes were round and looked extremely firm.

Margaret sat back in the chair, looked at me and pursed her lips.

Well, that ended that. We sat in silence for the next few minutes. The only sounds heard where the clanking of forks against plates as we all worked to eat every morsel of that delicious pasta, at least until a loud beep blared from Christopher's phone. He immediately put down his fork and looked at the screen. Suddenly like a man on a mission, he scowled and frantically began texting.

"Not again," Grace mumbled under her breath. She flung her napkin on the table. "I'm all done. Can I be excused?"

"No, dessert." Ben faced Margaret, sticking out his lower lip. "I get two remember, Mommy. I ate all my food."

"I'll start clearing," Mike said as he stood up and reached for Christopher's plate, which looked spit-shined clean. Christopher didn't even look up as he continued texting. He grimaced as his fingers darted across the screen.

"Why don't I help you, Mike?" I stood up and handed him my and Grace's plates. More than anything, I wanted to refill my wine glass. This dinner party was driving me to drink. That always seemed to happen when Margaret tried to set me up.

Suddenly, with his face flushed and water welling up in his eyes, Christopher stood up. "I'm sorry. I need to step outside for a minute." He scurried past Mike and me toward the front door as we looked around trying to figure out what happened. Margaret stood up as well with a confused look on her face.

"What's wrong, Mommy? Is Christopher sick?" Ben asked with genuine concern.

"I'm not sure, baby." She squatted down next to him and picked the napkin up off his lap, using it to wipe the lingering bits of sauce off his face. "Why don't you go upstairs with Grace while I go check on Christopher?"

"No, I want dessert." Ben protested.

"I promise if you go upstairs now, I'll bring you two desserts." Ben jumped up and down with excitement.

"Upstairs? Just when things were getting good." Grace reluctantly came to her feet.

"Take your brother upstairs now, young lady," Margaret said in her mom, you-better-do-what-I-say tone. I loved seeing her in mommy mode. It was so different from the Margaret I knew in college but very familiar all at the same time.

Ben ran over to Grace, who swallowed him up in her arms before walking over to the stairs.

Mike and I remained planted in the same spot, not sure what to do. Margaret came over to us. "I'll go check on him."

"What do you think is going on?" Mike asked.

"I hope it wasn't anything I did." I knew I could be sarcastic, but didn't think I was mean, at least not mean enough to make anyone cry.

"Oh, I'm sure it was." Margaret gave my arm yet another pinch. "Actually, I don't think it was you at all. I think he was texting with that stupid friend-slash-boyfriend of his and they must have gotten into it."

"So, should I go ahead and bring out dessert?" Mike inquired.

"Let's hold off for now." Margaret headed for the front door.

Mike and I made our way into the kitchen and dumped the dishes in the sink. Mike went back to the dining room to grab the rest of the plates. I heard a chime coming from my front pocket. I fished out my phone to see I had another message from Jordan. *Change of plans. I am taking care of things right now.*

I still had no idea what he was talking about. *Ok, I hope it goes well given the circumstances.* I didn't really know what else to say. I wasn't even clear on what the circumstances were.

Mike came back into the kitchen with another handful of dishes and my wine glass, which he briskly placed in my hand. Bless him. I really needed it. I really did hope everything was OK with Christopher. While there was definitely no love connection, he seemed like a nice, decent guy. But let's be honest, on par with Margaret's past matchmaking, we had very little in common.

Mike began rinsing off the dishes and placing them in the dishwasher. I looked back at my phone. I didn't have another message from Jordan. I flipped from the message screen to the home screen that listed all the guys online in the area. I noticed Jordan's picture was right next to mine. The order of the pictures correlated to how close in proximity you were from that person. If Jordan's picture was next to mine, that meant he was nearby. That must be a mistake. I clicked on his picture and it said he was only 200 feet away. The app was known for its glitches. I tried to refresh the screen, but nothing changed. Oh well, I would try again a bit later.

I heard the front door open. I tapped Mike on the shoulder and we went to meet Margaret in the dining room. She walked toward us, eyes wide. I couldn't tell if she was upset or trying not to erupt in laughter. Christopher was nowhere in sight.

"Where's Christopher?" Mike was shaking his hands in the air trying to dry them off.

"He's still outside. You're never going to believe what happened." She grinned, looking like she would burst if she didn't get the story out as fast as she could. "Can you believe his boyfriend, well now ex-boyfriend, just showed up and broke up with him. Christopher's devastated."

"Well, he did say things were *complicated*." I used air quotes.

They both chuckled. Margaret's eyes twinkled as she put her finger up to her chin, tilting her head down. "Well, it seems that Christopher could tell from the texts this is where things were going, so he begged that idiot to come over here right now in the middle of dinner, so he could plead with him to take him back."

"Now that's just sad." I slanted my head toward her. "And tell me again why you thought putting me in me the middle of this mess would be a good idea."

"But it all worked out." Margaret ecstatic, threw both her arms in the air. "Now you guys have no reason not to go out," Margaret said.

"Really, babe?" Mike rolled his eyes.

"You have got to be kidding, Margie. Were you not just at the same disastrous dinner with me an hour ago? The only saving grace was your amazing pasta."

"The pasta was magnificent as always," Mike chimed in.

Margaret smiled. "Well, you can't blame me for trying."

"Oh, trust me, I totally can." I gave her a playful shove and then pulled out my phone.

"Don't tell me you're getting on that stupid hook-up app again." Margaret reached for my phone. I raised my arms just out of her reach.

"I seem to be having better luck on it tonight then I did at this dinner party."

Margaret stuck out her tongue.

"That's kind of true, babe," Mike said.

"Hey, whose side are you on?" She peered at Mike.

Mike reached out and engulfed Margaret in his arms. "I am always team Margaret. Team Margaret all the way." He gave her a quick peck on the lips.

"So sweet! Ugh…" I stuck my finger in my open mouth like I was inducing vomiting. I looked back at my phone and saw that Grindr still hadn't updated. It still showed Jordan's picture right next to mine. Wait a minute. My heart fluttered.

"Margaret, what does Christopher's boyfr… I mean ex-boyfriend look like?"

"He's actually really good looking. Light-skinned black guy, a bit lighter than you, with really curly hair."

I clicked on Jordan's picture and held my phone up to Margaret's face. "Does he look like this?"

"That's him," Margaret shrieked. "Why do you have… "

I didn't even wait for her to finish. I darted to the front door and slung it open. The pungent smell of burning rubber greeted me as I stepped onto the porch and saw a car peeling out of the driveway. No way. Was Jordan just outside my friends' home on Vashon Island of all places and I missed him by mere seconds? No, I was not going to be defeated. Not yet. I ran down the driveway thinking I could somehow wave my hands and scream to get his attention, when a figure stepped from the other side of a hydrangea, planted just to the right of the driveway. The porch light didn't completely reach that area, but as the figure approached the driveway, I immediately recognized him.

"Hey, there." His chestnut brown, puppy dog eyes were even more luminous than in his profile picture.

"Hey, yourself." I smiled.

"Funny seeing you here." Jordan's curls were blowing in the light wind.

"Yeah, I was going to say the same thing." We smiled and looked at each awkwardly.

"So, I guess Christopher…" I wasn't sure how to finish that sentence.

"Oh ya, he's gone." Jordan pointed down the street.

"I see." We continued smiling awkwardly at one another.

I heard Mike and Margaret approaching.

"Mike, Margaret, this is my friend, Jordan." I stepped to the side. "Jordan, this is Mike and Margaret, two of my oldest friends."

Jordan waved to them. "Nice to meet you both." Mike waved back, but Margaret barely raised her hand.

"I want to apologize to you all for this crazy drama tonight. This was not at all my intention. Christopher was just out of control and threatening to smash in my headlights and all kind of things if I didn't show up."

Mike put his arm around Margaret. "No need to explain, we're starting to get the picture. Aren't we, babe?"

Thanks, Mike. He always knew what to say.

"Yes," she said quietly, staring down at the pavement before quickly looking up. Mike and I saw the wheels turning in her head. "You know what, Jordan," She moved toward him and grabbed his hand. "You've had a hectic night. Why don't you come inside for a moment?"

I pinched Margaret on the arm. Only Margaret could flip a switch so quickly and then continue matchmaking. At least Jordan was a much better prospect than Christopher. She did say I was going to thank her for tonight. I guess she was still trying to keep her promise.

"Well, Jordan, you're just in time for dessert. Do you like tiramisu?" *Not you too Mike.* I looked at him in disbelief.

"Yes, but I'm not sure…" He looked at me and then back at Mike and Margaret

"Oh, come on, I insist," Margaret said.

"Ok, sure," Jordan said, still a bit reluctant.

We turned around and walked back toward the house. "It's definitely been an interesting night," Mike said. I wasn't sure if he was being serious or sarcastic, knowing Mike it was the latter.

"Isn't that the truth? But oddly enough, I suddenly feel very alive." He smiled.

"Alive?" I blinked.

"Yep, Alive and Kicking." He totally knew what he was doing. Both Margaret and I stopped in our tracks. We looked at each other and then at Jordan.

"Oh, no." Mike recognized the look in our eyes.

Jordan started us off. He knew just what to do. "Ewwwww, Ohhhhhh"

Then I joined in, "*Alive and Kicking*"

Margaret joined in too. "*Stay until your love is, love is, Alive and Kicking*"

Once we reached the front door, even Mike couldn't resist.

"*Oh, Alive and Kicking*

Stay until your love is, love is, Alive and Kicking"

We filed into the house and raised our voices to really belt out the lyrics as the door closed behind us. Ok, so maybe, in spite of herself, Margaret finally got it right this time.

Victor Evans lives on Vashon Island and works as a college professor, teaching journalism and mass communication. He is a former entertainment journalist and has worked at numerous media organizations, including Entertainment Weekly, MTV, CNN and BET. He is currently finishing his new middle-grade mystery, Evan Sinclair and the Case of the Missing Baseball Bat, which follows the sleuthing adventures of 13-year-old Evan who will do anything to hang with the cool kids. You can follow his and Evan's latest exploits at www.victordevans.com. When Victor is not teaching or writing, you can find him on his farm with his partner wrangling chickens.